Chapter One

It was 11:30 pm; Alexis woke up to a loud beeping noise. She rolled over to see a flashing red light coming from her dressing gown pocket. 'What's happening?' She thought, as stumbled out of bed and over to the door where her dressing gown was hanging off the corner. She took a device out of her pocket. "Girls, we have an emergency, get to HQ now. John". A message on the screen read. Alexis ran out of her room and into her sisters' room, "BAILEY, CHARLIE, WAKE UP!" She whisper-shouted, nudging her sisters. Charlie groaned and sat up, wiped her eyes and yawned. "What time is it" she mumbled mid-yawn. "ITS 11:35" Alexis whispered. Charlie sighed, "Why did you wake me up then?" "I GOT A MESSAGE OFF JOHN, HE NEEDS TO SEE US NOW, HE SAYS ITS AN EMERGENCY" Alexis whisper-shouted again. "Damn, we better get ready to go then" Charlie said, climbing out of bed. "Wake Bailey up" Alexis instructed, before she ran out of her room and into her mum's room. She turned the light on and nudged her mum "Mum, you need to drive us to HQ, John has called an emergency meeting! Quick let's go!" Alexis shouted. Alexis' mum jumped out of bed, "WHATS GOING ON" She shouted, as she stumbled around the room, grabbing her bag and putting her coat on. "I don't know but we need to go!" Alexis said, running back out of the room. Everyone ran downstairs and out to the car. They climbed in and began their journey to the Limebarn Shopping Centre. "What's going on Alexis?" Charlie asked. "I don't know, John's message just said we needed to go to HQ now, and that it was an emergency" Alexis replied, shrugging. Bailey raised her eyebrows, "Okay, this better had be important and not just a joke, waking me without reason is never a good idea" she groaned, her head flopping back onto the headrest. Alexis and Charlie laughed, "We know" they simultaneously replied. Everyone started laughing.

"You look like right numpty's going to an emergency meeting in your PJ's" joked the girls' mum. "Yeah, but when emergency calls… we're super agents mum, not receptionists!" joked Alexis. Alexis and Charlie laughed.

About 10 minutes passed, Alexis and Charlie were talking about past missions, while Bailey was asleep and beginning to snore. After another 5 minutes, Baileys snoring was now echoing throughout the car. Alexis groaned, kicking her leg. Baileys eyes shot open and she jumped up. "What the hell" she shouted in confusion. "Shut the hell up with the damn snoring, me and Charlie are pretty much shouting to each other and we still can't hear over your obnoxiously loud snoring" Alexis chuckled. Bailey sighed, before laying her head back and closing her eyes. She was back to sleep in no time.

Ten minutes later, Charlie was now asleep as well. Alexis leaned forward, "Thanks for this mum, you know we love you right?" she said to her mum. Her mum smiled. "Off course I do, and I love you girls too. What made you randomly say that?" "Because you've helped us and supported us throughout this whole super-agent thing and I know it can't be easy on you considering you had such a bad experience when you was an agent yourself, I just wanted to make sure that you know that we really appreciate the support." Alexis smiled. Alexis's mum smiled. "That's a lovely thing to say Alexis! You know I'll always support you girls" Louise replied.

A couple of minutes passed, "Alexis..." said her mum. Alexis sighed, "What mum?" Alexis' mum said, "Don't you think you should tell Danny?"

There was a pause.

"I wish I could, you know I do, but I can't." Alexis sighed. "I really don't want to get into this right now." "I know you don't love, but he is your boyfriend and he's your best friend… you've been together for over two years now, and there's no doubt you can trust him, hell, even I trust him! I know you're old enough to make your own choices but you can't hide this from him any longer, it's not fair. The longer you put off telling him, the harder it will be." explained Alexis' mum.

Alexis sighed. "Eurgh, I hate it when you're right... Okay, I get the point, I'll tell him soon okay? Now how long are we going to be? We've been in the car for ages now!" Alexis said as she slumped back into the seat. "We're almost there now love, about 10 minutes at the most. Why don't you have a quick nap? I'll wake you up when we're there"

"Okay" said Alexis, then she closed her eyes.

Chapter Two

"Alexis!" the girls' mum shouted. "Alexis! Bailey! Charlie! WAKE UP WE'RE HERE!" she shouted again. Alexis opened one eye, "What?" she mumbled. "We're here love, wake your sisters up" their mum turned the engine off, opened the car door off and stepped out of the car. "WAKE UP! WAKE UP BAILEY! WAKE UP CHARLIE! WAKE UP!" Alexis shouted as she nudged Bailey and Charlie. Alexis sighed, "That's it!" Alexis shuffled into the driver's seat and beeped the horn.

"BEEEEEEEEEEEEEP!"

Bailey and Charlie sat up quickly and their eyes shot open. "WHAT'S GOING ON!? WHAT'S HAPPENING?! ARE WE BEING ATTACKED?!" Bailey shouted. "Shut up Bailey" said Charlie as she punched her in the arm. "What was that for?" said Bailey as she kicked Charlie. "STOP FIGHTING! We're here! Now hurry up and get out of the car we're late as it is!" Alexis shouted.

The girls and their mum all shuffled out of the car and ran into the building into the reception and through to the office, then into the stock cupboard at the back. Alexis began to move the book shelf at the far end of the cupboard to the side, starting to reveal a large door. "Some help, guys? I'm an agent, not a body builder" Alexis said, stepping back, circling her shoulders, arms and neck before shaking it off and moving back over to the shelf. "Super-agent actually" Charlie replied sarcastically. "Anyway, I thought you was taking a boxing class at the gym?" their mum asked. "God mum that was so last week" Alexis replied, rolling her eyes.

When she had moved the shelf completely away from the door on her own, she turned to her sisters and mum. "Thanks for the help guys, honestly I really appreciate it" she smiled sarcastically. She then typed in a key code on the panel, and a tray ejected out. She stuck her thumb on it, and there was a faint beep. The door then began to slowly slide open. "Why can't the shelf move like this too?" Charlie asked. "Gotta get that cardio in" Bailed chuckled.

When the doors had opened, Alexis began walking in, closely followed by the others. After travelling down a few corridors and up a few flights of stairs, they arrived at a pair of huge sliding doors. Alexis put her thumb on another touch panel, and again the doors slowly slid open. It revealed a huge lobby. "What is this all about, where do we go now?" their mum asked. "This is HQ mum" Charlie replied as they all walked in.

"Oh, ok. Not been to this new 'HQ' before, back in my agent days it was just a cellar in a warehouse and we called it 'the office'" Their mum explained, looking around in amazement. "You know, I'm so excited you girls are letting me come to HQ with you. Usually, you make me wait outside in the car!" she said excitedly. Bailey looked at her mum "I think you need to calm down mum, you can't go HQ like this, you need to enter in a professional manner!" She joked. The girls started laughing, "I can't help it! Things have changed so much since I was an agent!" their mum said. "Yeah mum, it's not the stone age anymore!" Alexis said. Alexis, Bailey and Charlie started hysterically laughing. The girls mum looked at them "Excuse me! I was NOT born in the Stone Age you cheeky girl!" she replied. Alexis stopped laughing, and said "Yeah, 70's... stone age... same thing really!" Then she started laughing again. The girls mum crossed her arms and stared at them, but after a few seconds she gave in and joined in the laughter.

They ran straight into the board room and ran to the front and sat in their seats. "Sorry we're late, traffic was bad" said Alexis. "It's fine girls, who's this you brought with you" John said to Alexis. "This is our mum, she used to be an agent" Charlie replied quickly. John walked over to the girls' mum and held his hand out. "Hello, I'm John, I run the agent base". The girls mum shook Johns hand, "Nice to meet you John, I'm Louise, the proud mother of ABC Triple Threat" she gloated.

"Well, take a seat Louise, you're welcome to stay and observe the meeting" John said as he walked back over to his seat at the head of the table. "Well girls, here's the deal. We appear to have a bit on an outbreak here in Limebarn" He hinted, trying not to give too much away. "What do you mean outbreak?" Charlie asked. "Oh my god it better not be contagious" Bailey added in disgust, pulling her jumper over her nose and mouth. "It's an outbreak idiot, obviously it's going to be contagious" Alexis joked. She turned to Jon, "What type of outbreak are we talking here? And have we started looking into finding a cure?" she asked. "Just zombies, no big deal" Jon replied, waving his hand dismissively. Alexis' face dropped…

Chapter Three

"Basically, Last Tuesday we had received a call from the police.
They said that they had received a call from the very
concerned owner of an empty warehouse at the edge of Lime barn.
Apparently, 3 bodies had been found dismembered, it looks they had
been "ripped apart" by some sort of large animal. Or so they
thought... When the police got to the scene of the crime, upon
examining the bodies, one of the officers was brutally attacked by a
man, apparently, he came out of no-where and locked his jaw around
the officer's arm, before taking several swings at him, leaving him
with huge gashes on his torso and face. According to a witness, the
attacker had bright red eyes, sharp teeth, and hands with long, bony
fingers with razor sharp nails. When the witness came forward, they
were extremely agitated about a potential zombie outbreak, and the
police disbelieved them to the extent that they had the witness
sedated and taken to a psychiatrist. The officer who was attacked,
sadly lost his life. The officer's partner shot the killer on the spot,
but apparently, it took a whole round of bullets to stop him. Even
then he/it still wasn't dead, and had to be shot in the head. The body
was brought to us for examination. I couldn't believe it myself when
Kevin from the lab put the report on my desk. When examined, it
was confirmed that the corpse had blood red eyes, sharp teeth and
the blood of the corpse was frozen stiff along with the muscles and
there was excessive damage to the organs, the lab are still confused
to how it was even managing to function. Almost as if he was
completely dead on the inside. The head examiner reported that upon
examining the eyes, he suddenly felt very intimidated, even
though the body was in fact dead. He was unable to finish the
examination because he was too frightened". Jon explained.
Alexis was too speechless to reply, as was her mum and Bailey, but
Charlie managed to get a few words out "What the hell? Are you
telling us zombies are real? Surely this has to be a joke?"

John laughed, and then stopped abruptly. "No girls, I'm being 100% serious, and it gets worse" he said. Alexis looked at John in disbelief, "How could this possibly get any worse?" she asked sarcastically. "Since then, 5 other dead, savaged bodies have been found and reports of 'Non-human' figures have been reported to be running in and out of that same warehouse. The whole area has been cordoned off by police and is under constant surveillance. As you well know, any case like this is out of the hands of the police and is handed over to us to handle. I think it's safe to say that this may be the start of a very big problem, I've heard whispers from other agents and other bases, calling it the start of a 'zombie apocalypse', but we aren't allowed to officially call it that till we can verify and we have evidence to back it up, because as you can imagine, if we declare code red to the public, and announce a zombie outbreak, we are going to look like right loonys" Jon continued. "How much more evidence do we need? Do we need to be bitten ourselves? How about taking a selfie with one of those things? Would that suffice?" Alexis asked in anger. Jon dismissed her comment, "For now, I thought it best that you girls and your mum would like to move in here so you are completely protected from anything that may happen in the outside world, and we can work around the clock to find a solution for this problem before it spirals even further out of our control." Jon suggested.

The girls' mum raised her hand, "May I say something?" John replied "Yeah, go for it you don't need to raise your hand, you're included in this meeting too." The girls mum smiled, "I'd rather we didn't move in here, I'd rather we'd stay at home, can't we get any protection there?" John laughed, "You don't need to be monitored by security if that's what you meant, your girls are fully trained with all models of guns and have a fully registered fire arm license declaring they can carry a fire arm. Also, we can have a supply of guns and bullets delivered to your home or your own protection, and if you'd like, you can re-take your fire arm training course again so that you are trained to use a gun and so that you are licensed to own and carry a fire arm. Although, you'd only be certified to use and carry a hand gun" Jon offered. The girls' mum looked speechless.

A couple of seconds passed before she was able to get any words out, "Excuse me? Your telling me my daughters, who are aged 17, 15 and 12 are fully licensed to use all models of gun? Are you also telling me that they can carry a gun around with them?" The girls mum said in disbelief. John looked at the girls, "Why haven't you told her?" "We knew she'd react like this" Alexis sighed. She looked at her mum, "Mum, it's not as if we carry guns around with us! We'd never do anything that reckless, you know that. I just think that considering the situation we are in now, getting stocked up on protection, and getting you trained and licensed as well could be a good idea" she explained. There was a long silence.

A couple of minutes later, the girls mum spoke. "I don't believe you, I need some proof, this is all just too much to take in" She said, pacing he room. "Come on girls to the studio. Let's show your mum what we mean, and how sensible and professional you are in the presence of fire arms, maybe that will put her mind at rest a little" John explained. He, the girls and their mum walked over to the firing studio and Alexis, Bailey and Charlie got themselves kitted up with protective gear, and got ready to enter the studio. "You have to stay behind this screen because you're not insured" John said to the girl's mum as he escorted her over to the back room. They both looked through the screen at the girls.

A couple of minutes later, Charlie walked into the studio first. She picked up a gun, loaded it and began shooting the targets. "The aim of this exercise is too test and monitor their targeting skills" John said to the girls' mum. "As you can see, Charlie is progressing really well and her target skills are improving, but she is still a little out, but at 18/25, her skills are way above average." He continued. There was a silence. "Great job Charlie! You're getting so much better!" John said in the microphone. Charlie stuck her thumb up. "Next in the studio is Bailey" he instructed. Charlie walked out of the studio and as Bailey walked in, they high-fived, and the shooting began again.

A couple more minutes later, and John looked to the girls' mum, "Considering Bailey is at such a young, tender age, her target skills are already very good. She's progressing constantly, and her current personal best is 16/25 which is astounding for a 12-year-old, especially when some of our other agents have been doing this for years, and struggle to get close to that score" he explained.

"Bailey you're doing great! Your target skills are getting better every time we do this practice! I'm so proud of you, keep it up!" Bailey stuck her thumbs up and left the studio. "NEXT UP, ALEXIS!" shouted John. John turned to the girls' mum, "Now for you to be truly amazed" he smiled. Alexis walked into the studio, and the shooting began. A couple of minutes later, John turned to the girls' mum. "Now, the first time that Alexis did this practice was over 7 years ago. She got it straight away, and ever since, she has continued to astound us. She hasn't missed a single target for over 6 years! She is the best agent we have EVER had to do this practice, 25/25 for over 6 years. This is why she has been awarded the title of Super-agent; she is a 17-year-old with the highest rank of agency that the base has ever seen. She's a credit to you, you should be so proud and we're so glad to have her as our head agent." He said confidently. Alexis' mum looked astounded. "Wait, what do you mean by head agent?" she asked in confusion. John smiled "She has a higher rank than I, and anyone else in the history of this base does. She was awarded with this honor just last week, there was a huge ceremony here at the base… I'm surprised she didn't tell you" He said. "It also means that when I retire, she won't only be a Super-Agent; she will run this whole base." Louise's jaw dropped, "Wow that is amazing! I am so proud of my girls!" she gloated. "Alexis, you're amazing kid! Come on out so me, you, your sisters and your mum can have a discussion about what happens next." John shouted. Alexis stuck her thumb up and left the studio. The girls took off the protective gear, and they all went back to the board room.

Chapter Four

"Right, about the gun situation, I've spoken to the suppliers, and here's what I can offer you. Firstly, Louise, you can complete a fire-arm training course tonight which will license you to carry a hand gun only, and your agent title will be returned to you. Also, by the end of tomorrow, you will each have a month's supply of 5 hand guns, with 1000 bullets per gun. Sounding good up to yet girls?" said John. The girls and their mum all nodded. "You look shocked Louise" joked John. "This is a lot to take in" Louise replied. "Also, each of the Triple Threat girls will get another 4 models of gun, 5 of each and 1000 bullets per gun. This is because super agents do a different fire-arm training course which is exclusively for higher ranking agents, and this gives them a license to own all registered models of gun. They will be specially delivered to your house tomorrow" Alexis, Bailey and Charlie smiled. "But due to fact that you girls are still classed as under age, this depends on whether your mum will sign this contract accepting the order of the guns" John said, as he passed over the contract and a pen to the girls' mum. She read the contract, then she turned to the girls, "Well girls, shall I sign it?" she asked. Alexis, Bailey and Charlie all nodded. "Louise, do we have a deal?" asked John. She looked at the contract, took a deep breath and signed on the dotted line. "Deal" she said.

"Okay girls, you can go into my office and make yourself at home, you can help yourself to whatever is in my fridge, go on my computer, read the notes from this case so far, read the notes from the examination of the corpse, look at the pictures that were taken and all of the notes from past cases are on there too. I'm going to take your mum to the studio to do her fire arm training course. I want you to stay this room, and do not go outside. It's not safe out there. We'll be back in about 2 hours" John said sternly. "Girls make sure you stay in here and stay out of trouble like John said, we won't be too long, okay?" she said. The girls nodded, "Yes mum". The girls mum walked over to the door and left with John, who closed the door behind them.

"This is so crazy!" Bailey shouted, as she slumped back into the sofa in the corner of the office. Alexis walked over to John's desk and sat in his chair and put her feet up. "Yeah it is!" she laughed. She reached into her pocket. "Oh crap, I left my phone in the car" she said as she jumped up, "I'm gonna go and get it, who's coming?" she asked. "I will" Bailey replied, as she walked over to the door. "Wait guys, mum and John are right, it's not safe out there!" said Charlie nervously. "Stop being such a baby Charlie! If it makes you feel any better, John has some hand guns in the bottom draw in case of emergency, we'll take one each!" said Alexis. Alexis and Bailey walked back over to John's desk and Alexis opened his bottom draw and took 4 guns out. "Why four?" asked Bailey. "In case of extreme emergency" joked Alexis, she handed a gun over to Bailey and Charlie. "Hide them; we can't let anyone see us with guns!" she said, as she put the guns in each of her dressing gown pockets.

"Let's do this!" she shouted, as she grabbed her mum's car keys.

The girls left the office and walked down to the entrance of the building, "It's so much easier to get out of the building than it is to get in" Bailey pointed out. Alexis and Charlie laughed. When they got to the entrance, they looked out of the glass doors, "It's all clear" Whispered Bailey. "Wait!" shouted Charlie, she ran to the reception and took the key for the door off the hook behind the desk. She ran back over to the door, "Okay, let's do this!" said Charlie. She pressed the push to exit button and the door opened "RUN!" whispered Bailey, "The car's over there!" she continued. The girls ran over to the car and Alexis unlocked and opened the car door and they all jumped in, locking the doors from the inside. Alexis grabbed her phone and the girls sat back and began to catch their breath back. Suddenly, a shadow walked past the car, "What the hell was that" whispered Bailey. "I don't know, turn all of the car lights off, inside and out and hide" Alexis whispered. They peaked over the bottom of the car window, and saw a shadowed figure walk towards the building, "Who the heck is that and what are they doing?" asked Bailey, who was beginning to panic. "I don't know, let's just hide in here for a while and see if they go" Alexis whispered.

About half an hour passed and the girls were panicking. "Alexis, have a look again, have they gone?" Whispered Bailey, who had tears in her eyes. Alexis peaked over the bottom of the window, "They're just standing in front of the doors and staring into the building" Alexis whispered. Bailey started crying, "I knew we should've listened to Charlie and just stayed in the office like mum and John said" She whimpered. "Calm down, everything's going to be fine, we'll just keep trying to ring mum and John, don't worry Bailey", Alexis said, as she put her arm around her.

Another fifteen minutes passed. "What are they doing now?" Bailey asked, mid-sniffle. "They've not moved" replied Alexis, who was still peeking out of the car window. "What are we going to do? We don't know who this is or why they're here, mum isn't answering her phone and neither is John, and we're stranded" Charlie asked. "There's only one thing we can do" Alexis said. "What is that?" asked Bailey. "I'm going to have to go and find out who they are and what they want" Alexis said. Bailey shook her head, "No you can't do that, it might be one of those things, it's too dangerous" she said. "Well we can't just stay here and do nothing" Alexis said. "What's the plan?" asked Charlie. "I'll get out of the car, as soon as I get out, you lock the doors behind me, I'll go and find out who they are and what they want" Alexis said. "But they might be a psycho" Bailey whimpered. "Yeah, but they could also just be lost and looking for directions" Alexis pointed out re-assuringly. "Are you sure this is safe?" asked Bailey. "I don't know, but I have the guns anyway" Alexis said. "Please don't go Alexis, it's not safe" Bailey pleaded. "She's a super-agent Bailey; she is perfectly capable of taking on whoever that is" Joked Charlie. Alexis laughed, "I'll be fine, don't worry" Alexis said, in attempt to re-assure Bailey. Alexis opened the car door quietly and slowly, and then she stepped out. She smiled at her sisters. "Be careful" whispered Bailey, "I will don't worry; just keep trying to ring mum and John!" Alexis whispered back. She slowly shut the car door and Bailey locked it from the inside.

Alexis began to walk quietly towards the building, as she got closer, and the figure was getting clearer, she began to get a feeling that something wasn't right. A chill ran down her spine and the hairs on the back of her neck stood up. She took a deep breath, "Hello, are you okay there?" she asked quietly. There was no reply. She repeated herself, and there was still no answer. A couple of minutes later, the person spoke up "I was looking for my friend" they said, as they continued to look into the building. "Oh, the shopping centre is actually closed now, does your friend work here?" Alexis asked. The person laughed and shook their head. "No, my friend was killed a few weeks ago, I was told to come here for some answers" the person said in a slightly louder voice. "Oh right okay, maybe you'd be better off contacting the police, you won't find any answers from here I'm afraid" Alexis suggested. The person then lowered their head, looking at the ground. Alexis put her hands in her dressing gown pockets and gripped the guns. "I was told to come here and speak to someone called John? My friend was killed in the warehouse incident" it spoke clearly. "Oh, are you a friend of the officer that was killed?" Alexis asked, her voice beginning to shake. The person laughed again, "you're getting warmer" they joked. Alexis gulped, "Who are you?" she asked, as she started to back away slowly. The person lifted their head, "Didn't your mum tell you never to talk to strangers?" they chuckled. Alexis took a deep breath and stopped moving, "I said who are you?!" she asked in a louder tone. The person looked back at the ground, "I'm a friend of the person who killed the police officer" the person said. Alexis pulled the guns out of her pocket and slowly put them behind her back. "Why are you here? Like I said, if you're looking for answers, you should be talking to the police" Alexis asked, her voice shaking even more.

The person turned around, and Alexis' jaw dropped. She stared into the person's blood red eyes, his skin was so pale. His hands were so big, the fingers almost to a point. He smiled, showing razor sharp teeth. "Revenge? Closure? You see, I'm not really sure... you see, all I know is my friend is dead and I'm not too pleased about it" he said, shrugging. "What are you?" Alexis mumbled. The person looked down, then back up and stared Alexis in the eyes...

"I'm your worst nightmare"

14

Bailey and Charlie looked out of the car window in shock, "Bailey, tell me I'm not imagining things" Charlie muttered, "we need to help her!" Bailey shouted, as she pulled down the car window, "ALEXIS RUN!" Bailey shouted, Alexis was frozen with shock, the person took a step towards her, "you should listen to your friend Alexis", they said. Alexis began to step backwards quicker as the person began to walk towards her faster. Alexis swung her arms in front of her and pointed the guns at the person. He laughed, "Lets be honest you're not going to shoot me" he joked, Alexis smiled, "You have no idea what I'm capable of", the person walked over to her and looked her straight in the eyes, "you should have run while you had the chance" he whispered. Alexis gulped, taking a shot. Without so much as a flinch, he threw Alexis back, and she landed on the floor. A gun-shot rang through the air and Alexis screamed... she lay on her back, holding onto her shoulder. The person laughed, looking down at his T-shirt... a dark liquid seeping through. "Well that wasn't very nice" he teased, grabbing her by the collar of her dressing gown, before throwing her back onto the floor, she groaned as she turned onto her side, still holding onto the guns. As she tried to get up, he just kicked her back down. "Your turn to die now, little girl" he smiled, as he leant over her.

Bailey and Charlie opened the car doors and jumped out, running towards Alexis. "Alexis!!!!" Bailey screamed. The man laughed, "Oh, look, here are your little friends, coming for back-up are they? How cute" he picked Alexis up by her the arm and stared at her, "Now to finished what I started" he said. Alexis laughed and lifted the gun from behind her back and shot the man in the forehead, he fell back and as he released Alexis from his grip, she fell back to the floor. "Oh shut up will you"
she groaned. She then began to cry as she continued to hold her shoulder.

Chapter Five

Bailey and Charlie helped Alexis to get back to the car, Charlie took her dressing gown off and wrapped it around Alexis' arm "We need to apply pressure to stop her losing so much blood... Bailey, you keep trying to ring mum" Charlie said. "It's no use, they aren't picking up". Bailey replied, panicking. Alexis began to slip in and out of consciousness. Bailey started crying, "Quick, we need to take her to the office, there's no point in us just staying here, there will probably be a first aid kit there" she whimpered. "Okay, let's go then, help me get Alexis" Charlie said, Bailey grabbed the car keys and opened the car door, she grabbed Alexis, gently lifting her out of the car, balancing her on her feet, whilst Charlie jumped out of the car and locked the door. They carried Alexis over to the entrance of the building and all the way through to the office. "They need to make a quicker way to get to HQ for emergencies" Bailey said. When they got there, they carried Alexis into John's office and lay her on the sofa, "Bailey, quick, go and get Mum and John!" Charlie shouted, Bailey ran out of the room. A couple of minutes later, she ran back in with John and their mum. They ran over to Alexis, "WHAT HAPPENED!?" the girls' mum shouted panicking, tears filling her eyes. "It's a long story, we need to her to the hospital she's already lost a lot of blood and she is still losing more" Bailey shouted. John quickly lifted Alexis off the sofa and carried her down to his car. "You take the girls to the hospital in your car and I'll take Alexis in mine, that way I can lay her on the back seats" John said. Louise, Bailey and Charlie ran over to the car and got in. John lay Alexis on the back seats of his car, he leant over her "Alexis, if you can hear me, we're going to get you to the hospital so we can get you some help, stay strong" he said softly, stroking her face. He closed the door and jumped in the front seat and turned on the engine and opened the window "Louise, follow me, we're going to the private hospital, it's about five or ten minutes away" he shouted, he began to drive with the girls not far behind.

When they got to the hospital, John carried Alexis from the car to the entrance. The girls and Louise ran in a couple of seconds later. They looked around "what the hell, this just looks like a house!" Louise pointed out. "I know, it's a hospital used only by the base, we can't exactly explain the situation to a normal hospital can we?" John replied quickly. He put Alexis on a hospital bed and a doctor walked over to them, "What's happened here?" he asked, John looked at Bailey and Charlie. Bailey began to cry again, "Basically, Alexis was in a struggle with some random man, there was a struggle and Alexis pulled out 2 guns, she got thrown, landed on the gun and shot herself in the shoulder, just please help my sister!" Charlie said quickly. "Okay, we need to take her for a scan to see if the wound has caused any major damage" the doctor said. "Louise and Bailey, you go with the doctor. Charlie, you can stay with me and explain exactly what happened" John ordered. "We'll take her to a cubicle and assess the damage, and then we will take her for a scan" the doctor explained, Alexis was then rushed into a cubicle, closely followed by Louise and Bailey.

"Okay then, explain", John said to Charlie. "Okay, so, Alexis left her phone in the car and she wanted it but I said we should stay in your office like you told us too, but then she said she's getting it anyway and she took your emergency hand guns for protection. I went with her and Bailey and we ran to the car. We saw a shadow so we hid, then we looked and we saw a person walking over to the entrance of the shopping centre. He just stood there for over half an hour, so Alexis went and found out who the person was and what he wanted. It turned out he was one of those zombie things. There was a struggle and the zombie lifted Alexis and threw her like, 4 foot into the air and she landed on her hand which was covering her shoulder to try and cause less damage for when she landed but she didn't let go of the gun so she shot herself in the shoulder. Then the zombie tried to attack her so she shot him in the forehead and it killed him. We couldn't get hold of you or mum so we took her back to the office but she kept going in and out of consciousness so we don't know what exactly happened or what they were talking about" Charlie said quickly, pretty much not even taking a breath...

She took a deep breath. John's jaw dropped. "Whoa, okay, first, you should've stayed in my office like me and your mum told you too, second, you're telling me that there is a dead zombie lying outside the shopping centre?!" he asked angrily. "Yes" Charlie replied timidly.

John quickly pulled his phone out of his pocket and started dialling. "Hello, Chris, there was an incident and there is now a body lying outside of the shopping centre, you need to go and move it right now as fast as you can. Take it to the lab and lock it in a body box, then get all the CCTV from the lower level and outside the shopping centre from the past 12 hours and destroy it! I will explain everything tomorrow!" he said, ending the call and putting his phone back in his pocket. He turned to Charlie, "Okay now that is sorted, lets go and see how Alexis is" He said. They walked over to the cubicle but she wasn't there. John saw a nurse and ran over to her, "excuse me, where is Alexis?" he asked, "Alexis has been taken to theatre, the scan results show her shoulder dislocated when she fell, and the bullet lodged itself in the gap, she's in theatre having the bullet removed. Follow me I will take you to her mum and sister" the nurse replied.

John and Charlie followed the nurse. When they got to the family room, Charlie walked over to Bailey to comfort her. Louise stood up and left the room with John, "How is she?" he asked. "She's lost a lot of blood, she's in theatre at the moment. The nurse said she's stable, last time I asked they said they were almost finished, it's only a minor procedure. Apparently, when she fell her shoulder dislocated quite badly and the bullet lodged itself in the gap, so they are removing it, then they are re-locating the shoulder and stitching it up, she's going to be fine. There is no major damage" Louise replied. John smiled, "that's great news", "It could've been a lot worse, you promised me nothing like this would happen to her again" Louise said angrily. "I did what I could, she disobeyed us both it was out of my hands" John said. Louise sighed, "we can go and see her when she's out of theatre, so she can wake up to a familiar face" she said.

An hour later, the doctor came into the room, "Alexis is out of theatre, you can come and see her, she hasn't regained consciousness yet but she will do soon", the doctor said. Louise, John, Bailey and Charlie walked into the room where Alexis was, they sat down next to her bed and a couple of minutes later, she began to stir, she turned her head and opened her eyes slightly, making a quiet groaning noise. Louise stood up, leant over her and stroked her cheek "are you okay love?" she asked. Alexis mumbled and blinked a few times. "What happened?" she mumbled. "You got attacked and shot yourself in the shoulder, then you passed out, your shoulder slightly dislocated when you fell and the bullet lodged in the gap, but your all better now, the bullet is out and the doctor put your shoulder back into place" The girls' mum explained, Alexis smiled, "Not bad for a days work ey?" she joked. Bailey, Everyone laughed. Bailey and Charlie climbed onto the end of the bed, "We were so scared" Charlie said. Alexis looked at them, "Told you I'd be okay". Bailey looked at Alexis inquisitively, "Does it hurt?" she asked. Alexis laughed, "Nope, can't feel a thing".

A couple of minutes later, Alexis turned to her mum, "What time is it?" she asked. "Its 8:30 love" her mum replied. Alexis raised her eyebrows, "really?" she asked. Her mum nodded. "Mum..." Alexis said. "Yes?" her mum replied. "I want to see Danny" she said. "Okay love, I'll ring him if you want me too and I'll ask him to come and see you?" Her mum said. Alexis smiled, "I was thinking, I need some clothes, a tooth brush, some toothpaste and some money to get some food, and you need to sign for the delivery, so could you go home and get me my stuff, sign for the delivery, then go and pick Danny up and bring him here?" She asked sweetly. Louise laughed and then sighed, "Okay love, but do you want to ring him first, you need to explain things to him, and today is the perfect time to tell him your secret." Her mum said. Alexis looked at John, "John can I tell Danny?" she asked, John smiled, "I knew this time would come, yes you can tell him, but he will have to be sworn to secrecy?" he replied. Alexis smiled and nodded, "we can trust him, I can promise you that" she said confidently.

Alexis, John, Louise, Bailey and Charlie chatted all night, discussing what happened, discussing potential future strategies, and before they knew it, it was 10:00am. Louise turned to Alexis, "It's time to ring Danny" she said. Alexis took a deep breath. "Okay, can I use your phone John? I don't have much credit left" she said. John nodded and passed Alexis his phone, she dialled his number and put the phone to her ear…

Danny: "Hello?"

Alexis: "Hey Danny, it's Alexis"

Danny: "Oh hi babe, what's up?"

Alexis: "Don't freak out, but I'm in hospital"

Danny: "What!? What's happened!? Why are you in hospital?"

Alexis: "It's hard to explain over the phone"

Danny: "Can I come and see you?"

Alexis: "Yes please"

Danny: "Which hospital are you at?"

Alexis: "I'm at a private one, my mum has to go home to get me some stuff so she said she'll pick you up and bring you here"

Danny: "Okay"

Alexis: "Go to my house at 11:30, and my mum will meet you there"

Danny: "Okay I will do, do you need or want anything?"

Alexis: "I'm okay thanks"

Danny: "Okay, I'll see you soon, I love you"

Alexis: "Love you too"

Alexis handed the phone back over to John, "Okay mum he'll be at our house for 11:30, don't tell him anything! You should probably set off now, in case there's traffic" She said to her mum. Her mum laughed "Even when you've been shot your still bossy! Okay love I'll be back soon" she said.

About an hour later, two men arrived at the hospital. "We're here to see John" one of them said. John stood up and shook both of their hands. He introduced them to Alexis, "Alexis, these are your body guards, they will be standing outside the door while you're here, in case your new-found friend decides to pay you a visit" He said. Alexis laughed, "First of all, he's dead, and second, You're joking, right?" she asked. John shook his head, "This is going to make it just that bit harder to explain all of this to Danny" she muttered, as she slumped back into the bed.

Another hour passed and the girls mum walked into the room, passing Alexis, Bailey and Charlie a bag each. "Here you go, clean clothes, clean underwear, your purses, your tooth brush, tooth paste, hair brush, and some other bits and bobs are in there! And I've got the same for you two!" She rushed to say. "I've also got a bag in the car with some essentials... food, toiletries, valuables and so on. I'm starting to warm up to the idea of staying here till everything calms down" she joked. "I'll take Danny to the family room while you get ready... oh, and I found your Agent ID and your kit, so I packed them in there too, just thought it might make things a bit easier. John, you come with me and help me begin to explain things to Danny... Bailey and Charlie, you girls get ready, and help Alexis to get ready if she needs help." The girls mum continued, then she walked out of the room and the girls got dressed and cleaned themselves up.

When they had all finished getting ready, Alexis turned to Bailey "Go and get Danny!" she instructed. Bailey saluted her and ran out of the room, and Alexis got back on the bed. A couple of minutes later, Danny ran into the room, "Oh my gosh are you okay?!" He said to Alexis, she jumped back out of bed and hugged him tightly. He kissed her forehead, before hugging her tight. "Ouch, watch the shoulder" she said. She got back on the bed and Danny sat on the chair next to her and held her hand. Alexis turned to her sisters, "Can we have sometime alone to talk about things?" she asked, Bailey nodded, and her and Charlie left the room, shutting the door behind them. Danny looked down, chuckling, "What are you laughing at?" Alexis asked him. "My girlfriend is a ninja" he joked. "Wait, what has my mum been telling you? I'm not a ninja, I'm a secret agent" she asked in confusion. "Yeaaaa, secret agent, ninja, pretty much the same thing…" he joked. She laughed, "You know you can't tell anyone, don't you?" She asked, "Yeah I know, your friend John told me, he swore me to secrecy, your secret is safe with me you don't have to worry about that" he said. "Good" Alexis replied. Danny laughed, "So, you going to tell me how you got hurt?" he asked. "Did my mum not tell you?" she asked. "Yeah, she told me some of it, but I want to hear it from you" he replied. Alexis groaned, "Do I have to?" she asked. "Yeah you do" Danny insisted. "Okay here goes," She said, and she explained everything.

When she finished explaining, there was a short silence…

Danny started laughing. "It's not funny!" Alexis shouted. "I know, I know, but I can't believe you got attacked by a zombie and instead of shooting him, ended up shooting yourself!" he said. Alexis started laughing, "No I did shoot him as well" she said, pouting before letting out a chuckle. "Yeah, after shooting yourself first" Danny smirked. Alexis shook her head, smiling and looking down. "Okay, when you put it like that..." she said, they both laughed for a while.

"So you aren't mad at me for not telling you I was an agent?" He shook his head, "No I'm not mad… to be honest, I can't be mad, John told me how good your gun skills are, I definitely can't be mad at you if I know you're licensed to use a gun" He joked, Alexis started laughing, "No seriously, are you mad?" She asked. He wrapped his arms around her, "No, I'm actually so proud of you, your only 17 and you've been doing this since you was 9, right?" he asked. Alexis nodded. "That is amazing and I bet it's so much responsibility, I couldn't have done that, knowing that so many people would be relying on me… I honestly can't even imagine how hard that is must be" Danny said proudly, kissing her cheek. Alexis looked at him and smiled, "You have no idea how much that means to hear you to say that" she replied. "Oh and did John tell you about how I'm head agent?" She gloated. Danny shook his head in shock, "Yeah, I'm the head agent, I technically own and run the whole of the base, but John was hired to run things until I'm 21" Alexis said proudly. Danny's jaw dropped, "That is so cool, I'm so unbelievably proud of you" Danny gushed, squeezing her again. "Ouch" Alexis groaned. He released his grip quickly. "Sorry" he said. Alexis smiled at him again and hugged him tight, "Thank you" she said, Danny smiled and he kissed Alexis' forehead and held her tight.

A couple of minutes later, Alexis' mum and sisters walked in, followed by John, "The doctor said that you can go home now Alexis, as long as you take it easy" Alexis smiled. She jumped off Danny's knee, "Let's go!" she shouted. She looked at John, "Is Danny allowed to come to HQ?" she asked. John nodded, "Off course, let's go" he replied. They then left the hospital.

Chapter Six

When they got to the shopping centre, they travelled up to HQ. "This is so cool" Danny replied, looking around. "It's just a corridor Danny" Alexis chuckled, holding onto his hand. He smiled, wrapping his arm around her shoulder instead.

When they got to HQ, they walked over to the board room. Danny was looking around in amazement, narrowly avoiding walking face first into a large concrete column. "Easy does it" Alexis laughed, pulling him away. They walked into the board room, and when they had all sat down, John walked over to Alexis and Danny, "That isn't your seat anymore Alexis" John said, Alexis stood up and looked at him, "I don't understand" she replied. "That is Danny's seat now" John replied, Alexis' eyes lit up, "Are you saying what I think your saying?" Alexis asked, mid-smile. John nodded, Alexis started jumping around, Danny stood up and walked over to Alexis, "I don't get it, I'm confused" he said. Alexis smiled, "I'm going to train you and you're going to work alongside triple threat! YOU'RE GONNA BE AN AGENT DANNY!" Alexis squealed. Danny smiled "This is AWESOME" he shouted, fist punching the air. Alexis stopped jumping and stood still, "Wait, if Danny has my place at the conference table, where am I supposed to sit?" She asked in confusion. John pointed to the seat next to Danny's, which was the top of the table. "What? But I can't take over till I'm 21" Alexis said. John escorted Alexis out of the room and closed the door behind them, "Alexis, I've retired. The base is yours" he said. Alexis shook her head, "No, I can't run the base on my own, I'm not ready" she said, as she sat back on a chair. John sat next to her, "Yes you are Alexis, you're an amazing agent and you're going to run this base better than I ever have, I know this may have come as a surprise to you, but it's all been sorted. I had a web-conference with the other base leaders, we do it every month. I explained the situation and they have all agreed to lift the rule about having to be 21 to run a base. We all know that you're more than capable of running the base, and we have so much faith in you. Because my resignation isn't official until noon, I have decided that you will train Danny to become an agent and then he can help you run the base. I know this has probably come as a shock to you, especially because of what happened last night, but it's happening, in less than 45 minutes, you will be the leader of the Limebarn division" The both stood up and he shook her hand, before handing her his Head Agent ID card. She put it around her neck and hugged him, "I promise that I will make you proud, please stay in touch, you've always been like a father to me and I don't want this to be the end" she said, hugging him. "If only I was so lucky to be a father to you" he sighed. She moved away, and handed him her ID card, "No matter what, retired or active, you will always be an agent" Alexis smiled. John smiled, he then turned around and walked down the corridor, not looking back.

Alexis wiped the tears from her eyes, and opened the door, walking back into the conference room. "Where's John?" Bailey asked. "He's gone" Alexis replied, she walked over to the top of the table and sat down. "Gone where?" Charlie asked. "He's retired with immediate effect; this base is mine now" Alexis mumbled. Danny held Alexis' hand, "Are you okay Al?" he asked, Alexis smiled, "I'm fine, just a little over-whelmed" she replied. A couple of minutes of silence passed. Alexis stood up, "Right here's the plan, I can train Danny right here right now, and by the end of the day, he will be an agent, and he will work alongside triple threat. Bailey, Charlie, you two need to re-train mum, show her the new stuff, okay? By the end of the day, we will have a full team and we can sort this "zombie" situation out", the girls' mum raised her hand, "You don't need to raise your hand to talk mum, your part of the team now" Alexis said, "Am I hearing this right? Am I re-joining the base?" Louise smiled in excitement. "Yes" Alexis smiled. Louise's eyes lit up. "Wait, what about these boxes John gave us?" Bailey asked. Alexis smiled, "Oh yeah, you can open the boxes girls, I already know what's in them" she said. "How?" Charlie asked. "I've got sources, I've known for a while" Alexis smirked. "Wait, what sources?" Bailey questioned. Alexis laughed, "I'm kidding, I overhead Johns conversation with the architect" she replied. "But how? That was a secret meeting, they had it in the vault" Charlie laughed. "Okay okay, I used those new mic kits that John gave us,

I've got this whole building wired like a hot cake" Alexis smirked. "Tut tut" Danny replied, shaking his head. Bailey and Charlie opened their boxes, and inside both boxes was a small pink key. Bailey looked at Alexis, "What's this for?" she asked. Alexis smiled, "We all have our own offices now, and because John doesn't need his anymore, mum is going to be having Johns office" she said. The girls smiled. "That's so cool, I've always wanted my own office" Louise gushed. Alexis smiled, "Okay, time to get this zombie situation under control! Bailey and Charlie, take mum to the studio, get her trained up, I'll take Danny to meet the Science team and we can find out about what happened with that zombie, and get some more information. Then I'll take him to the studio, by time we're there, mum will have finished her training and I'll start training Danny, Okay?" Bailey, Charlie and the girls' mum nodded, they then stood up and left the room. "You ready to become one of us?" Alexis asked Danny, "Let's do this!" he replied, they stood up and left the room.

Chapter Seven

Alexis and Danny walked to the lab, which was located on the top floor. "You go in that room for now, I need to go and see what's going on with this zombie guy. Don't worry, you'll be able to see and hear what's going on, there's a window in the wall that is used when we're being observed, and the room is kitted out with microphones, just flick the switch next to the window" Danny walked into the small room and stood at the window, then he saw Alexis walk into the room and she turned and waved at him. She walked over to the forensic scientist and he told her all about the body.

"Why is it already starting to decay?" Alexis asked, holding her hand over her face. "I'm not sure, it's strange really, the body has reacted to death like an animal would. It was filled with all sorts of gases when we brought it in, but over the past 6 or seven hours it's just been constantly changing. Parts of the skin are already starting to decay" the scientist replied, pointing to the wrist, where patches of skin was missing, clearly showing the bones. "That's so weird, do you know what's causing it?" Alexis asked. "We have no idea, we are running all sort of tests on it, the samples have been sent off to a different lab because we don't have the facilities here to carry out such complex tests, we aren't used to dealing with stuff like this" he replied. "Sorry I'm going to have to leave, this smell is so overwhelming" Alexis replied, gagging slightly. "No problem, I'll give you a ring when the results come back" he replied. Alexis nodded, leaving the room.

She walked into the back room with Danny. "They are doing more tests on it as we speak" Alexis said, Danny raised his eyebrow "You don't even need to do tests, I can tell you right now that it's a zombie", he said, pointing into the room to the body. "And I can smell it from here" he replied, shaking his head. Alexis laughed. "Just being around it has made me feel so uneasy"

Alexis replied, shaking her head. Danny shrugged his shoulders, "I'm rubbish at science" he joked. Just then, the speaker activated, "We're ready to start the physical now" said one of the forensics. "Okay, ring me with any updates" Alexis said. The scientist gave her a thumbs up, and Alexis and Danny walked out of the room and back up to the lobby. They walked into Alexis' office and Alexis sat on the chair behind the desk and Danny sat on the sofa.

A couple of minutes later, Alexis noticed that the light on the computer was flashing, she turned on the screen and there was a box on which read "1 new email", Alexis pressed on it.

"You're going to die"

She stared at the screen, "What the hell" she mumbled, confused. Danny walked over to the computer and stood over Alexis. He looked at the message that was on the screen. "Does it say who it's off?" he asked. "Nope, there is no sender address" she replied. "That's not possible, there HAS to be a sender" Danny said.

Just then, the lights flickered several times. "What's happening?" Alexis asked, she jumped out of her seat and ran over to the phone, she dialled the number for the studio and Bailey picked up, "Hello" Bailey said, "Bailey its Alexis, have you almost finished?" Alexis replied, "Yeah, we've just finished targets, she got 12 out of 25" Bailey said. "She's still got it! Another couple of sessions and she'll be smashing 17 out of 25, easy" Alexis replied. "Without a doubt" Bailey replied. "Listen okay, something really weird has just happened, I'm bringing Danny down to the studio." Alexis replied. "Okay" Replied Bailey. Alexis ended the call and turned to Danny, "I've got a bad feeling that something is going to happen, call it agent intuition, so we're going to get you your gun license, then we will skip the rest of the training for now and get you registered on the database" Alexis said quickly, Danny nodded and they ran out of the room and headed to the studio.

When they arrived at the studio, Alexis got Danny geared up ready for the target test. She handed him a hand gun and hugged him, "You can do this!". She left the studio and joined her sisters and her mum in the over-view room. She stood at the window and turned on the speakers. "Okay Danny, when I give you the signal, aim at the first target, to increase your chances of hitting the target, bend your elbow slightly and stand to the side, okay? Then the impact of the shot won't be as strong so your hands won't buckle as much" she explained. Danny nodded, "Ready?" she asked. He nodded again, "Okay, go" Alexis shouted. Danny stood to the side and readied himself, he took a deep breath and pulled the trigger, a loud shot rang. Alexis looked at the target, "Come on, you can do better than that! You have 24 more shots; you have to get 11 to pass the test and get your license, move onto the next target" she said, Danny continued shooting at the different targets. When he finished, there was a long silence, then Alexis smiled, "YOU GOT 14! YOU PASSED!" she shouted. She ran out of the viewing room and into the studio and hugged him again; he lifted her up and swung her around. "See, I knew you could do it!" she said. She helped him take off his safety equipment and they walked out of the room and into the viewing room. "What now?" Danny asked. "Let's go back up to my office, I have something to show you all" Alexis said, they left the viewing room and returned to Alexis' office.

Chapter Eight

When they were all at the office, Alexis showed Bailey, Charlie and their mum the email. "What the hell, who sent you this?" Bailey asked. "I don't know there isn't a sender" replied Alexis, she looked at her mum who looked confused. "Well we need to make sure that you are properly protected, I'm not having my daughter being sent death threats" the girls' mum said. "That's not the only thing, just after me and Danny read the message, the lights flickered... don't you think that that's a bit too weird to be a coincidence?" Alexis asked.

A couple of minutes later, the girls heard a quiet smash coming from outside. The girls ran over to the window and looked out and looked down to find broken glass on the floor directly below. Before they could say anything, a light shone on the concrete suggesting that the light in the entrance had been switched on. Charlie gulped "There's someone in the building" she whispered. "Why are you whispering? We're 20 floors up they can't hear you!" Bailey joked. Alexis walked away from the window. "What if it's another one of those zombie things?" She asked. "I doubt that" Bailey replied. "But you don't know do you?" Alexis pointed out.

"LOOK THERES SOMEONE WALKING TOWARDS THE BUILDING" Charlie said. "Quick, turn the light off so that they don't see that anyone is up here" Alexis said as she walked back over to the window, Bailey ran over to the light switch and flicked it off. The lights went off and Bailey ran over to the window. The figure stumbled towards the building, dragging its feet as it walked. They watched the figure get closer and closer to the building, and then it suddenly stopped. It stood there for a couple of seconds before lifting its head. "Is it looking at us?" Bailey said. "No, it can't be. There's no light in the room so the window for this room won't be any more visible from the outside than any other window on the building" Alexis said, in an attempt to re-assure not only herself, but also her sisters, her mum and Danny. The figure slowly lifted its arm and pointed it in their direction, "MOVE AWAY FROM THE WINDOW NOW!" Alexis said quickly. Alexis, Bailey and Charlie moved away from the window and ran over to the other side of the room. "It saw us!" Charlie said. "It can't of, like Alexis said, it's impossible!" Bailey replied. Alexis paced around the room for a couple of minutes before, before walking over to her desk and sitting back on the chair.

A couple of minutes passed and no one said a word. Danny walked over to the window and looked down. "It's still pointing up here" he said quietly. He then walked over to where Alexis was sat. "Are you okay?" He asked. "Yeah, I'm okay, just trying to think of a good plan" she replied. He smiled, "That's my girl" he said, he then stroked the side of her face and kissed her cheek, before walking over to the sofa on the other side of the room.

A couple more minutes passed, and then Alexis jumped out of her seat and ran over to the window. She opened the window and stuck her head out, "WHAT ARE YOU DOING!?" she shouted. Danny ran over to the window and pulled her away, "More like what are *you* doing?!" he asked, concerned. She moved back to the window, "I know what I'm doing" she said. She then stuck her head out of the window again and looked down. The figure was still pointing towards the building. "WHO ARE YOU?" she shouted. The figure then lowered its arm and pointed towards the entrance of the building.

Alexis gulped, "Charlie, when you first saw the figure walking towards the building, how far away was it?" she asked Charlie. "He was quite far away, the other side of the car park I think" Charlie replied. "If whoever it was, was that far away, how did they smash the window?" Alexis asked anxiously. "They couldn't have" Bailey said. Alexis then turned and looked at Bailey and Charlie. "Then how did the window get smashed?" she asked… Bailey's face went pale, and Charlie raised her eyebrows, and then gulped. "There's already someone in the building" Alexis mumbled. She then walked back over to the window and shut it and locked it. "Why are you locking it, it can't exactly climb up the wall and through the window" Charlie replied, looking at everyone for re-assurance. She then snapped her head back at Alexis, "It can't, can it?" she asked. "I'm not sure, but thank you for that terrifying mental image, I'm sure we will all be sleeping great tonight" she replied sarcastically, shuddering, making sure the window was properly locked. She walked back over to her desk and sat back in the chair.

"What are you doing?" Bailey asked. Alexis started typing, "I'm seeing if there is anyone else in the building, making sure that no one is still clocked in. As each person enters and leaves the building, they have to swipe their card which signs them in and out of the building" Alexis said. She continued typing, and then clicked the mouse a few times. "Everyone has signed out" she said. Alexis then leant back in her chair, running her hands through her hair and letting out a sigh. "What do we do now?" Charlie asked. Alexis didn't reply, and the room stayed silent.

After a couple of minutes, Alexis spoke up. "We need to go and see who is in the building" she said, nervously. "Are you mad!?" the girls mum asked. "Yeah, I agree with mum for a change! That is a stupid idea Alexis!" Bailey said. "You asked me what we should do and this is it!" Alexis said, starting to get angry. "But what if, and I mean if, it's one of those zombie things? Do you not remember what happened last time you confronted one of those things!? You ended up getting shot!" Charlie pointed out. "I know, but we need to make sure that we are safe here! That zombie thing I confronted was really smart and that really isn't a good thing! It's only a matter of time before it, or them if there is more than one in the building, figures out a way to get up here!" Alexis shouted. She walked over to the door, "Are any of you coming then?" she asked. Danny stood up and walked over to her, "I'll go with you, I'm not letting you go on your own" he said, grabbing her hand. Alexis turned to the others, "Well!? Anyone else?" she asked. Everyone else stayed silent. Alexis snarled, "FINE!" she shouted. "Bailey, go and look out of the window and see if that thing is still there!" Alexis instructed. Bailey walked over to the window and looked out. "Nope, all clear" she said. "Great! So there are probably two of those things in the building!" Alexis groaned. She turned to Danny, "We need guns!" she said. Danny raised an eyebrow. She ran over to the desk and pulled 2 hand guns out of the drawer. She made sure they were both loaded, before putting the safety latches on. She handed one to

Danny, putting one in her pocket. "Good luck" Bailey said, "Yeah good luck!" followed Charlie quickly. "Whatever" Alexis said, rolling her eyes. "Be careful Al!" Her mum said. "Aye not so fast, we aren't going anywhere yet. Everyone into the conference room!" Alexis instructed. Alexis opened the door and looked in all directions. "ITS CLEAR!" she whispered, she than ran down the corridor and into the conference room, followed by Danny, the girls mum, Bailey then Charlie. Charlie slammed the door behind her. "That was intense!" Bailey said, leaning onto the table to get her breath back. "Lock the door" Alexis said to Charlie. Charlie locked the door. "Okay, follow me" Alexis said, she then walked to the far end of the room to a door that was labelled, "NO ENTRY", she reached into her pocket and pulled out a set of keys, unlocking and opening the door, and everyone walked in. Charlie closed the door behind her. Alexis put the bags on a table, took the keys back out of her pocket and threw them too Charlie, "Lock it" She instructed. Charlie looked at the keys "Which one?" she asked. "The yellow one" Alexis replied. Charlie picked the yellow key and locked the door, she then threw the keys back to Alexis.

"Sit down everyone" Alexis said, and everyone sat around the table. Alexis walked over to a big cupboard and opened it, revealing a large fridge which was full of food. "Who's hungry?" Alexis asked. "ME" everyone shouted. "Mum, come help me get everyone some food?" Alexis asked. Louise stood up and walked over to the fridge. "Wow! It's fuller than our fridge back at home" she joked. She then started to pull things out and carry them over to the counter, making sandwiches.

A while later, Alexis handed everyone a sandwich and walked over to the fridge, pulling out a can of fizzy drink and a bar of chocolate for everyone. "Can't go zombie killing on an empty stomach" she joked. Everyone laughed. She then sat at her seat, followed by Louise and everyone began eating, drinking, and talking.

After everyone had finished, Alexis stood up. "Okay, I've put this off for long enough, who's coming to actually see who's down there?" Alexis asked. Danny instantly stood up and walked over to her, "Me" he said, putting her arm around Alexis. Alexis smiled at him, and then turned to the others, "Anyone else?" she asked.

A couple of minutes passed. Then one at a time, Bailey, Charlie and the girls' mum stood up. "ME" Bailey said, followed by Charlie and Louise. Alexis smiled. "I'll make sure you are protected" Alexis said, she then walked over to the cupboard, which revealed a large steel safe box. She inputted the code, and it beeped. Alexis opened it, revealing a stash of hand guns. She handed everyone a loaded gun. "Put them in your pockets, let's not have any more silly injuries" she chucked.

Alexis opened the cupboard next to it, and grabbed 5 walkie-talkies. She handed everyone a walkie-talkie and a small black ear-piece each, "Put the ear-pieces in, and turn the walkie-talkies on" Everyone followed her instructions. "Okay, now, you hold down the button at the side whilst speaking, and whatever is said will be transmitted into the ear piece. Alexis lifted up her walkie-talkie, and held down the button on the side, and spoke into it. "See, everything that is said, will be transmitted to everyone's ear-piece, is everyone's ear piece working?" Alexis asked. Everyone nodded. "Okay, good" Alexis said. "The walkie-talkie also has coloured buttons on the back, each colour will mean a different thing, blue means 'suspicious', which is pretty self-explanatory, so if you witness something suspicious, press that. Yellow means 'noise', so if you hear an unusual noise, press that. Green means 'Sight', so if you see something that you think is strange, press that, and Red means 'Emergency', so if you have a proper emergency, as in someone's hurt or you're under attack, press that. Got it?" Everyone nodded, Alexis smiled; "Now we're ready to go, remember, only use the gun in emergencies!" Alexis said, everyone nodded. "When we leave the room, me and Danny will go left, and Bailey, Charlie and mum, you go right, follow the corridor right round and we'll meet at the other side of the building, at the door for the stop of the stairs, check every room, and *do not* go downstairs unless we're all there, let's stay together! Everyone clear?" Alexis asked. Everyone nodded again. "Okay, let's do this!" Alexis said. She opened the door and her and Danny went left, and Bailey, Charlie and the girls' mum went right".

Chapter Nine

"I still can't believe all this, you know?", Danny said out of
nowhere. Alexis laughed, "What part can't you believe?" "That
you're a super-agent, you own the whole base. Thinking about it
now, you are responsible for saving so many people's lives,
yet nobody knows that you constantly put your life on the line to
protect the country. No offence, but to others you come across as an
ordinary teenage girl, but you're so much more! You're a hero"
Danny said to her. "Aw, you're so sweet, but I'm not all that, it's all
part of my job" Alexis replied, blushing slightly. Danny stopped
and looked at her, "Alexis, other girls your age are going to parties,
drinking alcohol, taking drugs and getting in trouble... *You* are out
there saving people's lives and handling situations that no teenager
should have to handle. I'm not even joking, you really are something
special, I'm so lucky" He gushed. Alexis hugged him
tightly, "What was that for?" he asked. "For just making me feel a
whole lot better, you're right, it's not easy having this much
responsibility, I'm just so glad you know about everything now, and
that I know I have you to support me through all of this" She said,
smiling. Danny hugged her back, "I will always be here for you" He
replied. As Alexis and Danny continued walked, Alexis' walkie-
talkie beeped, and a red light began flashing. "It's red!" Alexis
grabbed Danny's arm and pulled him into a room, she shut the door
and locked it from the inside. She pulled out her walkie-talkie.
"Guys, can you hear us?" she said into the walkie-talkie, trying to
stay calm. "Yeah, we're in a room safe, but there's 2 of those zombie
things outside" Bailey replied. Alexis froze. Danny pulled out his
walkie-talkie, "Which room are you in? And are they acting
aggressive towards you in anyway?" He asked. There was a short
silence. "Not sure what room we are in, and they're banging on the
door, and they chanting Alexis' name!" Bailey replied. Alexis' eyes
began to water up, "How do they know my name?" She asked
Danny, "I don't know, but we're going to sort this out okay? We
need to go and find your sisters and your mum, you need to stay

calm and we'll talk about this when we're all together again, okay Lex?" Danny asked, Alexis didn't respond. He put his hand on her cheek and looked at her, "Okay?" he asked softly. Alexis nodded, "Okay". She wiped her eyes and picked up her walkie-talkie again. "Look around the room, what do you see?" Alexis asked. There was a short silence, "There's loads of cabinets" Charlie replied. Alexis turned to Danny, "They're in the research room, it's just around the corner, which means we're stuck as well" She said. "We're stuck; we're just around the corner from you, we need to create a diversion" Alexis said into the walkie-talkie.

After a short silence, Bailey replied, "What's the plan?"

"Ask them what they want" Alexis said, "Put the walkie-talkie near the door so I can hear what they are saying" She instructed.

And It began...

Bailey: "Why are you here? What do you want?"
Unknown 1: "Revenge"
"Why do they keep saying that" Alexis mumbled to herself. "Saying what?" Danny asked. "The one outside the shopping centre said he was looking for revenge too, but I don't get why they are coming here for revenge" she replied in confusion.

Charlie: "Revenge for what?"
Bailey: "What have we done to you?"
Unknown 2: "You killed our leader, so we killed your sister for revenge... Then you got us sent to prison, and your people killed our crew, so it's our turn again"
Bailey: "YOU KILLED DAISY?"
Unknown 1: "Yep, and we're back for Alexis, it's her fault all this happened"
Bailey: "WHY IS IT ALEXIS' FAULT?"
Unknown 1: *laughs* "Ask her yourself"

Alexis gulped. "Move away from the door and stop speaking to them" She instructed into the walkie talkie, her voice shaking. She stood up and turned to Danny, "I'm going out there" She said. Alexis pulled off her sling, tried moving her arm, flinching slightly, before trying again. She pulled out her gun, holding it to her side. "No you're not, are you mental?" Danny said, grabbing her wrist. "You're not going out there" He said. "I have too" Alexis replied. "They killed my sister" she said.

Alexis walked over to the door, Danny jumped up and grabbed her, "You're not going out there alone" She moved out of his grip, "You can't come with me, I'm NOT letting you end up the same as Daisy… Danny, you have to let me go and you have to promise you won't follow me, if they see you they will target you to get back at me, and they won't stop until you're dead" Alexis said, a tear running down her face. "What happened Alexis?" He asked her softly. "I can't explain right now, I have to do this, you have to let me" She said, fighting back the tears. He grabbed her and hugged her, "Please, be careful", he whispered. She hugged him back tightly, a tear rolled down her face. "I will, don't worry" she replied. "When I leave the room, lock it behind me and stay in here! Promise me you won't come after me?" She asked. "I promise" he said.

Alexis took a deep breath and put her hand on the lock. She slowly unlocked and opened the door and stepped out into the corridor quietly, and Danny locked the door behind.

Chapter Ten

Alexis crept to the corner of the corridor, peering round. Straight in front of her, she saw the two figures stood leaning against a door. They hadn't noticed her. Alexis raised a gun above her head and pointed it towards the ceiling, she pulled the trigger and a loud shot rang through the air. She then stepped around the corner. The two figures, startled by the loud noise, turned around and looked at Alexis. One of them laughed, "Well well well, look who it is, our little Lexy" he joked, they both laughed. "Well, not so little anymore are you?" he smirked. Alexis stayed completely silent. "Remember us? James and Ray?" One of them said. Alexis smiled, "How could I have forgotten you two idiots, how are you even alive? I was told you were dead" She spat. They laughed, "We wondered when you'd show your face" James said. "Why are you here?" Alexis asked. "Revenge", James replied. "Why do *you* need revenge?" Alexis asked. "Maybe because your little mates killed our crew?" Ray replied sarcastically. "Oh I'm sorry, news flash though, you killed my sister! What, did you expect? For us just to let you get away with that?" Alexis asked them. "Well, news flash" James mimicked. "You shouldn't have killed our leader! We were all working together to solve that case, you had no reason to kill him!" Ray shouted. Alexis snarled, "THAT WASN'T MY FAULT, I DIDN'T SHOOT HIM INTENTIONALLY, YOU GAVE ME A GUN AND TOLD ME TO SHOOT THE GUY WE WERE LOOKING FOR, IT'S NOT MY FAULT THAT YOUR 'LEADER' WANTED TO PLAY HERO AND GOT IN THE WAY, HE WASN'T SUPPOSED TO GET KILLED, I HAD NO REASON TO KILL HIM AND I HAD NOTHING AGAINST HIM, IMAGINE BEING AN 11 YEAR OLD GIRL IN CHARGE OF MISSION THAT BIG, IMAGINE BEING TOLD ALL THOSE STORIES ABOUT THAT GUY, HOW HE TORTURED PEOPLE, AND THEN COMING FACE TO FACE WITH HIM!" Alexis shouted, and then she took a deep breath to try and keep herself calm.

James took a step towards her and Alexis lifted her gun and aimed it in his direction. James stepped back. "I don't care if you killed him by accident or on purpose, the fact of the matter is *you* killed him so *you* must suffer the consequences" James spat. Ray grabbed James' arm, "Don't anger her man, she's got a gun" he said. "THAT DOES NOT MEAN YOU CAN KILL MY SISTER!" Alexis screamed. "We did everything you wanted us to, we got you all the money, we got you transport out of the country, all you had to do was let Daisy go and it was all yours! You wouldn't have got into any trouble with the police and you could've just left, so why kill her?" she shouted, tears rolling down her face. James laughed, "Do you think I care? Whether you got us everything we wanted or not, we were going to kill her anyway" He said. Ray turned to James, "I thought we was going to let her go?" he asked. "Obviously not man, our crew don't work like that, we don't give second chances" James said. Alexis lowered the gun, "So you're telling me, no matter what I did, you were going to kill her anyway?" she asked, beginning to cry. James laughed. "I've spent more than 5 years blaming myself for her death, and you're telling me this now?" She said, beginning to get angry again. "Yep" James smirked. Alexis laughed, "Well you know what boys? Since we're confessing things, I have a confession to make myself", Alexis smiled, leaning back against the wall, crossing her arms. "You know after you got put in prison? Well a lot of things happened. Think back to when you got that phone call off the base, when they told you that the rest of your crew resisted arrest, and attacked those officers, when they pulled guns on us all, so we had to kill them. Do you remember that?" Alexis asked. "Yeah, why does that matter?" he asked. "Well, let's just say, we weren't being completely honest" she smiled. "The day after you got sent down, we called a meeting with the rest of your crew to discuss our next steps, and how we were going to try and re-start the mission to catch the guy. For starters, we managed to catch the guy without your help, and next, little Alexis here was allowed to have a gun with me, coz I was so scared to be around them. The meeting started, and your crew had a lot of interest in what their options were. But all of a sudden, things turned nasty. Somehow, they managed to smuggle knifes into the meeting room, and they started swinging at us all, trying to kill us. One of the officers actually died, and others had fatal injuries but survived. Your little mate stabbed me in the shoulder… I got the okay from the officers, and one by one; I shot each and every one of them"

James and Ray looked astonished. James clenched his fists, "So, *you* killed our crew?" he asked. "Yep" Alexis replied. Alexis smiled at them as James started walking towards her. "Oh, well this changes everything doesn't it! Well love, it appears you missed one of our crew! He created a drug that turns us into beings that are beyond any medical discovery to date, he turned us into zombies! We broke out of prison and now we're back for revenge" He said. Alexis looked confused, "That's impossible, I killed all of your crew, no one that went in that room came back out…" She said. James laughed, "Oh darling, do you really think we'd send the whole crew on that mission? Do you really think we are that stupid" he smirked. "The person who organized it all, that arranged the whole mission, who planned the kidnapping, the person that invented the drug and is now out creating an army of us… The person who is going to make you wish you'd never been born" James spat. "Who did I miss?" Alexis asked. "JOHN" James shouted. Alexis' face went pale, "NO!" she shouted. He nodded, "Oh yes Alexis, your dear friend John set up the whole thing. He wanted to take over the base but he knew you was the one that was in line to take over, so he set up the mission, he brought you and Daisy out with the intention to kill you both, but it backfired and you survived and killed the rest of the crew. Then he was forced to act as if he was on your own side the whole time." James explained. "You're pretty quiet Ray, what've you got to say about all this?" Alexis asked him, "Nothing, I'm staying out of it", he replied. "Wise guy" she replied back. "I need to talk to John" She said, sternly. James laughed. "Not possible" he said. "Why not?" Alexis asked. "He's dead" James laughed. "Okay, that was my fault", Ray said, they both started laughing. "YOU KILLED JOHN?!?!" Alexis shouted. Ray nodded. There was a silence. "So, how was it in prison?" Alexis asked Ray. "It was alright, being in prison with your brother has its advantages, you have a lot of time to plan your revenge" Ray replied, him and James high-fived. "Oh, you two are brothers?" Alexis asked Ray. He nodded. Alexis laughed, "Well, this changes things" She said. "How?" Ray asked. Alexis smiled, she then held the gun out in front of her and then pulled the trigger. A loud shot rang. James fell to the floor. Alexis lowered the gun and stared at Ray, who was knelt down next to James and shook him, "James, get up!" he shouted, shaking him repeatedly. After a couple of minutes, Ray let go of James and stood up, he faced Alexis. "You killed him" he said, quietly. Alexis nodded and smiled. "You'll regret this" he said, then he ran off, Alexis pulled the trigger again but it missed Ray and hit the wall, and he ran around the corner and out of sight.

Chapter Eleven

Alexis stood staring at James' body for a few minutes, before putting the gun back in her pocket. She walked around the corner, over to the door that Danny was in and knocked on the door, "It's Alexis" she said quietly. The door unlocked and he opened it. She walked into the room and stood facing Danny, as he closed and locked the door behind her. She stared at him for a few seconds, before starting to cry. He wrapped his arms around her. They continued to hug for a couple of minutes, before she wiped her eyes and sat down, he sat next to her and put his arm around her. "Are you okay?" Danny asked her. Alexis nodded "Yeah, I'm just a bit shocked" she said quietly. "What was all that about?" He asked, "you don't have to tell me if you don't want to, I know that right now it might be a bit hard" He continued.

"Me and Daisy were twins, it happened when we were 11. We went away training with the base, and it went wrong. We got mixed up with some bad people so we had to go into hiding. But then they found us, and took Daisy as a hostage. We were given 24 hours to get her back, but we weren't fast enough so they killed her." Alexis said, trying to push back the tears. Danny stayed silent, "That's horrible Alexis", he said softly.

There was a short silence, then she continued, "Well, that's what I thought happened, turns out it happened a whole lot more different that we thought. You know those people that were out there? They are James and Ray, they were part of the crew we were working with to try and solve a case as part of our training. They looked after us whilst we were away, they even took us sight-seeing in the spare time we had. At the time, James was 18 and Ray was 20. They were part of a gang, or 'crew' that had information about the where we could find the man we were trying to track down. Do you remember that guy, I think he was called Marcus Jones? It was about 7 years ago, he went on a murder spree, he kept people hostage in a large dis-used warehouse and he kept them all tied up and tortured them, killing them slowly. He got arrested but somehow managed to escape police custody, so there was a worldwide manhunt and at one point, he was the most wanted criminal in the world. We were looking for him, but things went wrong, the leader of the 'crew' that Ray and James were in, got in the way when I was told to shoot the killer. He always wanted the glory of being the one that killed him, he wanted to be the hero. As I went to shoot him, he ran in front of me trying to shoot him first, and I shot him by accident. After that, the James and Ray disappeared, and me, Daisy and John started receiving death threats, so we had to go into hiding. Somehow, they found us, and they kidnapped Daisy, taking her as hostage. At the time though, we didn't know it was them behind it, and we were given 24 hours to get her back, and they demanded $5,000,000 in cash, as well as a helicopter to get them out of the country, and absolutely *no* police. We got the cash from the agent base in that country, and the police got us the helicopter. When we went to hand over the money, they killed her anyway. I never knew why and I always blamed myself. James just told me the story behind it. The reason they killed her is because they were thirsty for revenge for me killing their leader. I didn't even do it on purpose, but James just told me that they intended on killing Daisy anyway. Do you know what that does to a person? I blamed myself for almost 6 years, I had to see doctors and psychiatrists because of the shock and guilt I was experiencing, and it wasn't my fault. I miss her so much and if she was still alive we would've been joint owners of the base. I miss her Danny, I killed him, to get revenge for her. And it gets worse! Apparently, *John* was behind it all! And *he* created the drug/toxin that has been turning people into zombies. When they made enough of it to create their army, Ray killed him. Now, they're coming for me, Ray got away and he's going to go and tell the rest of them, this is all my fault"

Danny hugged her again tightly, "This isn't your fault, we're going to solve this together! I promise okay? You have me and I will protect you", he said softly, kissing her forehead. "Thank you, Danny" she replied.

A couple of minutes passed, and then Alexis pulled out her walkie-talkie. "Mum?" she said into it. There was no reply. "Bailey? Charlie?" she said. A couple of minutes later, Bailey replied, "Yes" she said quietly. "Did you hear all of that?" Alexis asked. "Yeah, we did" Bailey replied. "I'm so sorry" Alexis said, holding back her tears again. "You don't have to be sorry, you did the right thing" Bailey replied.

Danny stood up and held out his hand, "Let's go to your sisters and your mum" he said softly, Alexis reached out and held his hand. She stood up and they walked towards the door, unlocking it then walking out. As they turned corner, they saw that James' body had disappeared. Alexis ran to where his body previously was. There was something written on the floor in blood.

"You're next" it read.

Alexis banged on the door. "Let me in" she shouted. The door opened, and she stormed in. "WHERE HAS JAMES GONE?!" she shouted. Bailey, Charlie and their mum moved from behind the cabinets. "NO I'M NOT HAVING THIS! HE'S GOING TO DIE AND THE REST OF THOSE ZOMBIE IDIOTS ARE GOING WITH HIM" Alexis shouted. She then grabbed her gun and ran out of the room. She ran to the end of the corridor and looked out of the window. She looked down and saw James and Ray stood looking up. They smiled at her and then ran off. Alexis screamed. "THIS IS GOING TO END, NOW!" she shouted as she ran off, "ALEXIS WAIT" Danny shouted, he ran after her and then Bailey, Charlie and the girls' mum went after them. Alexis ran down to the main entrance.

When she got to the main entrance, she paused.

There were 5 zombies stood right in front of her.

"What are you lot? Back up?" she shouted. She pulled out the gun and shot them all repeatedly until all the bullets in the gun ran out, she then threw the gun at the wall, the impact so hard that it made a hole in the wall. She then ran out of the doors of the main entrance and towards her mum's car. She jumped into the car and turned on the ignition. 'Let's see if these driving lessons have paid off' she said to herself. She slammed down on the accelerator and sped towards the exit of the car park, as she got closer, she began to think. She slammed her foot down on the brake, causing the car to skid across the car park.

CRASH!

The car crashed into a gate and Alexis sat frozen in shock. A couple of minutes passed and she just sat staring out of the window, staring at the damage she had caused, feeling completely numb to everything. Then she heard shouting, and she looked in the side mirror to see Danny running towards the car, followed by Bailey and Charlie. Danny pulled open the door and stood staring at Alexis in shock. She held her arms out to him, tears running down her face, and he gently lifted her off the seat and out of the car and held her tight, "Never do that again okay? You had us worried sick! Especially when you crashed! I'm so glad you're okay I am not letting you out of my sight ever again" he said to her, lowering her down onto the floor and wiping her eyes. Bailey and Charlie both hugged Alexis, "Dude, calm it!" Bailey joked, Alexis laughed. "Yeah, that drift was sick, but be careful!" Charlie added. They all stood laughing. Alexis looked around, "Where's mum?" she asked. They all looked around, "she was right behind us, I swear!" Bailey shouted. Alexis' face went pale. "What if they have her?" Alexis said, her voice beginning to shake. "They won't, I bet she's stood in the entrance waiting for us!" Bailey added. Alexis clenched her fists, "DID YOU NOT SEE THE DEAD ZOMBIES LYING ON THE FLOOR IN THE ENTRANCE!?" she shouted. "Yeah, but they're dead, what can they do?" Charlie added. "I THOUGHT JAMES WAS DEAD ASWELL!" Alexis shouted. "Woah, calm down Lex, mum can look after herself!" Bailey said.

Suddenly, gun shots rang through the air. Alexis turned and looked at the building, and then she turned back and looked at Bailey, Charlie and Danny. Alexis then ran towards the building, "GET IN THE CAR, LOCK THE DOORS AND WAIT FOR ME, WE NEED TO GET OUT OF HERE!" Alexis shouted, whilst she was running. Bailey, Charlie and Danny jumped into the car and locked the door from the inside.

When Alexis got to the entrance of the building, she stopped for a minute, taking a deep breath and she walked in. She stared at the floor, at the bodies of the zombies that she had shot earlier on, they were scattered over the lobby, and there was fresh blood. "Mum?" Alexis whispered. Louise jumped up from behind the counter. "ALEXIS!" she shouted. Alexis jumped, "Woah! You scared me! Are you okay?" she asked. Her mum nodded, "Old Louise has still got the magic touch" she said, pointing to the zombies that were lay, dead on the floor. They both laughed. "Why was you hiding behind there if they are dead?" Alexis asked. "I thought I'd go into the back and check out the CCTV, you know, to see how many of those things are in the building" Her mum replied. Alexis smiled, "Good idea! What's the damage?" Alexis asked nervously, walking over to the counter. "7, 2 of them were James and Ray, who left a while ago, and the other 5 are lying over there on the floor, dead" she said.

Alexis' walkie-talkie then started beeping. She pulled it out of her pocket; it was flashing yellow and green. "They've seen and heard something" Alexis explained.

All of a sudden, the walkie-talkie started flashing red. Alexis looked at her mum "EMERGENCY!" she said. They ran over to the door at the entrance and looked out. There was a zombie knelt on top of the car, banging on the roof. Alexis quickly grabbed her walkie-talkie. "BAILEY, QUICK, YOU, CHARLIE AND DANNY START SHOOTING THROUGH THE ROOF OF THE CAR!" Alexis shouted into the walkie-talkie. She heard gun shots, but then a group of people ran into the car park and started attacking the car. "WE NEED TO DO SOMETHING" Alexis shouted to her mum. There was a very short silence. "QUICK, THROW ME THE PURPLE KEY OFF THAT HOOK!" She shouted to her mum. Her mum scurried over to the back of the reception, grabbed the key and threw it too Alexis.

Alexis caught the key and ran to the entrance. "MUM, WITH ME, NOW!" She shouted, her mum jumped over the counter and stood next to Alexis. "Right, when I say go, run out of the doors, to the left to the big metal doors. It's a couple of seconds away, when I get into the building and unlock the van, jump in! But I need you to cover me until I tell you to get in the van" Alexis explained. Her mum nodded.

"Go" she said. They ran out of the door, quickly to the left to the metal doors. Alexis looked at the door, "CRAP! There's a padlock!" she said. A couple of seconds passed. Her eyes then lit up. She pulled a gun out of her mum's pocket and pointed it towards the padlock, "put your hands over your ears!" She said to her mum. Alexis then pulled the trigger and shot the padlock, it shattered into small pieces and fell to the floor. Alexis then lifted the shutters and smiled at the big, shiny black van that was parked in there "Hello my child" she smiled. Her mum turned to her, "Erm Al, not trying to ruin your moment, but there's a group of zombies running towards us!" Alexis turned and saw them running towards her and her mum. She quickly unlocked the van, "Get in" she instructed. She jumped into the driver's seat and her mum jumped into the passenger's seat, she put the key in the ignition and started it up. "Do you even have your license yet?" her mum asked nervously. "Not quite" Alexis replied. Her mum held onto the handle on the roof, "LOCK THE DOORS!" Alexis instructed. Her mum did so. "Okay, let's go!" Alexis said, she slammed her foot onto the pedal and the car went speeding towards the zombies, knocking them all straight over, she then sped towards the car that Bailey, Charlie and Danny were in. She pulled up next to them and lowered the window. "QUICK, GET IN THE BACK!" She shouted to them. They all jumped out of the car and to the back of the van, slamming the door shut behind them. Alexis closed the window and locked the doors. "What took you so long!?" Bailey shouted, nudging Alexis jokingly. Alexis laughed, "What, did you really think I was going to *run* to your rescue? There was zombies surrounding you, we needed protection!" Alexis joked. Everyone laughed.

A couple of minutes passed, and everyone was sat talking. "So, what happens now?" Danny asked. "We need to go put the van back into the garage for now, then we need to go back up to HQ and figure out our next move" Alexis said. "Yes boss" Charlie joked, and everyone laughed.

HOLD ON TIGHT" Alexis shouted, then she slammed her foot down on the accelerator and span the van around, and back towards to building, slowing down as she got closer to the garage. She then slowly drove the van into the garage and turned off the ignition. Alexis and her mum both opened the doors and got out of the van. Her mum went to the back of the van and opened the doors and Bailey jumped out, followed by Charlie, then Danny, closing the door behind them. Alexis locked the van and started pacing around the garage. "What are you looking for?" Bailey asked. Alexis ignored her and continued looking, she looked in all of the cupboards, then started rummaging through the drawers. "AH-HAH!" she shouted, she then pulled out a padlock and key. "Let's go back to HQ" Alexis said, everyone walked out of the garage and stood outside, Alexis being the last one out, she closed the door and then shut the hatch, padlocking it shut, and putting the key in her pocket. They all walked back over to the entrance, went through the secret passages and went up to HQ.

Chapter Twelve

When they got back to HQ, they walked through the main lobby and into Alexis' office. Alexis sat behind her desk, and everyone else sat on the sofa's. She turned on the computer and started typing. "What are you doing now?" Bailey asked. "I need my driver's license so that I can legally drive. The last thing I need during a zombie outbreak is getting arrested for driving without a license" Alexis replied. "I think the police have bigger things to worry about than a secret agent without a driving license" Danny chuckled. "At this point your more help to Lime barn than the police are anyway" Louise pointed out. "That's true, but as an agent I've always been taught to do things by the book, so I'd rather be safe than sorry" Alexis replied. "You've passed your test already haven't you?" she asked Danny. He nodded.

After a couple of minutes typing, Alexis stopped and clicked the mouse a few times, she then knelt down to the printer and opened it up, clicked a few buttons then it started processing. When it had finished, Alexis walked over to the cupboard and pulled out a camera, "Danny, come here and take my picture" she said. He walked over and snapped a photo of her. "Thank you" she said, taking the camera back over to her computer, plugging it in. A couple of moments later, the printer started churning and beeping. She walked over to it, and a card popped out of the site. She wafted it in the air, before looking at it. "Congratulations to me" she smiled. Everyone laughed. She then printed off another card, handing it over to Danny. "Your official secret services member card, welcome to the team" she smiled. Everyone cheered.

She opened a drawer, pulling out another hand gun, loading it up and putting the safety on. "Where's the gun you had before?" Danny asked. "It's sticking out of a wall in the main entrance" Alexis chuckled. He raised an eyebrow. "I got a bit angry so I threw it, don't worry it's not loaded" Alexis smiled. He smiled, shaking his head. "We should probably grab that on the way out" Louise pointed out.

"Right, now to put a plan into place. 1st on the agenda, Danny, we need to make sure your family are protected." She said. Danny smiled, "My mum and my big brother Dylan are at home, my dad and my little sisters Kelly and Katie are in Spain, seeing my granddad" he explained. Alexis nodded. "Okay, we will go and pick up your mum and Dylan, then we'll explain everything to them and we'll go from there" She said. "Okay, 2nd on the agenda, our stuff. John said we're getting all of our new guns delivered to our house today didn't he? Mum, did you sign for the delivery?" She asked. "Yeah, they put them in the cellar" her mum said. Alexis smiled. "Right, here's the plan then. Danny, you take your van and go and pick your mum and brother up, get your passports, get them to get theirs, then you all need to pack up some stuff. Drive back here, and stay in the garage and wait for us. Keep your gun with you for protection. My mum will go with you to make sure you remember everything, and she can try and start explaining things to your mum" Alexis said.

Alexis looked at Bailey and Charlie, "Us 3 will go home and all of ours and mums stuff, then we will get all of our passports, then we will get as many guns as we can, okay?" she instructed, Bailey and Charlie nodded. "Anyone got any questions?" Alexis asked. Danny raised his hand, "Yes, I have a question" he said, Alexis looked at him, "Yeah?" she asked. "What do you mean *my* van?" he asked. Alexis smiled. "Well, the company has 4 vans, one for me, one for Bailey, and one for Charlie, and that leaves us with a spare van, which I am giving to you" Alexis said. Danny's eyes lit up. "Are you being serious?" he asked. "Yeah", Alexis replied. Danny smiled, "That's wicked!" he replied, Alexis smiled back at him. "Okay, lets go" she said. They all left the office and walked down to the main entrance of the building. Alexis ran over to the wall, yanking the gun out, and observing the damage it had caused. "Well damn" she smiled.

They walked out of the building and looked around. Alexis pulled the key out of her pocket and unlocked her garage, she then lifted the shutter up and unlocked the van, "Bailey and Charlie, get in the back" she said to her sisters. They got in the back of the van and shut the door. She turned to Danny and her mum, "You still got your guns?" she asked them. They both nodded. Alexis smiled, "Okay, Danny, we don't know where the keys are for the garages, so you gotta shoot the padlock to open it" Alexis told him. "Okay" he replied. He handed him a key. "That's your van now! 4th garage along, drive safe!" She said to him, he smiled. "Will do, you drive safe too!". He replied. "Me, drive safe? You kidding me?" Alexis joked. They both laughed. "Okay, try and get back here for 8:30, its 6.30 now, when you get back, wait in your van in your garage!" Danny nodded, "yes boss" he joked. Alexis laughed. Danny and the girls' mum walked over to the other garage, and Alexis got in her van and drove home.

Chapter Thirteen

Alexis, Bailey and Charlie's P.O.V

"Alexis..." Bailey said. "Yeah?" Bailey replied. "What actually happened on that mission you and Daisy went on?" Bailey asked. Alexis took a deep breath. "Well, according to James, it was all completely different than I originally thought. When everything went wrong and me, Daisy and John went into hiding, and by the sounds of it, I think John tipped the crew off about our whereabouts, and that's how they found us. At the time, we were told that if we gave them what they wanted, they would let Daisy go, but earlier today, James said that they were intending on killing her anyway, to get revenge for me killing their leader. When they came back and attacked the offices, they came with the intention to target the whole base because as far as they knew, it was the military part of the base that killed the other people in their crew when James and Ray went to jail. But, because I'm a total idiot, I let it slip that it was me who killed the rest of their base, so now, they are after me, which means they could potentially try and get to you two. But I won't let that happen, I'm not letting you two out of my sight, I'm not letting them do to you what they did to Daisy. I will look after you, mum and Danny, they're not going to beat us, we *will* win this" Alexis said.

After a couple of minute's silence, Alexis heard a sniffle, "Are you two okay?" she asked. "Yeah", Bailey replied. "Yeah, we'll be fine", Charlie replied.

A couple more minutes passed, "We're here!" Alexis said, she parked in the driveway and turned off the ignition. They all jumped out of the van, and Alexis walked over to the door of the garage. She typed in the pass code and lifted the garage door, walking inside and grabbed a key off one of the hooks and throwing it to Bailey. "You two go inside and start packing your stuff, I'll be up in a couple of minutes" Alexis instructed. Bailey and Charlie ran over to the door and unlocked it, running inside. Alexis walked back over to the van and parked it in the garage. She then jumped out and closed the garage door, before walking to the back of the van and opening the doors.

She propped open the door in the garage leading to the kitchen. She ran through the kitchen, down the hallway and upstairs into her bedroom, grabbing her suitcase out of her wardrobe and starting packing things. Clothing, shoes, essentials, toiletries, money… She then fastened her suitcase and ran into her mum's room. She grabbed her mum's suitcase off the top of the wardrobe packed the same type of things as she'd packed for herself before shutting it and pulling it into her room. She then ran back into her mum's bedroom and walked over to her bed side drawers, pulled out her mum's purse, and all of their passports. She carried them back into her room and put them in her suitcase.

After a few minutes, Bailey and Charlie walked out of their rooms with their suitcases. "Okay, we're ready" Bailey said. They all took their suitcases downstairs, and through to the garage, putting them in the back of the van. "Okay, we need to get the guns now!" Alexis said. "Be careful, don't drop them or bump them against anything!" she instructed. The girls all walked to the cellar and looked for the boxes, which they found hidden at the back of the cellar. "It's so creepy down here" Bailey said, flicking on the light. They each looked for the boxes with their names on. "Okay, there are 4 boxes each for us 3 and 2 for mum. We need to carry them one by one carefully to the van, but leave 1 of my boxes here, okay?" Alexis instructed, Bailey and Charlie nodded.

Twenty minutes later and the boxes were loaded into the van. "What time is it?" Alexis asked. Bailey looked at her watch "It's 7:45", she replied. "So, we have 15 minutes before we need to set off, we can probably fit an extra bag each into the van, so let's see if we have anything else we want to bring, we have no idea when we will be coming back home" Alexis said. "I'll get a box and get some food as well!" Alexis said. "Food? Now that's more like a job for me, don't you think?" Charlie joked. They all laughed. "True" said Alexis. "Okay, Bailey you go pack an extra bag for Charlie, you know what she likes… I'll sort out mine and mums!" Alexis said. At this point, Charlie was already in the kitchen, rummaging through the fridge and cupboards and putting things into a box. Alexis and Bailey laughed and walked out of the kitchen and up to their rooms.

Alexis got herself: Her phone charger, her scrapbook, her diary, scrapbook, her laptop and charger and a small tatty teddy bear that she got when she was a baby.

Alexis got her mum: Her photo album, her phone charger, her favourite perfume, her net book, her favorite shoes and her slippers.

Bailey got herself: Her phone and charger, her net book and charger, her scrapbook, and her favourite CD.

Bailey got Charlie: Her phone and charger, her laptop and charger, her favourite dress, her slippers and her teddy.

Alexis and Bailey took the bags downstairs and walked into the kitchen. Charlie was sat on the counter eating a sandwich, "Are you being serious?" Alexis asked, trying not to laugh. "Yeah, I made you two one too" Charlie said, she then pointed at two plates with sandwiches on, Alexis and Bailey looked at each other and smiled. They then grabbed their sandwiches and started eating them.

When they had finished eating, Bailey looked at her watch, "Okay, its 8:00 guys! Time to go back to HQ" she said. Alexis and Bailey grabbed the bags and Charlie grabbed the box of food. They put the bags in the back of the van, and then Alexis sat in the driver's seat at the front, and Bailey and Charlie sat in the two passenger seats at the front. Charlie was still holding onto the box. "Why didn't you put the box in the back?" Alexis asked. "So the food doesn't get damaged!" Charlie replied. "Are you serious? What would be more dangerous, the food getting damaged or the guns in the back?" Alexis replied sarcastically. "The food" Charlie replied. Alexis laughed, shaking her head. Bailey jumped back out of the van and opened the garage door. Alexis drove out of the garage and then stopped in the driveway. Bailey then shut the garage door and jumped back in the van and shut the door. "Back to HQ we go!" Alexis said. She then drove back to HQ.

When the girls got back to the shopping centre car park, Bailey jumped out and opened the garage and lifted the shutters. Alexis drove the van in and Bailey walked into the garage after her, shut the garage door and bolted it from the inside, then got back in the van.

Alexis pulled out her walkie-talkie, "Danny, mum, are you back yet?" she asked. There was a short silence, "We're on our way back now" Louise answered. "Now we wait" Alexis said. They sat in the van and talked until Danny, the girls' mum, and Danny's mum and brother arrived back at the centre.

Danny and Louise's P.O.V:

"So, Danny, who are we going to pick up?" Louise asked. "My mum and my big brother. My dad and my little sisters are on holiday in Spain, visiting my grandad" Danny replied. "Ah, I see", Louise replied. There was a short silence. "So, are you glad to be an agent again?" Danny asked Louise, "I'm not sure, being an agent again brings back a lot of memories" Louise replied. "Oh I see, is that a bad thing?" He asked. "Meh" she mumbled, "There's more good than bad". She replied. There was another short silence. "So, what about you, how'd you feel about being an agent?" Louise asked Danny. "Kinda buzzing, kinda worried" he said. "What are you worried about?" She asked him, "I'm just not good with confrontation, and there will be a lot of people relying on me. I don't know how Lex deals with all this pressure, especially with her being head agent" He pointed out. "She's a tough girl, she fights for what she believes in and she always makes sure that the people closest to her are safe. Plus, she has a good way of dealing with things" Louise said, proudly. Danny smiled, "Yeah I know, she really is an amazing girl" He smiled to himself said, he then blushed a little. "You two are so sweet together" Louise replied.

Ten minutes passed, "Here we are!" Danny said. He drove into the driveway, turning off the ignition. "Please will you leave the guns and stuff here, I don't mind if you bring the walkie-talkie, I just don't want to freak my mum out" Danny said. Louise smiled. "Off course" she said. They both placed their guns in the back of the van. Then they got out of the van, and Danny locked it.

"Mum, I'm home!" Danny shouted, as him and Louise walked into the house. His mum walked into the hallway, "Hi love" his mum replied. "Who's your friend?" She continued. "This is Louise, Alexis' mum" He said. His mum smiled, and held her hand out, "Hi, I'm Lisa, nice to meet you" she said, shaking Louise's hand. "Mum, we need to talk to you, it is *really* important" Danny said. His mum walked into the living room, and Danny and Louise sat down on the sofa. "I don't really know where to start, so much has happened over the last couple of days, even I haven't managed to get my head around it properly myself" He started. "I don't like the sound of this, is everything okay love?" his mum replied. "Well I went to see Alexis at the hospital, didn't I?" He asked his mum, "Ah, yes" she replied, she turned to Louise, "How is she?" She asked, "Oh she's fine, you know our Lex, she's a fighter! Thanks for asking" Louise replied, "Good" Lisa replied. Danny cleared his throat, "Well, whilst we were there, Alexis told me a really big secret, and it sort of changed things, and I'm only allowed to tell you because you not knowing could jeopardize your safety" Danny said. "What is it Danny?" His mum asked. "She's a secret agent, she works for the secret services. I know this may sound hard to believe, but I've been to the base, and they offered me a place on the team. Mum, I'm training to be an agent" he explained. "What? Are you being serious?" His mum asked. Danny nodded, "What a job to have, eh?" he smiled. "What happens now?" She asked. "You and Dylan need to come with us back to the base, things have happened and we need to stay safe" He asked. "How do I know this isn't all just a big joke?" She asked. "Mum, please, you and Dylan go and pack a suitcase with some stuff in it, Alexis will explain everything to you when we get there" He said sternly. His mum went pale, "You're being serious, aren't you?" She asked. Danny nodded. "Okay then, I'll go and tell your brother, what do we need to bring?" She asked. "Just some clothes and essentials and everyday things, and a few luxuries if you want, and you need your passport and so does Dylan. We don't know when we will be coming back home" he replied. His mum walked out of the room without saying anything. Danny turned to Louise, "I don't think she believes me" he said. "It'll all become clear when she comes to the base, you go and get your stuff, and I'll wait here, okay? It'll be okay Danny don't worry, Alexis will explain it all to them" She said to him, she then tapped his shoulder. He smiled at her and left the room, and Louise sat on the sofa and waited for them all to come back.

After about 10 minutes, Lisa and Dylan walked into the living room, they both put their bags on the floor. "Dylan, this is Louise, Alexis' mum" Lisa said. Dylan held his hand out, "Hi, I'm Dylan, nice to meet you" He said politely, Louise smiled at him, "Nice to meet you too" she replied. "Your boys are so lovely and polite" Louise said to Lisa. "I can say the same for your girls!" Lisa replied. "We did a good job" Louise winked. Lisa laughed. "So, I heard our little Dan has got himself quite the job?" Dylan said. Louise laughed, "Yeah he has" she said. "Is this for real or is this a joke? Be straight up with me, Danny always pulls this kind of crap, him and Lex are little sods for it", Dylan said to Louise, "I understand why you might think that, but I can assure you, Danny was being 100% serious" She said.

A couple of minutes later, Lisa and Danny walked into the living room. "Okay, you guys ready?" Danny asked. Everyone nodded. "Okay, let's go" He continued. They all picked up their bags and walked out of the front door, Lisa locking it behind them. "Where did this van come from?" Dylan asked. "It's mine" Danny gloated. Dylan high-fived him. "Nice one bro!" He said. Danny unlocked the van and climbed into the back, he pulled and opened the latch on the door which opened to 2 car seats. He put everyone's suitcases in the back, "Dylan and mum, you get in here, Louise in the front with me again", everyone got in their seats and Danny turned the ignition and drove them back to base. Louise's' walkie-talkie beeped. "Danny, Mum, you back yet?" Alexis asked. "We're on our way back" Louise replied.

Chapter Fourteen

"We're here" Danny said to Alexis through the walkie-talkie. "Okay, get all of your bags and come to my garage" She replied. "Okay". Alexis got out of the van and un-bolted the garage door, and Bailey and Charlie got out of the van and shut the doors. Alexis opened the back doors, ready to start unloading it. They waited for everyone else. The garage door opened and Danny, Louise, Lisa and Dylan walked in carrying their bags. "Sup Lexxxxxxxx" Dylan said, Alexis high-fived him, "Sup Dyllllllllllllllll" Alexis replied, mimicking Dylan.

"Bailey please can you turn the light on?" Alexis asked. Bailey walked over to the light switch and turned it on. Alexis walked over to the door at the far end of the garage, She typed the password in the keypad, and a door slid open. "This will take us and all of our stuff up to HQ!" Alexis said. "Mum, you, take Lisa and Dylan up to HQ, we'll start sending the bags up" Alexis instructed. Louise, Lisa and Dylan climbed into the lift and Alexis threw her mum a key. "We'll send the bags up a few at a time, will you just put them to one side, I'll send Danny up when I'm sending up the boxes. If anything asks you for a password, it's my birthday" she instructed. "Okay" Louise said, she then pressed the button and the lift doors closed.

First, they sent up Lisa, Dylan and Danny's suitcases up, a few minutes later, the lift came back down, and then they sent up Bailey, Charlie and Louise's suitcases up. Another couple of minutes passed and the lift came back down. Charlie was still holding the box of food. "CHARLIE, PUT THE FOOD IN THE LIFT!" she shouted at Charlie. Charlie frowned. She put the food in the lift, along with Alexis' suitcase and the girls' smaller bags. When the lift came back down after that, Alexis turned to Danny, "Okay, you go up and take the boxes with the guns up, we'll send up 4 at a time, then the last couple, carefully put them out of the way until we come back up, so we can explain things before we start whipping out machine guns" Alexis joked. "You have machine guns? That's so cool" Danny said. Alexis winked, "Head agent perks" she joked. Danny got in the lift, "Send up the first few boxes with me?" Danny suggested. "Good idea!" Alexis replied. She handed him 2 boxes, then he went up in the lift, and a couple of minutes later the lift came back down, then they put in 4 boxes and sent them back up, then they repeated this process two more times. When all the boxes had gone up and the lift came back down, Bailey and Charlie got in and went up. A couple of minutes later, the lift came back down for the last time, Alexis made sure that the garage was bolted shut, then she jumped into the lift and went up to HQ.

"Okay, leave the stuff here and come with me!" Alexis instructed, she left the room and everyone followed, she took them to the conference room and they all sat down around the meeting table.

"Now I will explain to Lisa and Dylan what's going on" Alexis said. She took a deep breath and then began explaining things.

"Okay, so I run this secret services base, this is the Limebarn Division. This is all new to me, I was just an agent until a few hours ago when our other head agent went rogue. It all started when I was younger, I was in school and me and my twin sister were called out of our lesson. We were told that my uncle had come to see us, and he told us that he was an agent and that he needed us to 'join the base'. We were confused and excited 10-year-old girls at the time, so we thought that becoming a secret agent was cool, so we agreed. We were signed out of school and taken home. Our mum explained to us how she used to be an agent and how it runs in the family, and that we had a choice, nothing was set in stone. We agreed, and the next day, my mum got a phone call saying that had to go to a meeting here at the base. We were picked up from our house and they brought us here. At the meeting, the co-owner of the base, John, told us we had an opportunity to train at a secret location in France, just after our 11th birthdays. We signed our contracts, and we were programmed onto the mission. When got there, we were introduced to a 'crew' that had claimed they had information on the whereabouts of someone we were looking for, a man who went on a killing spree, resulting in the death of 15 people. We trained alongside the crew, and on the side, me and Daisy secretly did a fire-arm training program to get us our gun license. One day, whilst we were there, we came received an anonymous tip-off on the killer's location, and we tracked him down. When we got there, we found him hiding in an abandoned warehouse and I was instructed by John to shoot him. The leader of the 'crew' we were working alongside thought otherwise. He wanted to take the glory. He wanted to kill the guy and be the hero. When I was about to shoot him, he got in the way and I accidently shot him. The killer and his gang escaped, and to make things worse, the crew we were working with then swore revenge on the base I worked for, so me, Daisy and John had to go into hiding. Somehow, the crew found out where we were hiding, and they kidnapped Daisy. They gave us 24 hours to get them what they wanted, otherwise they said they'd kill Daisy. The police stepped in, and assisted to help us get the ransom requirements. When we went to hand it over, we couldn't get into the building, so we had to break in. We didn't get there in time and they told us that they had killed her and we were never going to see her again" Alexis sniffled, as she began to cry. Danny held her hand, "Are you okay?" he asked her. She nodded and wiped her eyes. She took a deep breath and carried on. "The 2 main people left in the crew, James and Ray, went to jail for murder, and my base held a meeting with the rest of the crew to explain their options. This was a trick to get them all there so we could kill them, and it was me who killed them. Harsh as it may sound, they were involved in my sister's murder and they were also connected to a lot of other crimes that had happened previously. So I was actually doing everyone a favour. Also, the fact that they wouldn't tell us where they hid her body, meant we couldn't give her a proper send off, which as you can imagine, added to my anger. After that, I had to go back home and break the news to my mum and my little sisters. I can still remember the look on my mums face when she realized she waved off her twins and only one came back. After that, I continued training, and I trained hard. I was homeschooled by the base, and I did 2 days a week of school, and 4 days a week training. When I was 13, I went to a meeting to discuss my future at the base, and whilst I was there, I got told that I was being awarded a higher rank. Everyone in the room was shocked and I didn't understand why. Turns out, I was the first person in the history of the base that had been awarded the rank of "Super Agent", at that point, across the world there were only 3 Super agents, and I was one of them. I was shocked and then I was told that this means that when I am 18, I run the whole base. After that, I helped John, who was the co-owner of the base, to train Charlie and Bailey and then I awarded them with the "Super Agent" rank aswell. We were nicknamed the ABC Triple Threat. Now, onto more recent events. A couple of days ago, we were called into an emergency meeting, and we were assigned to a new mission. John claimed that zombie sightings were on the increase, and we obviously didn't believe him. Unluckily for me, soon after, I ended up coming head-to-head with one of them, and like an idiot, I ended up shooting myself as well as the zombie. That's why I was in hospital. After that, I brought Danny here and started his agent training too so he could join the base. The shopping centre was attacked by a few of them, and John retired. After this, I ended up in confrontation with James and Ray again, who have become 'zombies', and I was told a lot. It turns out, John was behind the whole thing. We don't know how true it is, but considering he went missing just as things turned nasty… We are in two minds whether to believe them or not. Obviously, we're all still in shock, but there are bigger things to worry about, as more and more zombies are being spotted, and we're worried that they are going to start attacking people in the community. We wanted to make sure that you, Lisa and Dylan are going to be protected properly, so we brought you here" Alexis took a deep breath and there was a short silence.

"I'm so sorry to hear that about your twin love, that must have been awful" Lisa said. "Thank you" Alexis replied. "You weren't joking when you said she was one of a kind, was you Danny?" she teased. Danny blushed. "What about my husband and daughters?" Lisa asked. "I contacted the Spanish base earlier, they have agreed that your family can stay at the base until things are back to normal, that is off course unless they wish to come back to Limebarn, which we can arrange. If your husband agrees, him and your daughters will be protected there. As far as we know, the outbreak is only in Limebarn, but considering this seems to be also be a personal attack, I have no idea how much they know about me, but if they aware of my relationship with Danny, I can't be 100% sure that they won't try and attack your family, I'm sorry to say. The base will pay for anything they need whilst they are there. Your other option is, we can arrange for you and Dylan to be transported to Spain to join your husband and daughters, and we will also accommodate for anything you need whilst you're there" Alexis explained. "You'd do all of that for us?" Lisa asked in shock. Alexis nodded, "You mean a lot to Danny and Danny means a lot to me, so we will do whatever it takes to keep you protected" Alexis smiled. "I'd rather stay here, as long as you can promise me that my husband and girls will be looked after whilst they are in Spain? And that me, Dylan and Danny will be looked after here?" Lisa said, Alexis smiled, "Of course, come to my office and you can speak to your husband in private" Alexis said, she stood up, and Lisa followed her out of the room.

A couple of minutes later, Alexis walked back into the room and shut the door; she walked over to her seat and sat down. No one spoke until Lisa walked back into the room.

A few minutes passed then Lisa walked back in, "He'd rather we went to Spain, I've convinced him to let Danny to stay here because of the circumstances, but Dylan, he would rather you join us" Lisa said. "I can't leave Danny here on his own with all these girls? Anyway, I'm 19, so I can legally do what I want" Dylan said. Lisa give him a stern look, "Alexis has enough to deal with, without you adding to it all" she said. Dylan looked at Alexis, "Can I stay?" Alexis looked at Danny, "It's fine with me if it's fine with you?" She said. Everyone looked at Danny. "Fine" Danny said. Dylan then jumped up out of his seat and ran over to Danny, he hugged him, and Danny moved away. "Thank you!!!" Dylan shouted. "It's ok bro" Danny replied. Dylan walked back over to his seat and sat back down.

Everybody sat and had a chat for a while, then Alexis spoke up, "Okay, everyone come into my office and we'll sort out Lisa's flight to Spain, and we'll talk about what to do next" Alexis instructed, she stood up and walked out of the conference room, but then she stopped. "Guy's wait, something doesn't feel right" She said. "I'm going to go and make sure this floor is secure, everyone STAY HERE" Alexis said quietly, everyone walked over to the other side of the room, "Charlie, when I leave the room, close and lock it behind me, and keep an eye out of the window in the door and if you see me running towards the door, unlock it, okay?" She instructed Charlie, "Okay" Charlie said, nodding. "Don't you think one of us should go with you? You can't fight them off on your own" Dylan said. Alexis pulled out a gun, then she laughed, "It's okay, I've got this" She joked. Dylan stared at the gun in amazement, "Is that real?" He asked. "Yeah obviously, I can't kill zombies with a fake gun can I?" She asked sarcastically. Dylan laughed. Alexis opened the door and walked out, she walked down the corridor, then she heard a noise. She carried on walking, and walked into her office, shut the door and locked it behind her. She sat behind her desk and started typing on the computer. After a couple of minutes, she picked up the phone next to her computer and started dialing. "Hey Pete, it's Alexis from base 1, I need a helicopter to come here as soon as possible to take someone to Spain, base 6, can you do that?" She asked into the phone. "Yeah, there's a helicopter out now, I'll radio them now and ask them, hold on a minute I'll get an ETA for you" He replied. There was a beep. A couple of minutes passed and Pete spoke into the phone again, "Okay Alexis, he is on his way now, get them onto the roof in 10 minutes and Rob will pick them up, you need anything else?" He asked. "Nice one Pete! And no, that's it, speak to you soon!" she replied. Pete laughed, "Speak to you soon kid!" He replied. Alexis then put the phone down. She stood up and walked to the door, unlocking the door and taking a step out. She made sure it was clear, then she shut and locked the door behind her, and ran down to the end of the corridor. She went into the room with all their stuff in, and she picked up Lisa's suitcase. She walked back out of the room and began to walk back to the conference room. She heard the noise again. She began to run and just as she was near the door, she heard whispering.

"Alexis, Alexis" it said.

She ran into the room and locked the door behind her. She handed Lisa her suitcase, "A helicopter is going to be on the roof in 10 minutes to take you to the base in Spain, where your husband and daughters will be safely waiting for you. We will stay in contact with the base in Spain to keep you updated, and so Danny and Dylan can contact you" Alexis said to Lisa. Lisa hugged her. "Thank you so much Alexis" She said. "It's okay" Alexis replied. Lisa sat back down. Everyone began chatting again.

Five minutes passed. "Okay, we need to get Lisa to the roof now, it will be here in 5 minutes, Danny you come with me" Alexis instructed, Dylan got up and hugged his mum, "Stay safe love" She said to him, "I will, you too mum. Love you" He replied. "Love you too love". Lisa then picked up her suitcase, "Okay, I'm ready" She said. Alexis and Danny stood up and walked to the other side of the room, Alexis unlocked the door and stepped out, she checked it again to make sure it was clear, "Okay, all clear" she said. Alexis and Danny stepped out and Lisa followed them, they walked up to Alexis' office and Alexis unlocked it.

"Alexis, Alexis" she heard again.

She quickly opened her office door and rushed Danny and Lisa inside, she then shut the door behind her and locked it. "Did you two hear that?" Alexis asked. Danny nodded, "Yeah, someone was saying your name" he replied. Alexis ran over to the filing cabinet, she opened it up and pulled out a box. She then carried the box over to the door for the back room of the office, they walked into the room and then locked the door behind them. Alexis walked to the far end of the room and press the keypad next to a big lift door. The lift opened and they stepped in. She chose the roof level, and the lift began to move. In a couple of minutes, it opened into a small room. Alexis turned to Lisa and handed her the box. She opened the box, revealing a wad of bank notes. "When you get to the base in Spain, ask for Rick and give him that money, he will then exchange it for Euros. That'll keep you going for at least 2 weeks. If it runs out, Rick will give you extra, but try to only use it for things you need, okay?" Alexis explained to Lisa. "Thanks again love, I appreciate this, you're a great girl" She said to Alexis, Alexis hugged her. "Stay safe in Spain, I'll see you when all of this is over, say Hi to your husband, and Kelly and Katie for me, and tell the people at the base I said hey too" She said. Danny then hugged his mum, "I'm proud of you Danny" she whispered to him, "Love you mum" he replied. "Love you too" she said.

Alexis' walkie-talkie then beeped, she pulled it out of her pocket. "We're here" Rob said. "Okay" Alexis replied. They then heard the helicopter landing. Alexis opened the door and her, Lisa and Danny walked out. When they got to the helicopter, The pilot helped Lisa to get in, and got her suitcase for her, he kitted her up with goggles and headphones. "Right, let's go!" he shouted to the other pilot. Lisa waved at them, "Stay safe!" she shouted to Alexis and Danny, they waved back and smiled at her, the door then closed. Alexis and Danny stepped back and the helicopter began to lift off. They waved to Lisa, and when she was out of sight, they turned and walked back to the little room. They climbed into the lift and went back down to the office. As she walked in, her computer was beeping. She walked over to the computer and looked at the screen.

"AND THE FUN BEGINS"

Alexis looked at the sender. She gulped. "It say's it is off John" She said to Danny. "But I thought John was dead?" Danny asked her, "So did I, I also thought James was dead, and those zombies in the entrance, but they weren't, the ones in the lobby didn't die until my mum shot them directly between the eyes" Alexis said. "So that's probably how they die" she continued.

She stood up and ran to the door, she unlocked the door and pulled it opened, "COME ON THEN, COME AND GET ME" she shouted, as she stepped out into the hallway. She started walking towards the room in that she found James and Danny followed her. Just as she turned the corner, she saw someone. They were stood facing the floor. Alexis lifted her gun and faced it towards them, she was about to pull the trigger when the person looked up. It was John. "Surprise" He said. He then laughed. "Oh, look who it is, the traitor" She said. John laughed. "So, you like my new look?" He asked, he smiled revealing his razor-sharp teeth. Alexis smiled, "Lovely" She replied sarcastically. "I thought you was dead?" She asked him. "Well, technically speaking, being a zombie, I am dead" John replied sarcastically. "So, what, you're back for revenge too?" Alexis replied. John nodded, "This base should be mine" John said, sternly. "Oh boo-hoo, you're jealous because I'm a better agent than you?" Alexis said sarcastically. John took a step towards her, Alexis pulled another gun out of her pocket and held both guns in front of her, pointing them at John. "You wouldn't shoot me" he spat. Alexis smiled, "There's a lot you don't know about me" she replied. John looked at Danny and smiled at him.

"James and Ray were glad to know about your little boyfriend here, he might come in handy" John said. Alexis smiled, "That's not likely to happen" she smiled. He then laughed, "You really are stupid, aren't you?" he asked her. She laughed back. "Nope, I am far from stupid" She replied. She then lowered the guns and shot both of John's knees, and he fell to the floor. "It's that the best you can do?" John asked. "Still no" she replied. She turned to Danny, "*This* is how you do it" she said. Danny looked confused, Alexis then walked over to John and pointed the gun at him, "Say night night" she smiled. She pointed the gun between his eyes and released the trigger. John fell back. Alexis store and stared at his body. "He was like a father to me" she sighed. "I'm so sorry he did this to you" he said, wrapping his arm around her shoulders. "When we got back from France, after Daisy's so-called 'funeral' he put me through intensive fire-arm training. He taught me how to take a shot and never miss", She said, furrowing her eyebrows. "He told me that now I never miss, I'd never loose" she sighed. "He was right about that" Danny replied. "What?" Alexis asked in confusion. "You'll never lose, he kind of did you a favour. Now you're an amazing agent and you are going to beat every situation you come face-to-face with" he said softly. She looked at Danny, "Thank you" she smiled, gently kissing him the lips. "1 down, god knows how many to go!" she joked. "How do we know he's dead?" Danny asked, looking down at John, lying on the floor. "Yeah, you have a point, Alexis walked over to his body, and shot him between the eyes. "There we go" she smiled. "You little psycho, have you no remorse?" Danny joked. "Nope, I'm all out" she winked. "That was for Daisy" she said to herself quietly. "She would be so proud of you babe" Danny smiled, kissing her cheek. They then walked back to the conference room.

Chapter Fifteen

"Okay, your mum is on her way to Spain" Alexis said to Dylan, "Sweet" he replied. Alexis laughed. "Why did we hear gun shots?" Bailey said to Alexis. "We bumped into John" Alexis said, rolling her eyes. "What? I thought you said he was dead?" Charlie replied. "Well, he is now" Alexis said, Charlie and Bailey raised their eyebrows. "What did you do that for?" Charlie gasped. "He was a zombie, he was running his mouth. Apparently, he did all of this because he thought the base should've been his" she spat. "Oh right" Bailey said. Alexis laughed. "We have a problem though" Alexis said. "What?" Charlie asked. Alexis sighed. "James and Ray know about Danny" she said. Everyone stayed silent. Dylan walked over and put his arm around Danny, "I'll look after you little bro" He said. Danny laughed. "More like I'll be the one looking after you" He joked. They started play fighting and Alexis, Bailey, Charlie and Louise laughed.

Bailey turned to Alexis, "Alexis, they know where we are, there's only a matter of time until they start sending those zombie things to get us, what do we do now?" she asked. Alexis shrugged. "John knows this place better than I do" she said, there was a silence but then she smiled. "But John is dead" she said. Bailey smiled, "Have we ever been on any higher floor than this?" she asked. "The studio is on the floor above us, but if you look at the building from the outside, there are floors higher up than this" Alexis pointed out. Charlie interrupted. "But didn't John say that they were under construction?" she pointed out. "He did indeed!" Alexis said. "John also said that everything we need is on his computer" She said. Alexis, Bailey and Charlie smiled.

They all left the conference room and Alexis locked it behind them. "Where now?" Bailey said. "Let's get our stuff and take it to my office" Alexis said. They all walked down the corridor to the room where all of their stuff was, grabbed their suitcases and took them too Alexis' office. "Mum and Dylan, stay in my office, we'll go and start getting the guns" Alexis instructed. They walked back to the room.

"Alexis, Alexis"... the whispering started again, they all stopped. "We're probably just hearing things" Bailey said, they carried on walking down to get the guns, they then grabbed a box each and took it back to the room, they then went back and got another box each, then when they went back to get the next boxes, they heard it again...

"Alexis, Alexis..." it said.

"Let's hurry and get the rest of the boxes" Alexis said in panic, they ran to the room and grabbed a box each. They ran, but when they got back, there was no one there. Just then, all of their walkie-talkies started beeping. They all pulled them out and they were all flashing red. "MUM WHERE ARE YOU" Alexis shouted. There was no answer. "MUM!!!!" Bailey shouted into hers. There was still no answer. They started searching around the room, but they couldn't find them anywhere. Everyone started to panic.

Alexis ran over to the computer, she unplugged the hard-drive. "What's that?" Bailey asked. "Everything that's on the computer was on this, so I can just plug it into any computer or laptop and all the data off Johns computer will be on there" she explained.
When they'd all left the office, Alexis locked the door behind her. They started walking down the corridor, when they heard the whispering again...

"Alexis, Alexis..."

Everyone stayed silent. Then they got to a 4-point turn. Alexis pulled out a gun and shot in all
directions.

Just then, they heard a bang. All their walkie-talkies started beeping again. Alexis pulled hers out, it was flashing red again. "Mum?" Alexis said into hers. There was a short silence, "No, it's Dylan"

Dylan replied. Bailey and Charlie looked at Alexis in panic, "Don't worry, we'll find them" Alexis said softly. Danny pulled out his walkie-talkie, "Bro, where are you?" he asked. "I don't know man, I'm in some room" he said. "Ask him what he can see" Alexis said. "What can you see?" Danny asked Dylan. "There's a load of cabinets, and they're guarding the door" Dylan said. "HE'S IN THE RESEARCH ROOM" Bailey said, "We were in there before!" Danny was about to start running. "WAIT!" Alexis said to him, he stopped. Danny looked at Alexis, panic in his eyes, "I have to find him" he replied. Alexis took Danny's walkie-talkie. "Where'd you get the walkie-talkie from?" Alexis asked. There was no reply. Just then, Baileys walkie-talkie started beeping, she pulled it out of her pocket. "Mum?" Bailey said. "I'm in your office Bailey!" Louise shouted quickly. Bailey and Charlie ran to Baileys office, and Danny turned and ran to the research room. "Lock the door" Alexis shouted to Bailey and Charlie, as they ran into Baileys office, closing the door behind them. Alexis ran after Danny, grabbing him before he turned the corner. She pulled her gun out, stepped out onto the next corridor. "All clear" she said in confusion. They ran down to the research room, "DYLAN?!" Danny shouted. There was no reply. He turned to Alexis, "Where is he?" he asked her. They started walking around the research room, then Alexis froze. "Danny" she said. Danny turned to her, "Yeah?" he said. She pointed at the side of the filing cabinet, "Aren't they Dylan's shoes?" she asked him, and she pointed down at the shoes. Danny froze. Alexis walked over to the shoes and looked down the back of the cabinets. There was a zombie lay there, blood all over the walls and the back of the cabinets. "Looks like he fought the zombie off the old-fashioned way" Alexis joked. Danny walked over and looked down and saw the dead zombie. "Wow" he said.

"DANNY!!!!"

"That's Dylan!" Danny shouted, Alexis ran out of the room, and Danny followed her. They turned and looked down the corridor and froze. They saw Dylan, and there was a zombie held onto him. "LET GO OF MY BROTHER!" Danny shouted. Just then, Alexis saw another zombie walk around the corner, "James, let Dylan go, it's me you want!" Alexis shouted. Danny grabbed Alexis' wrist and looked at her. "Don't let him hurt Dylan" he pleaded to her. "Don't worry, look to your right" she whispered. He looked down the corridor and saw Louise stood outside Alexis' office. Danny turned to Dylan, "You're going to be okay Dylan" he said re-assuringly. Dylan nodded. Danny started trying to distract the zombies. Alexis slowly put her hand in her pocket and grabbed the key for her office. She got it in her hand and threw it in her mum's direction. Then, she shot the wall, at the end of the corridor. "What are you doing?" One of them asked her. "Thought I saw one of your little friends" Alexis said, she then laughed. Danny watched Alexis' mum come out of the office, she was holding a large gun. She then locked the office and put the key in her pocket. Then she turned around and walked down the corridor so that she could walk round to sneak up behind them. Danny looked down at Alexis and smiled at her, she smiled back.

"So, you going to let him go, or am I going have to kill you?" Alexis asked sarcastically. He laughed. "Move a muscle, and I'll turn your little friend here into one of us" he spat. Alexis and Danny saw Louise. "Game over" Alexis smiled. "Now" Danny said. Then Louise shot the back of James' knee, and he fell to the floor. "DYLAN RUN!" Alexis shouted. Dylan ran towards Alexis and Danny, and James jumped up, disappearing again around the corner. "What about John? His body is still here?" Danny asked Alexis. Alexis rolled up her sleeves, walking over to John's body. She dragged him over to the window, opening it. "Can you give me a hand?" she asked. Danny ran over, and they lifted the body, throwing it out of the window. Just then, they saw James run out of the building. "You can have your mate back" Alexis shouted, before laughing and closing and locking the window again. She then walked over to the door that leaded to the staircase. She pressed the button next to the door, and a metal shutter began to lower on both sides of the door. "This shutter is bullet proof, bomb proof, and as a special feature, zombie proof" she joked.

They all walked down to Baileys office, and when they walked in, Bailey and Charlie weren't there. "Oh not this again" Alexis said. Then Bailey and Charlie jumped out from behind Baileys desk, "BOO!!!!" they shouted. Alexis, Danny, Dylan and Louise all jumped, then everyone started laughing. "Back to my office" Alexis instructed.

When they got to Alexis' office, Alexis walked over to her computer and opened the screen, plugging in John's hard-drive. She then walked over to all the boxes and opened the box with all the food in. "Tuck in everyone!" she said, grabbing a bar of chocolate. Charlie ran over to the box, followed by the others, and everyone grabbed themselves a snack.

"According to John's records, there is absolutely nothing on the higher floors, it's just empty space" Alexis said. "It can't just be empty space, John's been saying that it has been under construction for like 2 years" Bailey said. Alexis shrugged. "I don't know, I don't even know how we'd get up there, there's no stairs or anything leading upstairs" Alexis said. Everything remained quiet for a while. "So, what do we do now?" Bailey asked. Alexis turned and looked at Bailey, "We need to shut the gates to the car park to try and stop anyone getting in, and then we need to secure the building" she said. "So, we have to go back out there?" Bailey replied. Alexis nodded. There was a silence. "B-b-but... I'm scared" Bailey mumbled. "So am I" Charlie said. Alexis walked over to her sisters, "I'm not going to make you two come with me if you're not up to it" Alexis said. "But we're letting you down" Charlie mumbled, "We're a team" she continued. "I'd rather you two stayed here anyway, I'm not risking the same thing happening to you two as it did to Daisy" Alexis said. "Alexis... Don't" Bailey said. "Don't what?" Alexis asked. "You need to stop blaming yourself for Daisy's death, it wasn't your fault" Charlie said. "To be honest, I'd rather you all stay up here, I don't want to risk anything happening to any of you" she said. Alexis stood up and walked to the door, followed by Danny. "Not a chance, I'm going with you" he said. "But Danny…" she started. "But nothing" he said. She smiled. "And if Danny goes, so do I" Dylan said, standing up. "I'd rather stay here too love, if that's okay" Louise said. Alexis nodded. "Wait" Alexis said, she turned and faced the others. "Dyl" she continued. "Sup Lex?" Dylan replied. "You need a weapon" Alexis said, she walked over to her desk. She walked over to Louise and whispered in her ear. "Are you sure?" Louise said. "Yeah" Alexis replied. "Okay" Louise replied. Alexis turned to Dylan and Danny, "wait here, I'll be right back" Alexis said. She walked over to the door, and opened it, she looked left and right and ran down to the conference room. She went inside, she grabbed 3 hand guns, loading them up. She put one in each of her pockets, and held one in her hand. She then ran back to her office, closing the door behind her. She walked over to Dylan, handing him a gun. "I shouldn't be doing this, 'coz you are not licensed, but... yeah" Alexis said. Dylan smiled, "You being serious?" Dylan said. "I am giving you this for emergencies only! I don't want you using it unless it's an emergency. Same goes for all of you, even though the rest of us are licensed, I'd rather the guns were only used as a last resort. Obviously if you come face to face with a zombie, you need to use it but if you can avoid being seen by one, please do, we can't be making any more enemies and these zombies seem to already have some serious beef with me" Alexis said. Dylan nodded, "You can trust me, don't worry!" he said, attempting to re-assure her. "Okay" Alexis said. "Put it in your pocket" she said. He put the gun in his pocket. She turned to Danny, "You ready?" She asked him, Danny smiled, "Off course I am". Alexis walked over to the door and stood next to Danny, "Come on then Dyl" she said, he walked over to the door. Alexis looked at her sisters. "If anything happens, beep me, and if you move, let me know, keep your walkie-talkies on, and keep me updated!" Alexis said. "Oh, and make sure you have a gun with you at all time!" Alexis instructed. "Be careful Lex" Bailey said. Alexis smiled, "Aren't I always?" she replied. "No, seriously, be careful!" Bailey said. Alexis walked over to her sisters and they both stood up, and then Louise walked over to them and they all had a big, group hug. "I love you all" Alexis whispered. Danny and Dylan ran over to them, joining in the hug. Everyone laughed. Alexis, Danny and Dylan then walked back over to the door. Alexis opened it and stepped out, looking around. "All clear" she said. She looked back and smiled at her sisters and mum, then she stepped out and Danny and Dylan followed her, they began to walk down the corridor, and Bailey walked over to the door, locking it behind them.

"Alexis, Alexis..."

Chapter Sixteen

Alexis stopped and put her hands to the side, stopping Danny and Dylan from walking, she paused and there was complete silence for a couple of seconds. "What's wrong?" Danny asked. Alexis turned to him, "Did you hear that?" she asked. Danny looked at Dylan, then looked back at Alexis, "Did I hear what?" Danny asked. "Someone said my name again" she said quietly. Danny held onto her hand. "No one said your name, you're just tired babe, I heard it earlier today but it was probably just Bailey or Charlie trying to scare you... we need to keep going" she said. She sighed, "Ok" she said. She started walking again, Danny to the side of her and Dylan trailing behind.

"Daisy, Daisy..." she heard.

Alexis grabbed her guns out of her pocket and swung both arms in front of her. She looked around and then stood facing forwards, in complete silence. Danny looked at her, "Alexis, look at me" he said. She ignored him and didn't more or speak. "Alexis, babe, look at me" he said. She turned her head so she was facing him. "Yeah?" she replied quietly. "What's wrong?" He asked. She stayed quiet for a few seconds. "Can't you hear it?" she whispered, desperation in her voice. He looked at her sorrowfully, "Hear what?" he asked. "The whispering" she replied. He shook his head. She closed her eyes tightly, before opening them and looking at him again, "Why can't you hear it?" she whispered. "I don't know" he replied, feeling like he was letting her down. She lowered her arms and held the guns to her side; she turned to Danny, staring down at the floor. Danny put his finger under her chin and lifted it. "What's wrong babe?" he asked. A tear rolled down her cheek "I can hear people whispering mine and Daisy's name" she said.

His eyes widened as he pushed his fingers through his hair.

"Danny, Danny..."

Alexis quickly turned and faced towards the bottom of the corridor, the anger building up inside her. "WHO THE HELL IS THERE!?" she shouted. Danny and Dylan looked at her in shock. She then began running down the corridor, and down to the main entrance. She stopped and looked around. Just as she was about to run out of the doors to the car park, Danny grabbed her hand pulled her back, she snapped her head to look at him. Just then, a shot was fired. Alexis turned to the entrance and saw a zombie stood in the doorway, as it started bleeding from the chest. The blood was a dark red; almost black liquid, and it started melting the t-shirt. She lifted both of her guns, pulling the triggers, both hitting the zombie between the eyes. "Bullseye!" Dylan shouted. She snapped her head to him. "Sorry" he said. It was all silent, then Alexis turned towards the entrance, and took a step. Danny stood in front of her, "No" he said. "What do you mean, 'no'?" she asked. "You're going nowhere" he said. She raised her eyebrows, "And since when did I take orders from you?" she snapped, before she pushed past him and started walking towards the entrance. Danny reached out to grab her wrist but she pushed his hand away. "Go back to HQ" she said to them, still walking. Danny started walking towards her "I don't think s-", "Go back to HQ NOW" she shouted. Danny stopped. He turned to Dylan, "Come on bro" he said, walking back into the store cupboard. Dylan, deciding not to question, followed him.

Alexis walked out of the entrance, towards her garage. She got to the garage door, before pulling the keys out of her pocket. She unlocked the garage door and walked into the garage, turning the light on and grabbing a chain and a padlock off the worktop. She then unlocked her van, jumped and started the ignition. She drove out and towards the gates of the car park, before jumping out and walking to the gate. She looked out of the gates and saw a big group of zombies huddled up, towering over a body. She quickly grabbed the gate, closing it as quietly as she could.

CLING!!!

She lost grip of the padlocks, and they crashed to the ground. "Crap" she whispered, looking back up. The group of zombies were now stood staring at her. She quickly wrapped the chains around the gate, clamping them together with the padlock. She then looked up, to see that the zombies were now running towards the gate. She quickly ran back over to her van and jumped in, driving full speed to the entrance of the building, she swerved when she got to the doors, almost crashing into the wall. She jumped out of her van and quickly shut it, locking it and running into the entrance. She closed the doors behind her, before activating the shutters. They began to shut, and she turned to see Danny leant against the wall. "I thought I told you to go back to HQ" she said sternly, walking towards him. "Yeah, you did, but I had to make sure you was okay" he said. "I'm more than capable of looking after myself Danny" she said. She began to walk past him, before he grabbed onto her wrist and pulled her back so she was facing him. "What are you doing?" Alexis asked. "What's wrong with you, why are you being like this, I know you're scared, and so am I, but-""WOAH!" Alexis shouted, "Let me stop you right there. I'm not scared, I've just got a lot on my mind, and you asking these stupid questions isn't helping" She said, she then turned and began to walk down the corridor. Danny then turned and ran to her, standing in front of her to stop her walking anymore. "Get out of my way" Alexis sneered. "No" He replied. Alexis raised her eyebrows, "What do you mean n-""I said no" Danny interrupted. "Listen yeah, you work for me, which means you do what I say, got it?" Alexis said sternly. Danny raised his eyebrows, "Yeah, but you forgot the part where I'm not only your colleague, I'm your boyfriend too" he replied. "I know, but if I tell you to do something, I still expect you to do it" she replied. "Are you actually being serious right now?" Danny asked. "Yep" she replied instantly. "Why you being like this? We were fine before? What changed?" He asked. "I tell you I'm hearing things, and then you say that it's because, and I quote, 'I'm tired', I know what I heard Danny, you heard it too before so why do you assume that now I'm just imagining things?" She asked. He ran his fingers through his hair. "Listen Alex, I didn't mean that I thought you were making it up, I just-" Alexis interrupted, "Save it" she said, she then walked around him and walked to HQ, Danny sighed, trailing behind.

Chapter Seventeen

Finally at HQ, Alexis pulled out her walkie-talkie, "Where you guys?" she asked, a couple of minutes, she got a response, "Conference room", Alexis then walked to the conference room, and over to her sisters and her mum. Dylan walked over to the door, "Where's Danny?" he asked. "What do you mean where's Dan-", Alexis said, turning around to face the door. "He was right behind me" she said quietly. "Well obviously, he wasn't" Dylan said, getting frustrated. He pulled out his walkie-talkie, "Bro, where you at?" he said into it, there was no reply. "Danny, you there?" he said again. There was still no reply, he threw the walkie-talkie onto the sofa nearby, and turned to Alexis. "Why was he behind you anyway? You two are usually joined at the hip" he continued. Alexis sighed, "We had a bit of an argument" she said. "An argument about what?" he asked inquisitively. Alexis sighed again, "It was a stupid argument, and I was just angry, I didn't mean to-"Dylan interrupted, "So now, because of your 'stupid argument', my brother is missing?" he snapped. "Yeah" Alexis sighed. Dylan turned and walked to the other side of the room and he kicked the wall. Alexis put her head in her hands.

A couple of minutes passed and everyone was completely silent. Alexis then stood up and walked out of the room. She walked down the corridor and pulled out her gun, pointing it in front of her.

She carried on pacing the corridors, her mind racing…

What if he was hurt?
What if they'd got him?
What if he was dead?

Suddenly, her head started spinning, the whole room span round and round. She tumbled back, falling against the wall. She slid down the wall, sitting on the floor and grabbed her walkie-talkie, putting it to her mouth. She sighed… "Danny, where are you? I'm so sorry about before, it shouldn't have happened… I shouldn't have gotten so worked up about it all. You were right, I'm scared, I'm so scared, so much is going through my head right now. You need to know that I'm so sorry. I can't lose you as well, the reason I freaked out is because after I told you about what I heard, I heard someone whispering your name. That was the last straw… I can't do anything to bring back Daisy, but I will do EVERYTHING to protect you, like I'd protect Bailey, Charlie and my mum, you guys mean the world to me. I need you Danny please come back" A tear rolled down her cheek, she leant her head back against the wall and ran her fingers through her hair. A couple of minutes passed, and everything stayed silent, tears ran down her face.

"I will never leave you"

Alexis turned to see Danny stood at the end of the corridor, blood on his clothes. Her eyes lit up. She jumped up and faced him. "What happen-" "Zombies" Danny replied. Alexis smiled, "I thought they'd got you" she said, wiping away her tears. Danny smiled, "Well they haven't, and they won't" he said. "Why didn't you answer your walkie-talkie?" she asked. "I couldn't exactly fight off a zombie and chat at the same time" he joked. "But wh-", Alexis started. Danny interrupted. "You ask too many questions babe" he said, he then smiled and held his arms out. Alexis smiled and ran up to him, he lifted her up in the air, and she wrapped her legs around his waist as he held her up. Alexis put both hands on either side of his face, and then she leant so that their foreheads were together. "Did you?" Alexis asked, "Yeah, I heard what you said" he replied. "I meant all of it, you know that right?" she whispered. "I know" he replied. They both smiled. "I love you" Alexis whispered. "I love you too" he whispered back. Alexis smiled, before leaning in and kissing him gently on the lips. She then pulled away, before he leaned back in and kissed her back.

She poked his chest, "From now on, I am not letting you out of my sight!" she smiled. He kissed her, "Likewise" he replied. They both smiled. "Don't you think we should go back to HQ and let everyone know you're okay?" Alexis said. Danny shrugged, "I kind of hoped we could just stay here for a while, we don't really get much time on our own nowadays" Danny replied, holding her tighter. Alexis smiled, "I know, but everyone's really worried about you" She said softly. "But we don't know when we're going to be able to do this again, you know" he kissed her gently on the lips. "Spend time on our own" he kissed her again. Alexis smiled, "Tell you what, how about we go back now, and I'll sort something out" she said, "How does that sound to you?" she asked. Danny smiled, "Promise?" he asked, sticking his little finger out. Alexis smiled, she linked her little finger with his. "Pinky promise" she replied. They both smiled. "So, are you going to put me down so we can go back?" Alexis said. Danny smiled, then a couple of seconds later, he raised his eyebrows. "How about we have a bit of fun with Dylan, your sisters and your mum?" he asked, wiggling his eyebrows. "I like where this is going, what've you got in mind?" Alexis asked. Danny smiled, "We pretend I've been turned into a zombie, and I have hold of you pretending I'm going to bite you, you slam your foot on the floor, pretending your standing on my foot, and I repeat, *pretending*, then you run off, and turn and shoot near me? I'll pretend I've been shot and fall to the floor, then when they come over, I'll jump up and scare them?" He asked. Alexis laughed, "Oh my gosh, I can't wait to see the look on their faces" she said, before starting laughing again, "But wait..." she said, "What if Dylan doesn't find it funny? What if he gets annoyed with us for doing this?" She asked, he waved his hand dismissively, "He will find it funny, it'll just be revenge for all the times he's played pranks on me" he replied. She raised one eyebrow, "Do you think it'll work?" Alexis asked. He nodded, "I've got blood all over me already" he pointed out. "Okay, let's go then" Alexis said. "Wait" he said, "What now?" she said, she then sighed and put her hand on her hip sarcastically. "Alright little miss sassy, I was just gonna say, you forgot something" he said. She laughed. "What did I forget Danny?" she said. Danny smiled, he then grabbed her hands and pulled him towards her. Before he said anything, he leaned in and kissed her. Then he pulled away, they both smiled. "Okay, let's go" He said, he held out his out for her, she entwined her fingers with his and they started walking back up to HQ.

Chapter Eighteen

When they got around the corner from HQ, Alexis let go of Danny's hand. "Let's do this" she smiled. She walked around the corner and Danny grabbed onto her. "HELP!!!!!" She shouted. "BAILEY, CHARLIE, MUM, DYLAN, SOMEONE PLEASE HELP ME" she shouted. She then took a deep breath.

"HEEEEEEEELPPPPPP!!!!!!!!!"

She shouted. A couple of seconds later, everyone came running out. "DANNY!?" Dylan shouted. "OH MY GOD ALEXIS" Bailey shouted. Alexis pretended to cry. "Danny, I know part of you is still in there, please let me go, you don't want to do this" Alexis cried. Danny tilted his head to the side, "Shut up, you deserve everything you get" he spat, grabbing onto her tighter. She squealed. "Danny, please let go of her" Louise pleaded, tears in her eyes. Danny smiled. "Don't do this bro, that's your girl, let go, we will try and help you" Dylan said, taking a step towards them. Danny laughed, "She's not my girl" he spat. He then opened his mouth and leaned to Alexis' shoulder, pretending that he was about to bite her. "NO" Bailey shouted. Danny smiled and then bit her shoulder. Alexis screamed and slammed her foot down, slightly in front of his foot, but close enough to look real. Danny let her go and fell to the floor. Alexis ran over to her sisters. She then turned, just as Danny stood up, he wiped his face on his sleeve, "I'm going to rip you apart" he smiled, he then took a step towards her. Alexis then pulled her gun out of her pocket. "NO ALEXIS! PLEASE DON'T!" Dylan shouted. Alexis lifted the gun and point it in front of her; she then pulled the trigger, buckling her hands, pretending it happened from the power of the shot. Danny then put his hands over his stomach and fell to the floor. "NO!!!" Dylan shouted, he ran over to Danny and kneeled next to him. Alexis dropped her gun to her side, and put her hand over her mouth. "Oh my god what have I done?" Alexis asked. "Danny, come on, you can fight this, come back to me bro I need you, mum needs you, dad needs you, Kelly and Katie need you, we all need you, please don't die" Dylan pleaded. Alexis walked towards Danny and Dylan. "Oi, Danny, get up!" she shouted. Just then Danny opened his eyes and smiled. He jumped and brushed himself off, before giving Alexis a high five. "Wait, what?" Dylan asked. Danny wrapped his arm around Alexis' shoulder. "You, big bro, have just been PRANKED" he said. Alexis laughed. "What the hell Alexis?" Bailey asked in shock. Charlie started hysterically laughing, she walked over to Alexis, high-fiving her, "Nice one sis" Charlie said. Alexis smiled, Dylan looked at him, he started laughing, walked over and gave him a quick hug, "You got me good bro" he said, "well played" he continued, shaking his hand. Everyone started laughing.

"Right, time for action, get your butts to the conference room, or else!" Alexis shouted, and pointed to the conference room. Danny turned to her "Oh yeah, or else what?" he asked. Alexis put her hand on her hip, and Danny walked over to her "Babe, let's be honest, you're not as tough as you think" he joked. Alexis smirked, pointing the gun at him, "Oh really?" she smiled. Danny lifted his hands up and started walking backwards. "Yeah, that's right, do what you're told" she joked, walking towards him with the gun. Danny carried on walking backwards until his back hit the door. Alexis lowered the gun. She leaned towards him, "Now go inside" she whispered. Danny twisted the handle and started walking backwards into the room; he held his arms out and pulled Alexis towards him by her waist. He smiled, then leaned in and kissed her.

Dylan cleared his throat. Alexis turned around and Danny looked at Dylan, "You two finished now?" Dylan asked. Alexis laughed, moving away from him and walking over to the table. Bailey popped her head around the door, "Have they finished kissing now?" she asked. Alexis laughed, "Yeah" she said. Bailey, Charlie and Louise walked into the room, closing the door behind them. They all sat around the conference table. "So, what now?", Bailey asked. "We've spent so much time focusing on ourselves, we've completely forgotten that we're not the only ones in danger… Everyone is, we don't know how far this has spread, whether it's only in Limebarn, or whether it's national, or even worse, worldwide." Alexis explained. "So what do we need to do?" Bailey asked. Alexis shrugged, "Well, I think we can say it's definitely occurring in Limebarn, because this has been going on for weeks, hasn't it?" Louise asked. "Yeah, but it's been occurring slowly" Alexis replied, "Only thing we can do at this point is listen to the news" Danny suggested. "We could I guess, but how? There are no radios?" Alexis asked. "Some radios are accessible online?" Danny said. Alexis raised her eyebrows, "Okay, let's all go to my office then" Alexis said. Everyone stood up. Alexis jumped onto her chair. She then grabbed Danny's shoulders and jumped onto his back. He held onto her legs quickly. "Bloody hell" he said. Alexis laughed. She pointed to the door. "To my office!" she instructed. Danny bowed his head "Yes ma'am" he joked. He then started walking towards the door; he opened it, and walked down to Alexis' office. "Wait!" Bailey shouted. "What?" Danny asked. Alexis jumped off his back. "Can we not all just chill in our offices, we can communicate through the intercoms, that way, we can just chill until we figure out our next move, instead of all huddling in one office... Mum, you've got John's office, Alexis and Charlie and I have our own offices, Dylan and Danny can stay with Alexis obviously" Bailey explained. "I like the way you think" Alexis smiled. She turned to Danny. "Then you can ring your mum, see how she is" she suggested, "Yeah, that sounds good! I could do with some time to just relax, we can get all our stuff as well?" Bailey asked. "Even better! we can all get our luggage and our guns, that way I'll have more space in my office aswell! Bailey, my sister, you are a genius" Alexis explained. Bailey smiled proudly. "All in favour raise your hands" Everyone raised their hands. "Okay, everyone grab your bags, and grab the boxes with your names on, take them to your offices, and then when you're done, meet me back here" Alexis instructed.

Another hour passed, and everyone had sorted out their stuff, and taken it to their office, then they all met back in the conference room.

"Okay, all of the phones are connected, there's a piece of paper under the phone in each office with everyone's direct dial numbers. Apparently, each room has a fridge filled with everything you'll need, there's two weeks' worth of food in there, so make sure it lasts, otherwise, you'll be going hungry I'm afraid!" Alexis explained. "How could you possibly know that?" Charlie asked. "So I may have also snooped in the offices after I overheard John's conversation" Alexis admitted. Charlie laughed, shaking her head. "Any questions?" Alexis asked. Bailey raised her hands. "What about if we need to go to the toilet?" she asked. "Good question. Each office has an on-suite bathroom, fully equipped with towels, cleaning products, toilet roll, everything you'll need, each bathroom also has a toilet, bath, and shower. And we've all got our toiletry bags" Alexis explained. "How did John afford all of this?" Charlie asked. "Apparently, every base has a re-model every 2 years, where it gets kitted out with all the up to date equipment, modernized offices and emergency zones. All agents have their own offices fully equipped with kitchen and bathroom facilities for emergencies" Alexis explained. "And before you ask, I know this because John told me" she joked. Everyone laughed. "Okay, let's go" she smiled. "Everyone has their mobiles too, so if you move to someone else's office, please can you just send everyone a text so we know where everyone is" Alexis asked. Everyone nodded in agreement. "Let's go!" Alexis said, and they all left the room.

Chapter Nineteen

"Okay, it's almost finished" Alexis said.

BEEP!

A face popped up on the screen.
"Hey Pete!" Alexis said. "Hi Alexis, how're things?" Pete replied.
"Eh, okay at the minute" she said, "How about you, how's things in
Spain?" she continued. "Things are great, we've just completed
mission violet" he said. "No way! You've captured Larslo and his
gang? They've been on the top of the most wanted list in Spain
for *years*! Nice one!" Alexis smiled. "So, what's been going on
in Limebarn? Word is that you've got a zombie invasion on your
hands" Pete asked. "Yeah, guessing you're not being over-run by
them too?" Alexis asked. "Nope, I've spoken to few other bases, it's
just you guys that have the outbreak. I also heard about John, I'm so
sorry" Pete said. Alexis shrugged, "He's just jealous isn't he" she
joked, brushing off her shoulders. "Yeah, because he had to give up
his job to a 17-year-old girl" Pete joked. "Congrats on your
accomplishment by the way!" He continued. Alexis laughed.
"Where's Lisa?" she asked. "She's unpacking, wow that woman can
talk, she never bloody shuts up!" Pete joked, Danny walked over to
Alexis and knelt behind her, "Tell me about it" he added. Pete
laughed "Ah, so you're Danny I'm guessing?" Danny nodded. "The
one and only" he joked. Rick laughed. "I've heard a lot about you"
Pete said. Alexis looked away. "All good I hope?" Danny replied.
Pete laughed, "Alexis talks about you consta-" "Pete, please will you
go and get Danny's family?" Alexis interrupted. "Oh, yeah sure,
give me a few minutes" Pete said, then he walked out of the view of
the camera and went to get them.

"So, what've you been saying about me then?" Danny asked. "How
great you are" Alexis gushed. Danny smiled, "No really" he
said. "It's nothing bad" Alexis replied. "Do I need to start tickling

you?" Danny asked. "Do I need to get my gun back out?"
Alexis replied, as she went to reach into her pocket, "Alright, alright,
truce" Danny said, holding his hands up. Alexis smiled, "Yeah,
that's what I thought" she joked. Danny looked over to Dylan,
"What's up bro? You're quiet" he said. Dylan looked up. "I'm just
tired" Dylan said. "Same bro, you can have a sleep after we've
spoken to mum, dad and twinnies" Danny said. "Safe" Dylan
replied.

"Alexis" Rick said, sitting back down in front of the webcam.
"Yeah?" Alexis asked. "I've got the lads family, shall I put them
on?" Rick asked. "Yeah" Alexis replied, she turned to Danny and
Dylan "You can speak to them now" she said. Danny and Dylan
walked over to the webcam. "Okay, I'll leave you too it, I'm going
to go and see my mum and the girls, ring me on my mobile if you
need me, or if you've finished, I'm going to lock the door behind
me" Alexis said, as she grabbed her phone out of her bag. "Thanks
babe" Danny said. "Cheers Lex" Dylan said. Alexis walked down
to Baileys office, she knocked on the door. "Who is it?" Bailey
shouted. "Alexis" Alexis replied. Bailey unlocked the door and
Alexis walked it, shutting and locking it behind her. She saw her
mum and Charlie sat around the table eating crisps. "You lot are
always eating" Alexis said, as she walked over to the table. She
grabbed a packet of crisps and opened it. "Bit hypocritical?" Charlie
said, pointing to the packet of crisps in Alexis' hands. Alexis
shrugged and laughed. "So, why you here?" Bailey asked. "I've left
Danny and Dylan talking to their family" Alexis said, midway
through eating a mouthful of crisps. Alexis started looking around,
"If John was plotting against us, why did he go through the time and
effort of making us all these offices? I mean, look, these offices are
amazing" Charlie asked. "I'm not sure, I don't even think he was
plotting against us, I think James and Ray were just saying that to try
and get information out of us, we've got no evidence to suggest they
are telling the truth, they turned John into a zombie before we had a
chance to question him. I don't think they're telling the full truth"
Alexis pointed out. "Yeah, but what about all the stuff he said before
he tried killing us?" Bailey asked. "He had that toxic virus thing that
changed him, I'm not justifying what he did, and I'm not saying that
I don't think he was plotting against us. I think that there is more to
all of this than we think" Alexis said. "John hasn't always been as

nice as you girls think, he's got a dark side that you've not seen" Louise explained. "What do you mean?" Bailey asked. "Wait, how would you know? You only met him a few days ago" Alexis pointed out. Louise shook his head. "I've known John for a long time, he was an agent once and I can promise you girls, he isn't as nice as you think. Like I said, he has a dark side" Louise continued. "What do you mean a dark side" Charlie asked. Louise shook her head. "It's not relevant now, and I don't want to ruin your memories of him. He was a good leadership figure to you girls and I will always be thankful for that. We will talk about it after this whole nightmare is over" Louise explained. Everyone left it at that. Alexis shrugged, "I'm not sure, I just feel like we've only got half a story" she said. "What do you two think?" She asked. Bailey shrugged. "I agree with you, I think there's more to it" Charlie said.

It all stayed silent for a while.

"Well, we will have to wait and see, won't we" Alexis said, breaking the silence, they all nodded. Bailey's desk phone started ringing. "Baileys office, Bailey speaking" she joked. "It's Danny, where's Lex?" he asked. "She's in here, I'll tell her you've finished" Bailey replied. "Thanks, over and out" He replied, then Bailey put the phone down, chuckling to herself. She turned around to tell Alexis, but she'd already unlocked the door and gone.

Alexis knocked on her office door, a couple of seconds later, Danny opened the door, "Oh it's you, what do you want?" he joked. "Oh, okay, I'll just go" Alexis said, then as she turned to walk away, Danny snaked his arms around her waist and pulled her back, Alexis laughed. He rested is head in the crook of her neck and she leant her head to rest on his. "I'm so tired" Alexis mumbled, "Same" Danny replied. "I'm going to ring Bailey and tell her we're going sleep, Dylan, you tired?" Alexis asked. Dylan nodded, mid-yawn. Alexis walked over to her desk, picked up her phone and dialed the number for Baileys office.

Bailey picked up after a few seconds. "Yo Bailey" Alexis said. "Wassup girl" Bailey replied. "We're going sleep, so if you need us, ring the phone before you leave the office, but only if it's an emergency, we're all really tired" Alexis explained. "Yeah, we're tired here too, so I think we'll do the same" Bailey replied. "Alright, talk to you soon, nighty night, sleep tight, don't let the zombies bite" Alexis joked. Alexis then put the phone down. "How very original" Danny joked.

"The sofas are pull-outs, so they turn into beds" Alexis said. She walked over to one of the sofas, and pulled it out, "Oh look, there's covers and pillows inside! I love this office!" Alexis said. She pulled the pillows and covers out and pushed it down. "WALL-LAH, one double bed" Alexis said. Dylan copied what Alexis did, with the other sofa. "Ok, I'm going to go and put my onesie on" Alexis said. "What's a onesie?" Dylan asked. Alexis grabbed her bag, "You'll see!" she replied. She walked into the bathroom.

A couple of minutes and Alexis ran out wearing a Minnie mouse onesie, her hood up, a pair of black ears and a bow on the hood. "Ah, a onesie, I get it" Dylan said, half asleep. "Haven't you two got any Pyjamas?" Alexis asked, putting her bag under her desk. "Nope" Danny replied. Alexis turned to Dylan to ask him, but he was already asleep. Danny walked over to the sofa bed and took his shirt off, Alexis walked into the bathroom and took her toothbrush out of the cup next to the sink and put some tooth paste on it, and started brushing her teeth.

When she'd finished, she put her head down and swirled her mouth with mouthwash. She then looked up and looked in the mirror, and she saw Danny stood behind her. Alexis jumped. "Oh my gosh, you scared me, don't sneak up on me like that" Alexis said. Danny wrapped his arms around her waist. "Aw, are you cold?" Alexis asked. "Yeah" Danny replied, holding her tighter. "Well put a bloody top on then!" she joked. Danny laughed. Alexis leant in towards the mirror, "Eugh, look how many spots I've got" Alexis said, poking at her face. "You still look beautiful" Danny said. "Aw, thank you!" Alexis replied. She turned to him and wrapped her arms around the back of his neck. "I can't wait for all of this to be over" she sighed. Danny leant in and kissed her. "Okay, seriously, I'm really tired, it's 1 o clock in the morning and way past my bedtime" she mumbled mid-yawn. Danny nodded, "Okay, sleep time for my little zombie slayer" he joked. He walked into the office and lay on the sofa-bed. A couple of seconds later, Alexis staggered in, she slumped down onto the sofa and cuddled up to Danny, who then wrapped his arms around her. He kissed her forehead, "Night princess" he whispered, and they both fell asleep.

Chapter Twenty

RING RING! RING RING!

Alexis jumped up and rubbed her eyes, before walking over to her desk and picking up the phone. "What?" she groaned. "Are you 3 awake? It's Charlie" Charlie replied. "I am, the lads are still asleep" Alexis mumbled. "What do you want Charlie?" she continued, rubbing her eyes. "We went online and looked at the news, this is happening all over Limebarn, the authorities have closed off roads in and out of Limebarn" Charlie explained. "What? Really" Alexis asked, her eyes now wide open. "Yeah, really, check for yourself, it's on the LLN website" replied Charlie.
Alexis turned on the computer and went to the website.

BREAKING NEWS
Chaos continues to occur throughout Limebarn. Authorities are clueless as to what has caused the epidemic. The government have activated code red, closing off all entrances and exits to it. Scientists are saying that the virus isn't airborne, and it is only contagious through direct entrance to the blood stream. The epidemic has remained in Limebarn only, sister towns are barricading off roads in attempt to keep the infected away. We are asking that if anyone has any information, please contact us on 0213 444 6797. We will keep you all updated via our website.

IF YOU ARE ALIVE IN THE TOWN OF LIMEBARN, AND IF YOU HAVEN'T BEEN AFFECTED BY THE VIRUS, CALL 0213 444 6798 AND WE WILL ARRANGE TRANSPORT OUT OF THE TOWN AND YOU WILL BE TAKEN TO THE SAFE ZONE.

-

Alexis ran her fingers through her hair, "Wow, this is mad" she said. "I know" Charlie replied. "We need to have a meeting" Alexis instructed. "Should we come now?" Charlie asked. "Not yet, Danny and Dylan are still asleep, give us 10 minutes" Alexis replied. "Okay" Charlie replied.

Alexis put the phone down. She stood up and walked over to where Danny was still sleeping, and sat on the edge of the sofa-bed and poked him. "Babe?" she said. Danny opened his eyes slowly, "Mmmm?" he mumbled. "You need to wake up, we've got some new information, we need to have a meeting. The girls will be here in 10 minutes" Alexis explained. Danny slowly sat up and rubbed his eyes. "Okay, I'm up" he said. He sat on the edge of the sofa-bed and looked over to Dylan. "That morning hair though" Alexis teased, running her fingers through Danny's hair. He laughed. He then leaned over to kiss Alexis, but was pushed away by her hand. "Not gonna happen, morning breath" she said. She then walked into the bathroom and brushed her teeth. A couple of seconds later, Danny walked into the bathroom and did the same. When Alexis had finished, she walked into the office so that she could tidy up the sofa bed and make more room. She threw the covers back in the bottom, and picked up a pillow and threw it at Dylan. Dylan quickly sat up, startled. He turned to Alexis, "What are we being attacked?!" he shouted. Alexis laughed. "No Dylan, the girls are coming over for a meeting, you've got less than 10 minutes to get ready" Alexis said.

Danny walked back into the office and over to Alexis, "Will you kiss me now?" he groaned, pouting. Alexis laughed, "What's the magic word?" she asked. "Pleaseeeeee" Danny replied. Alexis smiled. "No" she said, before walking over to her desk. "Fine then" Danny said, crossing his arms pretending to sulk. Alexis looked over to him, "Oh puh-lease, as if I'm going to fall for that" Alexis joked. "Now, finish getting ready" she continued. Danny laughed, "I am ready" he said. Alexis looked at Danny, who was stood, shirtless, wearing a pair of tracksuit bottoms and a pair of hi-tops. "Danny, you're missing something" she said. He raised his eyebrow. "A shirt?" she said. Danny shrugged, "Don't feel like wearing one" he said. Alexis crossed her arms. "Put a shirt on, NOW!" she shouted. Danny laughed, "You gonna make me?" he asked. Alexis smiled, and she reached into the top drawer of her desk and pulled out a gun. She pointed it at him. "Do what you're told boy" she said. "Okay, okay" he said. He reached into his bag and pulled out a black t-shirt, putting it on. Alexis smiled and put the gun back in her desk. She looked back at Danny, to see him pointing two guns at her, and smiling. Alexis laughed. "Now, you come here"" he instructed. She slowly walked over to him, "What?" she asked, as she leant to one side, resting her hand on her hip. "Kiss me" he instructed. Alexis smiled, Danny put the guns on the table next to him. Alexis leant in to kiss him, but then quickly leant over and grabbed his guns off the table. She took a step back and pointed them at him. Danny stood and looked at her in confusion. "Never threaten me with guns again" she joked. She then turned and shot both guns at the dart board, which was hanging off the back of the door.

They both hit the bullseye.

She turned back to Danny and smiled, before giving the guns back to him. "Now, put them away before someone actually gets hurt" she joked. Danny laughed, putting one in his bag and one in his pocket. He walked over to Alexis' desk and looked at her computer. "Lex, come here a minute" he said. Alexis walked over to the desk. "What's u-" Danny grabbed her face and kissed her. Alexis smiled into the kiss. Dylan then walked back into the main office, "Why am I always the one that walks in on you two kissing?" he asked. "I don't know, bad timing?" Alexis joked, her and Danny laughed. Then there was a knock at the door, "It's us " Bailey shouted from outside. "Let them in" Alexis instructed. Dylan saluted her, and walked over to the door, Alexis smiled, before leaning in and kissing Danny again, as he lifted her slightly. "Oi, put my sister down Jackson!" Charlie shouted. Alexis and Danny laughed. "Make me" Danny said. Charlie then pulled her gun out and pointed it at him, "Do not make me ask you again" she warned. "Jeez, what is it with you chicks threatening me with guns?" Danny laughed, letting go of Alexis. She walked over to Charlie and high-fived her. "Nice tactics girl" she laughed. They both started laughing.

When everyone had sat down, Alexis started talking "Alright, here's the plan, we need to stop only thinking about ourselves, it's all fine

and dandy that we're all safe here, but the other people in Limebarn aren't. Our friends and other members of our family could be in trouble. What we're going to do, is ring everyone in our contact lists on our phones, if they answer, we find out where they are, if they are still in Limebarn, we go and get them, and bring them back here, where they will be safe for now. The rules are: no getting guns out unless it is an EXTREME emergency, and if they ask how we got access to the shopping centre, we'll say that my uncle owns it. We can't let them know that we work for the secret services, okay?" Alexis instructed.
Everyone nodded.

"It's going to have to be Danny and Dylan in one van, Me and Bailey in one, Charlie and mum in the other" Alexis instructed. Danny squeezed her side and looked up at her. "You'll be fine, don't worry" she whispered, kissing his cheek.

Everyone pulled their phones out and started dialing.

Half an hour passed, and everyone was sat back on the table. "Well?" Alexis asked. "Everyone on my contact list either didn't answer, their phone was off, or they were at the safe zone" Danny said. "Same" Dylan said. Bailey and Charlie nodded. "Same" they said in unison. "Your auntie Lisa and Uncle James are still at home, they're hiding in their basement, everyone else didn't answer" the girls' mum said. Alexis sighed. "Amy is hiding in her mum's room with her mum, brother, dad, sisters and her dog, Hannah and Harriet are hiding in their attic with their dad, and Shay is in the toilets in the supermarket, apparently, her and a bunch of people are barricaded in the toilets, and there's loads of those zombie things trying to get in" Alexis said. "We're going to have to all go together, and take three vans" she continued. Everyone agreed. "Danny and Dylan, you take Danny's van, mum and Bailey, you take Baileys van, but obviously mum will be driving, and Me and Charlie will go in my van" Alexis instructed. Alexis stood up. "Let's go" she said. They all grabbed their guns, mobile phones and walkie-talkies, and walked out of the office, locking it behind them.

When they got to the end of the corridor, Alexis pressed the button and the shutters lifted, they all crawled under the shutters, and Alexis typed in the combination, and the shutter closed behind them. They all walked down to the main reception.

"Charlie, go and open the shutters, we will go and jump into the van, then everyone else run to the garages… shoot the locks to open them, remember! First place we're going is 14 Portmend Road" Alexis instructed. Everyone nodded. "See you there" Alexis said. "NOW!" she shouted. Charlie pressed the button to lift the shutters. Her and Alexis then quickly ran and jumped into the van. Everyone ran out and too the garages. Alexis jumped out of her van and closed the shutters, before she ran and got back and got in the van. She heard shots being fired, and then she turned and saw everyone run into their garages. A couple of seconds later, the vans drove out of the garages. Alexis slammed her foot on the accelerator and they went speeding towards the gate, slowing down before she reached them. She looked out of her window, and there was no one outside the gate, she turned to Charlie, "At least we won't have trouble getting out" she said. Charlie smiled. Alexis jumped out of her van and unlocked the gate and opened it, allowing Danny and her mum to drive out, they stopped slightly outside the gates, Alexis got back in her van and drove outside the gates, before she got back out of her van and locked the gates. For the last time, she got in her van, and they drove off.

Chapter Twenty-One

When they got to the first address, Danny and the girls' mum were already parked outside. Alexis pulled up next to the vans, and waited. A couple of minutes later, her mum and Bailey ran out of the house, followed by her uncle James and aunt Lisa, they jumped into the back of Baileys van. Alexis lowered her window, "Amy and her family are at 56 Rowcorn Drive" she shouted. She then slammed her foot onto the pedal and she sped off, followed by the other 2 vans.

When she got to the address, Alexis pulled up outside the house and opened the door and jumped out of the van, followed by Charlie. They ran towards the house. Alexis pressed the key, locking the van, she got to the door and pressed the handle. It was locked. She started banging on the door. "AMY, ARE YOU THERE?" she shouted. "HELP" she heard someone shouted. "Stand back" Alexis instructed, Charlie took a step back, and Alexis lifted her foot and kicked open the door, sending it flying off its hinges. They ran up the stairs, and turned to find the right room. There were three people stood outside the bedroom door, they turned and saw Alexis and Charlie. They were zombies. Alexis pulled out her gun and shot them all between the eyes. She heard screaming coming from the room and she knocked on the door. "Amy, it's Alexis and Charlie, open the door, we're here to help you" she said. A couple of seconds later, the door, opened, and Alexis' friend Amy was stood there, staring down at the bodies, her jaw dropped. Alexis laughed, "Come on, we'll take you somewhere safe" Alexis said. Amy turned and looked back in the room "Quick, it's help" she said. "Follow me" Alexis said. Alexis ran down the stairs, followed by Charlie, Amy and her family. Alexis ran out of the door and towards the van, she pressed the car key to unlock it, and she opened the back doors, Amy and her family and dog jumped in and shut the door behind them. Alexis and Charlie jumped in the front seats. She opened the window, "MUM, you go and get Louis, he rang me on the way here, 102 Grayson Avenue, then go and wait outside the supermarket, DANNY, you come with me to get Harriet and Hannah, 19 York Street" Alexis said. Danny and the girls' mum sped off, "Alexis?" Amy mumbled. Alexis turned "What's up?" Alexis said. "What's happening?" Amy continued. Alexis shrugged, "I honestly have no idea" she replied. "Where'd you get the gun from?" Amy asked. Before Alexis could reply, Amy's dad spoke up, "Told you she was a bloody thug" he said. Alexis laughed. "Well, this thug just saved your life, so shut up" she said. Amy laughed. "You can't talk to me like that" Amy's dad shouted. "She's right dad, she's just saved our lives, so leave her alone" Amy shouted back. Her dad shut up. Alexis slammed her foot on the pedal and drove off.

When they parked up outside Harriet and Hannah's house, Alexis was about to jump out, before Amy's dad spoke up again, "Do you even have your driving license?" he sneered. "I thought I told you to shut up" Alexis spat. She got out of the van and slammed the door. She noticed that Danny's van wasn't there so she jumped back in the van and grabbed her phone. She dialed Danny's number, "Where are you?" she shouted. "I've just pulled up outside the supermarket" he said, then the phone went off. Alexis' eyes widened. "What's up?" Charlie asked. "Danny's at the supermarket" she mumbled. Before anyone had anytime to respond, she jumped out of the van "stay there" she shouted, before running into the house. She ran up the stairs and stood underneath the attic door. "QUICK, IT'S ALEXIS, COME OUT, WE NEED TO GO NOW!" she shouted. A couple of seconds later, the attic door lifted, and Harriet's mum jumped down, followed by Harriet and Hannah. "Thank you so much!" Harriet's mum said. Alexis smiled, she ran down the stairs, and they followed her, she jumped into the van, and they jumped into the back. "Hey Harriet, hey Hannah" Amy said. Alexis then slammed her foot on the pedal, and they sped to the supermarket.

Chapter Twenty-Two

Alexis and Charlie pulled up outside the supermarket and got out of the van, locking it after them. They walked over to their mums van, and she lowered the window. "Ready to g-" Alexis started. "Danny and Dylan are already inside" their mum interrupted. "Well, let's go and help them then" Alexis said. "We heard gun shots, then everything went silent" Bailey continued, and before anyone could say anything else, Alexis turned and ran towards the supermarket.

When she got to the entrance, she saw Dylan limping towards the exit, "OH MY GOD DYLAN, ARE YOU OKAY?!" Alexis shouted, walking over to him. Dylan fell to the floor, "No, Danny" he muttered, putting his head in his hands. "What's happened?" Alexis asked. "We got here, and they were all over the place, we fought them off eventually, and we found the others hiding in the bathroom, we walked in, but they thought we were zombies because we had blood on our clothes, so they started attacking us, one of them smashed Danny in the face and he fell to the floor and they all started kicking and punching him, and when I tried helping, they grabbed me and two of them started attacking me with golf clubs, when I fought them off, I turned, and Danny wasn't there. I thought he might've got up and left, so I went looking for him, and then that's when you found me, please find him Alexis" Dylan explained, flinching. Alexis went over to him and helped him up. "Come on, we'll get you to the van" she said, she put his arm around her shoulders and helped him to walk towards the doors, "MUM, COME AND GET DYLAN, CHARLIE AND BAILEY, WITH ME, NOW, BRING YOUR GUNS" she shouted. A couple of seconds later, they all came running towards the exit. Louise helped Dylan walk over to her van, and he jumped in the back, Charlie give Alexis her gun. "You ready?" Alexis said. Bailey and Charlie nodded.

They walked towards the door to the bathroom. Alexis pulled out both of her guns, and so did Bailey and Charlie. Alexis kicked the door open, startling everybody who was inside. They all looked towards her, one of the people ran towards her with a baseball bat, and Alexis held the guns out in front of her, "If anyone dares touch any of us, I will shoot you, understand?" she shouted. They all moved back. "Where's Danny?" she asked. "Who the hell is Danny?" someone shouted, then, one of the people pointed behind her. Alexis turned, and saw Danny slumped back against the wall, his face cut and bruised, cuts and bruises on his arms. She ran over to him and knelt beside him, "Are you okay?" she whispered. He nodded. Alexis stood up and held her arms out. He grabbed onto her hand and she pulled him up, he groaned as he put his arm round her shoulders to stop himself falling back down, Charlie walked over to him and he put his other arm around her shoulder. Alexis looked at him, "We'll get you fixed up" she said, kissing his cheek softly. Danny nodded, fear in his eyes. "Bailey and Charlie are going to take you to my van, and my mum will make sure you're okay" she said. "No, I'm not leaving you" he groaned. "I'll be okay, I can deal with this lot" she spat, looking at them. She leaned in and softly kissed him. Bailey walked over to where Alexis was stood, and Danny moved away and put his other arm around her shoulders, they turned towards the door and walked out.

Alexis turned towards everyone else. "Where's Shay?" she shouted. "She's not here" one of the people said. "What do you mean, she's not here?" Alexis shouted. "She got away" they continued. "Oh, okay" Alexis said. Alexis turned towards the door. "So you only came here to help her? What about the rest of us?" one of the people shouted. Alexis turned towards them, "Why should I help any of you, Danny and Dylan came to help you, and considering you battered them, I wouldn't have thought you wanted help" She pointed out. Everyone stayed quiet. "Yeah, that's what I thought, oh, and do you want to know something? We could have stayed in hiding, we were safe and in a secure place, but instead we put our lives at risk to help the other people in our community, and what for? For you to attack us" she pointed out. "We're sorry," they all said, at different times. "It's not me you have to say sorry too," Alexis said. "We'll apologize to him aswell, just please help us" someone shouted. Alexis sighed. "Come with me" she said, she walked out of the bathroom, and towards the exit. As they got to the entrance, Alexis turned and saw a group of zombies running down the road towards them. "Everyone, move back" she whispered. Everyone did so. She pulled the doors closed behind her.

She pulled out both guns, pointing them in front of her. All the zombies were at bottom of the stairs that lead to the supermarket. "So, you must be Alexis?" one of them said, Alexis smiled, "The one and only" she joked. The person turned to the others, "So, which one of us is going to have the honour of ripping her apart?" he asked, they all laughed. Just as he turned back to face Alexis, she pulled the trigger, the bullet hitting him directly between the eyes, "Not you" she said. He fell to the floor, the others stood over him, saying nothing, startled. Alexis smiled. They all looked back up at her, before turning and running down the street. She laughed. "Wimps!" She shouted. She then saw someone walk to the bottom of the stairs, looking up…

"Alexis?" They mumbled.

Chapter Twenty-Three

Alexis looked closer, it was Shay.

"Shay!?" Alexis shouted. "W-w-what's happening?" she mumbled. "I don't know, I really don't, I'm just so glad that you're okay" Alexis replied. She ran down the stairs and hugged her. "I'm so scared," Shay whispered. "You don't have to be scared anymore, I'll look after you," Alexis whispered back. Shay smiled. "So, what's with the guns?" Shay asked, looking down at the guns that Alexis was holding. "I found them…" Alexis mumbled. "Oh really? The truth please, Alexis" Shay said. Alexis sighed. "Alright, but you can't tell anyone" Alexis said. Shay ran her finger across her lips, "My lips are sealed," she said. "I'm sort of a secret agent," Alexis said. "Sort of?" Shay repeated, then laughing. "Well, I am an agent" Alexis continued. "What type of agent? Is that the same as a secret agent? Like, in the secret services?" Shay asked in shock. Alexis shook her head, "Yeah, I kind of run the secret services Limebarn division" Shay stayed silent for a few seconds, "Kind of?" she asked. Alexis laughed, "Alright then, I do run the secret services," she said. Shay didn't say anything.

A couple of minutes passed, and it was silent. "Well, say something" Alexis said. "I don't know what to say" Shay replied. "Well, are we going to just going to stand here, targets on our backs? Those zombies could come back at any time" Alexis asked. Shay laughed. "Come on then, to the van!" Alexis said. She ran back up the stairs and opened the door. "Come on everyone, to the vans" Alexis said. She walked down the stairs and everyone followed her. When she got to the vans, she stopped. She then counted everyone. "Okay, there are 11 of you, so 5 of you get in the second van, 6 of you get in the third van" she instructed. She walked over to the second van and 5 of them got in the back. She shut the doors and walked over to the third van, and the remaining 6 got in the back. Alexis turned to Shay, "Do me a favour? We don't have anyone to drive the last van, because Danny and Dylan cannot drive now, thanks to them lot thinking they were zombies and attacking them" she shouted, looking at the people from the supermarket. "So will you please drive it? You only have to follow us?" she asked, "Fiiiiine" Shay replied, dragging it out. Alexis smiled, "You're the best," she said. Shay got in the front of the van, and lowered down the window. "I've got to go and make sure Danny and Dylan are okay, so wait until I signal you, then follow behind my mums van" Alexis instructed. Shay saluted her, "Yes boss" she joked. They both laughed.

Alexis walked over to the first van, she opened the back and jumped in. "Mum, you need to take the second van, Shay's going to drive the third one and Danny and Dylan are staying here with me, you've got some of the people from the supermarket in the back" Alexis instructed. Her mum nodded. "We'll go with mum," Bailey said, Charlie nodded. "Okay, go on then" Alexis instructed, Louise, Bailey and Charlie got out of the van, and jumped into the second van, Alexis closed the doors. "Are you two okay?" Alexis said quietly. Dylan and Danny nodded. Alexis moved over and knelt next to Danny, who was slumped against the seat. "Are you sure you're okay?" she whispered. Danny nodded. "Yeah, just in a bit of pain" he replied. "Look at me" Alexis whispered. Danny looked up at her; she could tell that he was in pain. "Everything will be okay, there's a pharmacy in the shopping centre, when we get there, we'll sort you out, okay?" she whispered. Danny smiled and nodded. She put both hands on either side of his face and gently kissed him. "Do I get a kiss?" Dylan groaned. Alexis laughed, kissing his cheek. "That'll do" he smiled. "Behave man" Danny joked. She then stood up and got out of the van, shutting it behind her. She walked to the front of the van, jumped in and started the ignition. She lowered the window, stuck her head out, and looked behind her. "Let's go!" she shouted. Then she started driving to the shopping centre.

When they got to the shopping centre, it was still all clear. Alexis pulled up next to the gates, followed by the others. She jumped out of the van and pulled the keys out of her pocket, unlocking the locks on the gate. She pushed the gate open, before walking over to her van and getting in, and drove into the carpark, followed by Louise, and then Shay. Alexis then walked back over to lock the gates. When she got to the gates, she saw a small group of people running towards them, Alexis quickly grabbed the gate and slammed it shut. "NO, PLEASE DON'T LOCK IT, PLEASE HELP US!" one of the people running shouted. She looked closely, and they weren't zombies. She pushed the gates open again quickly and let the group into the car park. Alexis turned to them "What was you running away from?" She asked. "We were being foll-" One of the people started, then they pointed out of the gates, Alexis turned, and saw a large group of zombies running towards them. She then quickly shut the gate and started locking all the chains back around it, "QUICK, YOU LOT, RUN TO THE ENTRANCE AND WAIT NEXT TO THE DOORS!" she shouted, the group of people ran towards the building. Alexis finished padlocking it all back, and ran over to her van, she jumped in and started the ignition, she slammed her foot down and went speeding towards the entrance, the other two followed. She parked in front of the doors, and turned off the engine and jumped out, she ran to the shutters, and typed in the combination, before grabbing her keys out of her pocket, and unlocking it. She pressed the button and the shutter started opening. She ran over to her van, turned on the ignition, and sped into the reception, crashing through the back wall and into one of the shops "Shit" Alexis mumbled. Both vans followed her, parking in the reception. Alexis jumped out of her van and pushed through the rubble, and got to the entrance, the group of people ran in, then she looked out to see the zombies trying to get into the gates. She quickly closed the doors and pressed the button, lowering the shutters, locking them. "Thank you so much" one of the people said. "Yeah, thanks" another one said. Alexis smiled. "I'm Alexis, by the way" she said. One by one, they all introduced themselves as Lauren, Paul, Josh, Ben, Frankie, Deana and Allie. "Wait, you all go to my school, right?" Alexis said. "Oh yeah, I thought I recognized you! You were in the year above, right? The girl who used to fight all the time?" Frankie said. Alexis laughed and nodded. "Is that the one?" Ben whispered to Josh. Josh nodded. "Is who the one?" Alexis asked. "Josh used to have a huge crush on you, he's totally into bad girls" Ben said. Josh blushed, "Thanks for that mate" he said. "It's okay bro" Ben teased. Alexis laughed. "Well, I'm flattered" she joked. "Aren't you the one who's dating that guy who went to our school, Danny Jackson?" Allie asked. Alexis nodded. "Lucky girl" Frankie said. Alexis laughed.

They carried on talking for 10 more minutes, "Okay, I'd love to stay and chat, but I need to go and check on everyone, you guys can go and chill in the shopping centre, the supermarket is open so you can get some food and drinks" she said. "We can't just take anything we want" Paul said. "I know, don't worry, I've sorted it with the owners, only take what you need, the shop is still being monitored by CCTV though so be careful, if you take the mick then the owners might kick you out, there has to be enough for everyone" Alexis warned. "What do you mean 'you've sorted it'?" Frankie asked. Alexis smiled, "Ah, that's for me to know, and you to never find out" she joked "Yes boss" Frankie replied. "See you round?" She continued. Alexis nodded, "Yeah definitely, and don't worry, you're all safe here" she replied. "Thanks" Josh interrupted. "It's okay" she smiled. They all walked off, and Alexis walked over to the back van. She opened the back doors, "Okay everyone, you have access to the supermarket, get yourself a drink and some food when you need too, the owners have given me authorization. No taking the mick though or you'll get kicked out" Alexis said sternly. "You can't threaten us," One of the people said. "Oh, I think you will find I can" Alexis replied. "If you've got a problem with my rules, tell me now and I'll open the shutters and let you back out" Alexis spat. The person smirked. "Oh, and I've got the whole shopping centre monitored by CCTV, so I'll know if you cause any trouble" Alexis replied, smiling at everyone. Everyone nodded. "I'm Alexis, by the way" she introduced. They introduced themselves as Luke, Lola, Maisy, Ida, Vicky and Sarah.

They all then walked off.

Louise, Bailey and Charlie then jumped out of the front of the van, and locked it behind them, and Shay jumped out of the other van and locked it. Shay gave Alexis the keys for the van, "Thank you Shay! You're a star!" Alexis said. Shay smiled, "No problem" she replied. "So, what happens now?" She continued. "We just stay here basically, until I can get conformation that this whole situation is sorted" Alexis replied. "Is it okay if I stay with you guys? I don't know anyone else here" Shay asked nervously. Alexis nodded, "But you have to do exactly what I say, I'm not doing it to be bossy, I'm doing it to protect us all, okay?" Alexis asked. Shay saluted her. "Yes boss" she replied. "Hi Mrs Smith" She said, waving to Louise. Louise laughed. "Hey Shay, and none of this Mrs Smith talk, call me Louise" she replied. Shay nodded, "Gotcha". "Hey Bailey and Charlie" Shay continued. "Hey Shay" they replied in unison. Alexis turned to Bailey. "You, Charlie and mum go up to HQ, I'll be there soon, me and Shay need to go and help Danny and Dylan" She instructed. "Okay, meet you there" Bailey replied, and her, Charlie and Louise walked off and up to HQ. Alexis and Shay then walked over to Alexis' van. She opened the back doors and they climbed in. "Come on, we're going up to HQ" Alexis instructed. She went to help Danny up, before he fell back down, groaning and flinching. She jumped out of the van and towards the back room behind the reception desk in the entrance, she came out holding two folded up wheelchairs, she opened the wheelchairs and put them next to the van, "Shay, you get Dylan and help him into the wheelchair, I'll get Danny" she instructed. Shay walked over to Dylan and held her arms out for him to grab, "Ooh, who's your friend here?" Dylan smirked, looking at Alexis. Shay laughed. "This is Shay" "Sup Shay" Danny said. "Heya Dan" she replied. "Hey, I'm Dylan, nice to meet you" Dylan said, sticking his hand out for her to shake, Shay laughed and shook his hand, "I'm Shay, nice to meet you too" she replied. Alexis and Danny laughed. "Dylan, you can flirt later, we need to get you up to HQ" Danny teased. Dylan blushed. "Whatever" he replied. Alexis and Danny laughed again. Dylan grabbed Shay's arms and she pulled him up, before helping him out of the van and into the wheelchair, Alexis did the same with Danny. Alexis then grabbed the bags out of the vans, and locked her van, putting the keys in her pocket.

"Follow me" she instructed. She started walking towards HQ, pushing Danny along, Shay and Dylan followed close behind.

When they got to Alexis' office, they walked in. "Okay, time to get you two fixed up" Alexis said, looking towards Danny and Dylan. Just as she was about to continue talking, she remembered that she had left some people in her mums van. "Bloody hell, I almost forgot, there were people in mums van too" Alexis said. Her mum threw her the van key. "Right, I'll go and let them out and explain everything to them, Charlie, you come with me and, and when we get to the entrance, you go to the pharmacy and get us some more medical supplies. We need plasters, bandages, tissues, cotton wool, antiseptic cream, surgical tape and pain killers" Alexis instructed. She wrote everything down on a small piece of paper and handed it to Charlie.

When they got to the entrance, Charlie walked off towards to the Pharmacy.

Chapter Twenty-Four

ALEXIS' P.O.V

Alexis unlocked the van, before returning the keys into her pocket. Suddenly, the door of the van flew open, hitting Alexis in the face and knocking her back "WHAT THE FUCK" she shouted. The people jumped out of the van, slamming the door after them, and they all stood in front of her. Alexis wiped her nose with the back of her hand, to see that it was covered in blood. "Thanks a bunch" Alexis shouted sarcastically, holding her nose. "You shouldn't have been in the way, it's your own fault" a woman replied. Alexis looked up at her, "Listen yeah, I've just saved your life, so if you think you can speak to me like that, you can fuck off back out there with all those zombies" Alexis said angrily. The woman grabbed Alexis. "Who do you think you're talking too?!" the woman spat. "You, obviously" Alexis replied. The woman then swung her arm back and then punched Alexis in the nose, causing her nose to begin gushing with blood. Alexis wiped her nose on her sleeve. She then put one hand over her face, and used the other hand to punch the woman back, the force of the punch causing the woman to fall backwards onto the floor. Alexis then leant over the woman, "Tell you what, I'll let you have that one, but if even dare touch me again, those zombies will be the least of your problems", Alexis sneered. The woman laughed, "Oh yeah, and what are you going to do?" she asked. Alexis laughed, before standing up and pulling her gun out of her pocket, she aimed it a few millimeters away from the woman's head, before pulling the trigger. The sound of the shot startled everyone, and the woman squealed. Frankie and Allie then pulled her back, "Woah, cool off girl" Frankie said. Alexis laughed, before facing the other people, and the woman stood with the others. "Here's how it is, you've all got access the supermarket, you can take a reasonable amount of food and drink, and other necessities. I find out you're taking more than you need, if you've gone into any of the restricted shops, or if you cause any trouble, you'll be out of here quicker than you can say the word zombie. Got it?" Alexis shouted, her hand still over her nose. Everyone nodded, the woman walked up to Alexis and stood directly in front of her. "Got it?" Alexis sneered. The woman nodded. Alexis then pushed her backwards, "Now get out of my face" She sneered. The woman spat in her face. Alexis looked at her in shock, she wiped the spit of her cheek, before punching the woman square in the mouth, before shoving her into a wall, then throwing her over the counter. "I swear to god, touch me again and you will die" she screamed, as she tried lunging at her. The woman stood back up, groaning and stumbling into the shopping centre. "Chemist is over there" Alexis shouted. The woman turned to lunge at her, before someone grabbed her and pulled her away. Alexis laughed. "Oh yeah, I'm Alexis by the way" she shouted. Everyone introduced themselves, except the woman that attacked her, as Rick, Jade, Logan and Jackie. "What about her?" Alexis sneered, pointing to the woman. "That's Dana" Rick said. "Right" Alexis replied. Alexis turned and walked off towards Frankie and Allie. "Nice punch girl" Frankie joked. Alexis laughed. "You should get that seen too" Allie said. "I'll be fine" Alexis replied. Charlie walked behind her "Okay, got every- WOAH what's happened to you!?" she shouted. "Long story, let's just go back to HQ" Alexis replied.

CHARLIE'S P.O.V

When Charlie got to the pharmacy, she grabbed a basket on her way in and scoured the isles for the things on the list. She was looking down an aisle, when she spotted a first aid kid on the top shelf. She reached up for it, but it was too high up. Just then, she saw an arm reach up and grab it. She turned around to confront them, when she saw a tall dark haired boy stood in front of her, he handed her the first aid kit, "There you go" he said, smiling at her. "Thank you" Charlie replied. "I'm Luke" he said, introducing himself. "I'm Charlie" Charlie smiled. "You're one of the girls that saved us, right?" Luke asked. "Yeah, I was there, but that was mainly my sister" Charlie replied. "You still helped that guy after he got beaten up, so in my eyes, you're as much of a hero as your sister" he replied, attempting to re-assure her. Charlie smiled, "Thanks that means a lot" she replied. Luke smiled. "So, where are you hanging out, whilst you're here?" Luke asked. "Oh, erm, I just walk around really" Charlie replied. "Same" Luke replied. "Who are you here with?" he asked. "My mum, my sister Bailey, my sister Alexis, Alexis' boyfriend, and his brother" Charlie replied, "How about you?" She asked. "Sounds cool, and I came here with my mum, but now I've ended up on my own" he replied. "Why are you on your own, where's your mum?" Charlie asked. "She doesn't pay much attention to me, as soon as we got here, she told me to go away and go find someone else to hang around with, she doesn't care where I go" he sighed. "That's horrible, especially in these circumstances" Charlie replied. "Yeah, but I'm used to it" Luke replied. "Anyway, what's a pretty girl like you doing in here?" Luke asked. Charlie laughed. "You've got a cute smile" he continued. "Thank you" she replied. Luke leaned on the wall, "So, you say you're here with your sister's boyfriend, what about you, you got yourself a boyfriend on the outside?" he asked. "No, I'm single" Charlie said, before laughing. "How?" he asked. Charlie raised her eyebrow, "What do you mean?" she asked. Luke smiled, "I mean, you're so pretty, and you seem like a really nice girl, so how have you not been snatched up yet?" he asked. Charlie blushed a little, before smiling, "I don't know, must be a mystery" She shrugged. Luke laughed, "Must be" he replied. They both started laughing. "We should totally hang out more whilst we're here" Luke said. Charlie smiled, "Yeah, we should" she replied. "And you never know, we could sort out this 'no boyfriend' problem of yours" Luke winked. "Well, that depends on you, doesn't it?" Charlie replied. "What about me?" Luke asked, confused. "Are *you* single?" she asked. Luke laughed, "I am" he replied. "Well then, maybe we could sort out this 'no girlfriend' problem of yours while we're at it" Charlie replied. Just then, they heard a shot, Luke jumped slightly. "What the hell was that?" he asked. Charlie laughed, "It's probably Alexis, she's a bit trigger happy at times" she joked. Luke laughed. "I should go" Charlie replied, Luke sighed, "Do you have to?" he asked. "Yeah, I need to go and make sure Alexis is okay" she replied. "Okay, but what about the stuff on your list?" he said, pointing down to the list in Charlie's hand. "OH YEAH, I FORGOT, PLEASE WILL YOU HELP ME?" she asked quickly, Luke laughed, "Sure, what do you need?" he asked. "Plasters, bandages, tissues, cotton wool, antiseptic cream, and pain killers" Charlie replied. "Okay, well that first aid kit covers the plasters and bandages, you get the cotton wool and tissues, and

I'll find the antiseptic cream and pain killers for you" he replied. "Thank you" Charlie said, before running down the aisle and grabbing as much stuff as she could.

When they got everything on the list, they met back in the aisle where they met. Luke gave Charlie the stuff, "Thank you so much" Charlie said. "I'll see you round then?" Luke asked. "Yeah" Charlie replied. Just as he was about to walk off, Charlie shouted him, "Luke!". He turned around, "Yeah?" he replied. "Come with me" she said. Luke smiled and walked towards Charlie. "Want some help with those?" he asked. Charlie smiled and handed him the basket. "Come on then" Charlie said, and she walked towards the entrance, Luke following behind.

When she got to the entrance, she saw Alexis talking to some people, she walked over to her, "Okay, got every-" Charlie started. Alexis then turned around, and Charlie saw all the blood on her face. "Woah, what's happened to you?" Charlie asked. "Long story, let's just go back to HQ" Alexis said.

No one's P.O.V

"Wait" Charlie said. Alexis looked at her, and saw Luke stood next to her, "Alexis, this is Luke" Charlie introduced. Luke smiled at her, "Hey, are you okay?" Luke asked her. Alexis smiled, "Yeah, just had a bit of a fight" Alexis replied. "I did first aid at school, do you want some help with that?" Luke asked. "Yes please, that would be great" Alexis replied. "We need some tissue" Luke said, Charlie quickly opened the tissues she had just got, and passed him a few. "I need you to sit down, and tilt your head back" Luke instructed. Alexis walked over to the reception, and jumped up and sat on the edge of the counter-top. She then tilted her head back, and Luke pinched the bridge of her nose, Alexis flinched slightly. "I'm sorry if this is hurting you, I don't think you've broken your nose, I think having a nose bleed" Luke explained, then gave her the tissues, "Here, you just have to pinch the bridge of your nose to stop the bleeding, and just hold some tissue over it for a few minutes" he continued. Alexis did as he said.

A couple of minutes later, and Alexis put lowered her head and moved the tissue, "Is it still bleeding?" she asked. Luke looked at her, "Nope, it's stopped" he replied. Alexis smiled, "Thank you so much" Alexis said. "It's fine" Luke replied. "I don't think it's broken, just be careful and try not to get into any more fights" he joked. "Easier said than done" Alexis replied. "Charlie, can I talk to you in private?" Alexis asked. "Sure, Luke, can you give us a minute?" Luke nodded, and walked over to the wall opposite them. Alexis smiled at Charlie, "So, who's your friend?" Alexis asked. "He helped me in the pharmacy, he's really nice isn't he?" Charlie asked, glancing over at Luke. "Yeah, and he's alright looking too" Alexis teased. Charlie laughed. "I know yeah, and he was proper flirting with me too!" Charlie said. Alexis smiled, "Ooooh, boyfriend material maybe?" she asked. Charlie laughed, "Definitely" she replied. They both laughed. "Hey, Alexis, would it be okay if he stayed with us?" Charlie asked. Alexis looked over at him, "Sure, but we can't train him" Alexis said. "Thank you!" Charlie replied, hugging her. "But, we've got to swear him to secrecy, I'm guessing you want to tell him, you know, about who we really are?" Alexis asked. "Yeah, I don't think he'd tell anyone" Charlie replied. "He'll still need to sign one of those declaration of privacy agreements that John has the staff signing" he explained. Charlie nodded, "No problem, we can print one off when we get to my office, I saw them on the computer" she explained. "Okay, who's he here with?" Alexis asked. "He came with his mum, but apparently, she doesn't care where he is as long as he stays out of her sight", Charlie replied, "Ahh, one of those parents?" Alexis said. Charlie nodded. Alexis looked over to Luke, "Hey Luke, can you come over here for a minute?" she shouted. Luke walked over, "Sup?" he asked. "Do you want to chill with us?" Alexis asked. Luke smiled. "Yeah, I'd love to, is that okay with you?" he replied. Alexis smiled, "Yeah, that's fine, come with us" Alexis said. "Thanks" Luke said. Alexis jumped off the counter, and started walking towards HQ, Charlie and Luke trailing behind.

When they got to HQ, Luke stopped and stared. "Where are we?" he asked. "Charlie, you take him to your office and start explaining things to him, I'll go and sort Danny and Dylan out" Alexis instructed. Charlie and Luke handed the stuff over to Alexis. "Come on then, this way" Charlie instructed, grabbing Luke's arm and linking it with hers.

Chapter Twenty-Five

ALEXIS' P.O.V

Alexis walked into her office, "Sorry I took so long" she said. "What happened to you?" Danny asked, looking at the blood and bruises on her face. "Oh, I got into a fight, where are mum, Shay and Bailey?" Alexis asked. "They went to Bailey's office for a nap" Danny replied. Alexis put the stuff down and walked over to Danny, she knelt next to him. "Are you okay?" Alexis asked, stroking his cheek with her finger. "Yeah, I'm fine, are you okay?" he replied. "I'm fine" Alexis replied. Alexis looked over to Dylan, "How you holding up Dyl?" she asked. "I'm fine now, just got a bruised knee from what I can see" Dylan replied, "It just hurts a bit" he continued. Alexis threw him the painkillers, "Here, take some of these" she said. "Cheers" Dylan replied.

Alexis turned her attention back to Danny, "Where does it hurt?" she asked. "Just my chest" Danny replied. "Alright, take your top off" Alexis replied. Danny smirked at her, Alexis laughed, "Oh, behave, I just need to see if you have any open wounds" she replied. Danny laughed; he then took his shirt off. Alexis scanned him over, "Nope, you should be fine, you may just have some bruised ribs" she said. Dylan threw him the painkillers, "Take some of these bro, they're good, they're already kicking in" Dylan said. Danny took 2 of the tablets. "You can put your shirt back on now" Alexis said, throwing his shirt at him. "Yeah, I can, but I'm not going too" he replied, he then laughed and threw the shirt back at Alexis. Alexis laughed. "Come over here and give me a cuddle?" Danny asked, holding his arms out. Alexis smiled, she walked over to him and sat on his knee, and he wrapped his arms around her. "Oh, guess what" Alexis said. "Mmmm?" Danny replied. "Charlie found herself a friend" Alexis replied. "What do you mean?" Danny asked. "A boy she met in the pharmacy" she replied. Danny laughed, "In the pharmacy? how romantic" Danny joked. Alexis punched his arm,

"Shut it you, she seems to really like him, she's brought him up here" she said. "Are you going to tell him?" Danny asked. "I'm not, Charlie is, she has to make sure he stays out of trouble, and she has to make sure that he doesn't tell anyone" Alexis explained. "Charlie's smart, she wouldn't bring him up here unless she knows she can trust him" Danny replied. "Yeah good point" Alexis replied.

A couple of minutes passed. "So, what's the plan now boss?" Danny asked, playing with her hair. "Well, we need to see if you can walk" Alexis said, she stood up and held her hands out, he grabbed onto her hands and she pulled him up, he wobbled a bit, but then stabilized himself. He put his arms around her shoulders, "Come on then, let's go and meet this friend of Charlie's" he said. Alexis laughed. She took a step forward, and he did the same. "Oh, it's fine, I can walk" he said. He took his arm from around her shoulders, and hobbled around the room, holding onto his chest. "All good" he said, wheezing a little. "Take it easy" Alexis laughed. She held her hand out, "Come on then muppet" she joked. He held her hand and they walked to Charlie's office.

CHARLIE'S P.O.V

"So, you've got your own office, do you work here?" Luke asked. "Sort of" Charlie replied. "What do you mean 'sort of'?" he continued. "I'll explain it to you when we get to my office" Charlie replied.

When they got to Charlie's office, she unlocked the door and they walked in. Charlie walked over to her desk and sat on the edge, "Sit down" she said, pointing at the chair next to her, he walked over and sat on the chair. "I don't even know where to start..." Charlie said. "Just go at your own pace, there's no rush" he replied. "Basically, I work for the secret services, and this is where we are based. This is the Limebarn division, this is where the secret services originated from" Charlie explained. Luke stayed silent. "Say something then" Charlie said. "I-you-wha-how?" Luke replied. Charlie laughed. "How what? Did I become an agent?" Charlie asked. Luke nodded. "I was employed by the head agent" Charlie replied. "What do you mean by that?" Luke asked. "We have a head agent, she runs this base. Each base has a leader" Charlie explained. "Where is she then? Because shouldn't she be the one keeping this all under control? Instead of leaving it to you and your sisters? I mean, you're doing a great job, but I can't even imagine how hard it is" Luke replied. "She is here, it's Alexis" Charlie continued. Luke's jaw dropped. "What? Alexis is head agent?" he mumbled. Charlie nodded. "But how? She's not even that old" he asked. Charlie laughed. "I know, but she's been working here for over 6 years, she knows this place better than anyone" Charlie explained. "What, how old is she?" Luke asked. "17, almost 18" Charlie replied. "Wow, so she's been working here since she was 11... That's crazy, she must be really good at her job" Luke replied. "Yeah, she is, you've seen the way she handles situations" Charlie pointed out. Luke nodded, "I can't even imagine how hard it must be for her" he said. "She's strong, she can handle the pressure" Charlie continued. Luke nodded. It stayed silent for a while.

"So, let's talk about you" Luke said. "What about me?" Charlie replied. "What's your role here?" he asked. "I'm a super agent" Charlie said proudly. "What's one of them?" he replied. Charlie laughed. "Did you ever hear about that huge report on that team of 'spies' a while ago? The ABC Triple Threat?" she asked. Luke nodded. Charlie smiled. "What about it?" he asked. "ABC..." Charlie replied, trying to hint to him. He looked at her in total confusion. "Alexis, Bailey, Charlie" she said. Luke's eyebrows raised. "You?" he mumbled. Charlie nodded. "We are the TRIPLE THREAT ABC" she said proudly. "Oh my god" he replied. Charlie laughed again. "Yeah" she replied. "You're amazing" he replied. He then blushed a little. "Thank you" she replied. "I still can't believe my girlfri- you are a super agent" he said. "I know, it's really hard to belie- wait, what did you just call me?" She said. "Nothing" Luke said, starting to blush. "You did, you called me your girlfriend" Charlie smiled. "No, I didn't mean that, I meant my friend that is a girl" Luke said quickly. "You sure about that?" she asked. "Yeah, unless, you know, you want to be my girlfriend?" he asked. "What if I do?" Charlie replied. "Is that a yes?" Luke said, smiling. "Well, that depends, doesn't it?" Charlie replied. She smiled. Luke stood up and stood in front of her, "On what?" he replied. "If you want me to be" Charlie replied, looking up at him. "What if I do?" he replied, smiling. "Well you better show me a sign" she replied. "What kind of sign?" he asked, leaning closer to her. "Depends what you have in mind" Charlie replied. Luke smiled; he then leaned in and kissed her, after a couple of seconds, he felt her kissing back. "So does this mean you're my girlfriend?" he asked. Charlie stood up in front of him and looked up at him, "Looks like it, doesn't it" she replied. He smiled and held her hands. She smiled back at him. "You do know you can't tell *anyone* about anything I've told you, right?" Charlie asked. "I know, your secret is safe with me" he replied. Charlie smiled. Luke leant in to kiss her again, before Alexis and Danny walked in.

Chapter Twenty-Six

Alexis and Danny walked into Charlie's office, and saw her about to kiss Luke, "Woah woah woah, what's going on here?" Alexis interrupted. Charlie looked at her and smiled, "Busted" she said. Luke laughed. "Yeah, busted, care to explain?" Alexis said, tapping her foot. "Erm, well, you know, yeah" Charlie mumbled. "Was I supposed to understand that?" Alexis asked. Charlie laughed. "Hey Danny" Charlie said. "Sup girl" Danny replied. "This is my boyfriend, Luke" Charlie replied. Alexis' eyebrows raised, "BOYFRIEND?!" she shouted. Charlie nodded. Alexis smiled, "Nice going girl" she replied. Charlie laughed. Luke smiled, "So you approve?" he asked. "Yeah, I knew this would happen" Alexis replied. Charlie and Luke laughed. "How you gonna tell mum?" Alexis asked. "Like this" Charlie replied. She walked over to the phone on her desk, and dialed Baileys office number. "Hello?" Bailey said. "Hey Bailey, put mum on" Charlie replied. "Hello?" Louise said. "Hey mum, it's Charlie, I have a boyfriend, Okay, bye" she said, and before her mum had a chance to respond, Charlie put the phone down. "Done" she said. They all started laughing. "Come on then guys, let's go to my office and plan our next move" Alexis instructed. Everyone stood up and walked out of Charlie's office, Charlie locking it behind her. When they got to the office, they opened the door, to see Shay and Dylan kissing. "OH MY GOD HOW MANY TIMES AM I GOING TO HAVE TO WALK IN TO A ROOM AND SEE PEOPLE KISSING?" Alexis shouted. Everyone laughed. "Now you see what we have to put up with, with you and Danny" Dylan replied. "Yeah" Charlie said, backing up Dylan's statement. Alexis and Danny laughed. "Yeah, but we've been together for ages, we didn't even know you and Shay, or Charlie and Luke were together, until we walked in on you kissing" Danny replied. "Yeah" Alexis said, mimicking Charlie and backing up Danny. "Whatever" Dylan said. "So, are you guys together aswell?" Alexis asked Dylan and Shay. Shay looked at Dylan, "Are we?" she asked. "Damn straight" Dylan said. Shay smiled. "Okay, well tell you what, no kissing around my mum or Bailey, they'll kill us all! plus Bailey's a bit trigger happy at times, takes after her big sis" Alexis joked. Everyone laughed.

BANG!

The door flew open, "CHARLIE SMITH, WHAT DO YOU MEAN YOU HAVE A BOYFR-" Louise shouted, stopping when she saw Charlie stood with Luke. "Hi, I'm Louise, Charlie's mum" Louise said, introducing herself to Luke. Alexis and Danny laughed. "Hi, I'm Luke" he replied. "Nice to meet you" Louise replied. "You too" Luke continued. "Well, my girls always go for the lookers, don't they, first Danny, now you" Louise said, looking at Danny and Luke. "Mum!" Alexis shouted. "Thanks Louise" Danny smiled. Luke laughed, "Thanks" he said. Alexis and Charlie looked at each other and laughed. "What? I'm just saying..." Louise said. Everyone laughed.

Bailey walked into the room eating a bar of chocolate, "WOAH" she shouted. "What?" Alexis asked. "Am I hallucinating, or am I seeing 3 couples?" she said. Alexis laughed. "Does this mean more kissy kissy?" Bailey replied. "No, it doesn't, because around us, they will have to learn to control themselves" Louise said sternly. "Hey hey hey, I'm perfectly controlled" Danny replied. Alexis laughed, "As if" she replied. Danny winked at her, "Oh, behave" she said. Everyone laughed. "So, what do we do now?" Bailey asked. "Well, we should probably go and make sure everyone's okay down there, and ensure that bitch Dana isn't causing trouble" Alexis sneered. "Alexis Smith, Language!" Louise shouted. "Have you seen what she has done to my face?" she asked. Louise gasped, walking over to Alexis, looking at her face. "What the hell? Are you okay love?" she asked. Alexis nodded. "What did she do?" Louise asked, walking over the fridge-freezer and pulling out an icepack. She handed it to Alexis, "Thanks" she said, as she rested it on her cheek, flinching. "She slammed the van door into my face then punched me a few times" Alexis explained. "Just you wait till you see what I did to her though" Alexis smirked. Louise nudged her shoulder and laughed, "That's my girl" she smiled. Everyone laughed. "Let's go then" Charlie said. "WAIT!" Alexis shouted. Everyone turned to look at her. "Does everyone have a weapon?" Alexis asked. Bailey,

Charlie, Danny, Dylan and Louise held a gun up. "Luke, stay with Charlie, Shay, stay with Dylan" Alexis instructed. Luke and Shay nodded. "Okay, let's go" Alexis instructed, and they all walked down to the shopping centre.

Chapter Twenty-Seven

When they had reached the entrance, they stopped. "Okay, just act normal and try to blend in, if anything kicks off, inform us on the walkie-talkies and we'll get to you as soon as we can, keep each other updated on your location. We'll split off into 4 teams, Me and Danny, Bailey and Mum, Charlie and Luke, and Dylan and Shay, and remember, no guns" Alexis instructed. "Everyone okay with that?" she asked. Everyone nodded. "Okay, split up" She instructed, and everyone went their own way.

Alexis and Danny walked into the main hall of the shopping centre, and Alexis saw the group of teenagers that she had met before, sat against the wall. She grabbed Danny's hand and walked over to them.

"Hey Alexis" Frankie shouted. Alexis smiled, "Hey guys, this is Danny" said Alexis, introducing Danny. Danny smiled, "Hey" he said. Frankie turned to Alexis, "We were looking for you before, where did you go?" She asked. Alexis shrugged, "Just walking around" she replied. Frankie tilted her head to the side, "We looked everywhere for you" she replied. "I was just browsing, we just didn't cross paths" Alexis replied, starting to get nervous. Allie cleared her throat, "What are you hiding from us?" she asked. Alexis turned to Allie. "Nothing" she replied. "Really?" Frankie asked. Alexis clenched her fists, beginning to get angry. "Why are you asking me these questions? I barely even know any of you, I don't have to explain myself" Alexis sneered. Danny grabbed onto her hand tighter, "Calm it" he whispered, kissing her cheek. "Woah, cool it girl, we were just wondering" Frankie replied, confused at Alexis' sudden outburst. Alexis rubbed her eyes, "I'm sorry for snapping, I'm just tired, you have every right to ask me questions" Alexis replied. "What's going on?" Ben asked, Alexis turned to Ben, "What do you think?" she replied. "Well, I think we're having a zombie apocalypse" Ben replied. Frankie, Allie and Deana laughed. Alexis turned to them, "No, don't laugh, he could be right" she pointed out. "What, for real?" Frankie asked. Alexis nodded. Everyone stayed quiet. "Does that mean we're trapped here?" Josh asked. Alexis shook her head, "No, we're not trapped, it's just safer here" Alexis replied. "How are you so sure?" Allie asked. "I just know what I'm talking about" Alexis replied, attempting to re-assure not only everyone else, but also herself. "We saw a hell of a lot of those zombie creatures, they're going to figure out a way to get in here" Frankie replied. "How many did you see?" Alexis asked. Josh spoke up, "We saw a load of them coming out of a warehouse near Range Road School" he said. Alexis turned to him. "How many would you say?" she asked, her palms starting to sweat. "At least 50" he replied. Alexis gulped. "What happened after you saw them coming out of the warehouse?" she asked. "We were just walking down the road, on our way to a garden party, and they started running towards us, and as they got closer, we could tell something wasn't right, so we turned around and just started running, and we ended up here, but about half way here, we turned to look back and they had all split up into smaller groups and ran in different directions, so we kept running until we got here" he explained. Alexis gulped. "Where did they split into groups?" she asked. "At the roundabout, a group went down Littlefield drive; a group went down Warshaw Road, one group turned and went the direction they came from, and a group followed us" Ben interrupted. It stayed silent for a few minutes.

Danny turned to Alexis, "Don't you live on Littlefield drive?" he asked. Alexis nodded. "They've gone to my house" Alexis mumbled. "But it's fine, there's no one in your house" he replied, trying to re-assure her. "Why would they be targeting you?" Allie asked. Alexis shrugged it off casually, "I'm probably just being paranoid" Alexis replied. "What's going on Alexis?" Frankie asked. "I'm not sure" she replied. Danny tugged at her arm. "Let's go find everyone" he said, to stop her saying everything else. Alexis nodded, "We'll see you later" she said. "Oh wait, do you want my number? In case you need me?" Alexis asked. "I do!" Josh said instantly. Alexis laughed. Josh, Frankie and Allie nodded and pulled out their phones, Alexis told them her number, and then she waved and her and Danny walked away.

Alexis pulled out her walkie-talkie. "Hey guys, we need to have a meeting, now" she said. Then her and Danny walked up towards HQ.

When they got up to HQ, Alexis and Danny walked into the conference room, to find that everyone was already there waiting for them. They sat down. "Right, we were talking to those teenagers that were running from that group of zombies earlier, and they told us that they saw a load of zombies coming out of that warehouse near Range Road school, so my guess is that that's where they are hiding. The plan is, Me, Danny, Bailey, Charlie and mum will go and find out what's going on... Shay, Luke and Dylan, I need you to stay here and look after things, and make sure that no trouble starts" Alexis instructed. "If Dana kicks off, literally just shoot her I don't even care" she laughed. "Alexis, is it okay if I stay here? I really don't want to do this" Bailey mumbled, tears in her eyes. Alexis walked over to Bailey and hugged her, "You stay here if you don't want to come, I'd rather you stayed here anyway" she whispered. "Thank you" Bailey whispered back. "Yeah, can I stay too? I don't think I'm quite up to that" Louise continued. Alexis nodded. "Charlie, Danny, are you okay to come with me?" Alexis asked. They both nodded. "Okay, we'll keep in touch through the walkie-talkies, I'll keep you all updated" Alexis replied. Everyone nodded. Charlie gulped. "Are you okay?" Alexis asked Charlie. "Yeah, I'm fine" she mumbled back. "Charlie, I know there's something bothering you, what is it?" Alexis asked. "I don't think I'm up for this" Charlie sighed. Alexis smiled, then hugged Charlie. "Thank you" she whispered. "Guns?" she asked Danny. He nodded. "Okay, time to roll" Alexis said. "You sure you're ready for this?" she asked. Danny grabbed onto her hand "Let's do this" he replied. "Do you really have to do this?" Bailey asked. Alexis nodded, "We both know the answer to that" Alexis replied. Alexis ran over to Bailey, Charlie, her mum and Shay, and hugged them all. "Be careful love" Louise instructed. Alexis nodded. Dylan walked over to Danny, "Stay safe bro" he said, giving him a hug. "Will do bro" Danny replied. Dylan cleared his throat and looked at Alexis, tapping his cheek. Alexis laughed, running over and kissing his cheek again. Everyone laughed. Alexis walked to the door, followed by Danny, and turned and waved them goodbye, before walking out of the room, shutting the door behind her.

When Alexis and Danny got to the entrance, they walked into the main part of the shopping centre. "EVERYBODY" Alexis shouted. Everyone ignored her and kept on talking. Alexis pulled out her gun and pulled the trigger. Everyone stopped talking and turned to her. "Everyone, stay in this part of the centre, we're going to block off the entrance from here to the main reception. Me and Danny are going to see if anyone else needs help, and to hopefully try and get some answers" She shouted. Everyone stayed quiet, before Frankie spoke up. "Be careful" she shouted. Alexis smiled and nodded.

She and Danny then walked into the main reception, before lowering the shutters, and locking them, and then throwing Danny the keys. Danny walked over to the entrance doors, and unlocked them, lifting the shutters. Alexis got in the van, and drove out of the entrance doors, and stopped just outside them. Danny then walked out of the entrance, closing the shutters behind them and got into the van. Alexis then drove to the main gates and stopped. She looked out to see that there were no zombies surrounded the gates. "They must all be at the warehouse" she said to Danny. She got out of the van and unlocked the gates and opened them, allowing Danny to drive the van out of the gates. She then locked the gates behind him, and jumped back into the van. "You ready for this?" Alexis asked. Danny nodded. "LET'S GO" she shouted. She then slammed her foot down onto the accelerator, and sped off towards the warehouse.

Chapter Twenty-Eight

When they got to the roundabout, Alexis stopped. Instead of carrying on towards the warehouse, she turned down Littlefield Drive, and pulled over in the driveway of her house. Alexis jumped out of the van, followed by Danny, and locked the van behind her. She pulled out her gun and walked towards the door, she saw that the front door had been tampered with. She gulped, and pushed the door open with her foot. She then walked inside, Danny following close behind, and they began checking the rooms. She walked into the living room, and on the floor, saw all of the framed photos smashed up in the middle of the floor, covered in blood. She walked over to them and knelt next to them. She picked up the picture of her and Daisy, which was from their first day of year 3. She pulled the picture out of the smashed frame, and put it into her pocket. "Erm, Alexis" Danny said. Alexis stood up, and turned to see Danny staring at the wall, which had writing on it. She walked over to him, and looked up at the writing.

"*Everything you have been told is a lie*" it read.

"What does that mean?" Alexis asked. Danny shrugged. She pulled out her mobile phone, and took a picture.

Just then, she heard a noise. She turned to see a zombie stood in the doorway of the living room. "Move out of the way!" Danny shouted. Alexis then dropped to the floor, and Danny shot the zombie directly between the eyes, causing it to fall onto the floor. It didn't move. Alexis stood back up and ran over to Danny. "Nice shot" she said, giving him a high-five. "Let's check the rest of the house" She continued... She slowly walked into the kitchen, and saw that there was another message written on the wall.

"Everything didn't happen the way you think it did" **it read.**

Alexis took a picture of that wall as well, before walking out of the kitchen, and up the stairs, followed by Danny.

First, she walked into her mum's room. Everything was just how they left it. Alexis then began searching the room for another message. She then shut the door to find it written on the back.

"Thing's will become clearer soon" **it read.**

She took a picture, then she walked into Baileys and Charlie's room. Everything had been pulled out of their drawers, and the drawers had been smashed up. She turned to Danny and he shrugged. Just then, Alexis saw a drop of red fall onto the carpet next to her. She looked up to see another message written on the ceiling, she nudged Danny, and Danny looked up.

"You were so young and naive" **it read**.

She took a picture of that message, before walking out of that room and into her room, followed by Danny. Everything had been smashed up. All of the pictures off her wall had been ripped up, her picture frames had been smashed, and everything was ruined. "Who would even do this?" Alexis asked. "It's probably James or Ray" he replied. "Yeah, you're probably right. I wonder why there isn't a message in here" Alexis pointed out. Danny was just about to reply, when Alexis heard a familiar chime. Her eyes widened, and she ran out of her room, she then walked down the end of the hallway, to the door at the end. She put her hand onto the doorknob, but then quickly took it off. "This is Daisy's room, and that is her jewellery box" she said to Danny. Danny put his hand on her shoulder, and turned her around, he then put his hands on either side of her face and smiled at her, "You can do this" he whispered.

"Nobody's been there since......in ages" Alexis mumbled, tears in her eyes. She then turned around and put her hand on the doorknob again. She left it on for a couple of seconds, before taking it back off. "I can't do this Danny" she whimpered. Danny put his arms around her waist and rested his head on her shoulder, "I'm here baby, you can do this, I know you can" he whispered. Tears rolled down Alexis' face. The chime then ended. Alexis then took a deep breath and put her hand on the doorknob, and turned it, she then slowly opened the door. In front of her, on the wall, read another message.

"Your sister isn't dead" **it read.**

Chapter Twenty-Nine

Alexis' legs collapsed under her, and she fell to the floor crying. Danny ran into the room and over to the wall. He then turned to Daisy's bed and his face went pale. Alexis didn't see, and she pulled out her phone and dialled her mum's number. She soon answered. "Hello?" her mum said. "Mum guess what?", "what?" her mum replied. Before she could say anything else, Danny interrupted her. "Erm, Alexis" he mumbled. Alexis looked up at him. He then walked over to Daisy's bed, Alexis stayed frozen on the spot. He then walked back over and stared at the bed again. "What is it?" Alexis asked. "What's happening Alexis?" her mum asked. She ended the call. Alexis then saw a girl walk into the doorway.

It was Daisy…

She stood there, staring at Alexis. "Daisy?" Alexis mumbled, starting to cry again. Daisy smiled, "Hey sis" Daisy replied. Alexis then collapsed back onto the floor, and blacked out.

Alexis was woken, her name being shouted. She opened her eyes to see Danny looking down at her. "Lexy? Babe?" he said. He helped her sit up and leant her against the wall. "What happened?" Alexis asked, rubbing her eyes. "You passed out, you were out cold for about 10 minutes, I was starting to get so worried" he said, stroking her cheek. "I had the craziest dream" Alexis mumbled, before rubbing her eyes again. "What was it" Danny asked. "I had a dream that Daisy was still alive" she replied. Danny smiled, as he turned and faced into Daisy's room. "It wasn't a dream" he said. Alexis then turned to see Daisy stood in the doorway. "Oh shit" Alexis whispered. Daisy smiled and walked over to her. She held out her hand, and Alexis held onto it, and Daisy pulled her up. Alexis then stood and stared at her for a few seconds, before raising her hand and putting it on her face. "Oh my god" Alexis whispered, tears pouring down her face. Daisy smiled. Alexis hugged her, and held onto her tight. "I thought you were dead" Alexis cried. "I know, but I'm here now, and I'm never leaving again" Daisy replied. Alexis then stood back and wiped her eyes, "I can't believe this" Alexis mumbled. She then turned to see Danny staring at her smiling. "What you smiling at?" she asked. "Which one are you?" Danny joked. Alexis smiled. "She's alive Danny" she said. "I know babe" he replied. Daisy smiled, "I've missed you so much" she said. Alexis smiled. "I've missed you too, so much" Alexis said. They then hugged again. "WE NEED TO TELL MUM" Alexis shouted. Daisy smiled. Alexis then pulled out her phone, and on the screen, it read:

15 missed calls

She looked down the missed calls, to see 6 off her mum, 2 off Bailey, 2 off Charlie, 2 off Shay, and 3 Dylan. Then her phone started flashing, saying "1 voice mail" she then held her phone to her ear.

*"We know where you're hiding, you better keep an eye on those sisters of yours, you wouldn't want a repeat performance of the Daisy situation... *laughs* Leaving them alone and unguarded wasn't such a good idea"*

Alexis then froze, before collapsing again.

She was then woken up a couple of minutes later by Daisy. "Lex, LEX!" she was shouting. Alexis opened her eyes, "Mmmmm?" she groaned. Daisy helped her up, "Girl, I wish you'd stop passing out, are you *trying* to give us a heart attack?" she asked. "What's happened Lex?" Danny asked. Alexis then pushed herself up. "They're going after Bailey, Mum and Charlie" she said. "What did they say?" Daisy asked. "That they know where mum, Bailey and Charlie are and they are going after them next" Alexis said, tears running down her face. Danny held onto her hand, "We'll find them, don't worry" he whispered. Alexis didn't respond. "Lex, I think I know what they are planning" Daisy replied. Alexis turned to her, "What?" she asked. "They're going to try and do the same with them as they did with me" Daisy said. "What do you mean?" Alexis asked. Daisy explained. Alexis nodded. "We need to get to HQ" Danny said. Daisy grabbed a bag and threw it over her shoulders,

"What's that?" Daisy asked. "Oh, I packed some things up when you passed out, because I guessed that we weren't going to be staying here. I grabbed some of your stuff, because obviously, my old stuff isn't going to fit me now" Daisy explained. Alexis laughed, "Nice thinking sis" Alexis replied. They all then ran down the stairs and out of the door. Alexis unlocked the van "Get in the back" she instructed to Daisy, she jumped in the back and Alexis and Danny jumped into the front, and they sped off to HQ.

Chapter Thirty

When Alexis got to the main entrance of the shopping centre, she slammed her foot down on the brake, causing the van to jolt. "What the hell?" Daisy asked. "Look" She said, pointing to the entrance. The gate was wide open, and there was a group of zombies surrounding a body. "What if?" Alexis mumbled. "No, don't think like that" Danny interrupted. Alexis handed Daisy a gun, "You still know how to work one of these, right?" she asked. Daisy laughed. "Alexis, your lack of confidence in me is insulting" Daisy joked. Alexis laughed. She turned to Danny, "You ready?" she asked. "Yeah I am" he replied. He pulled out 2 guns. "Right, I'll drive at them, and when they move away, jump out and start shooting, okay?" Alexis instructed. "Okay" Danny replied. Daisy nodded. Alexis then slammed her foot onto the accelerator, before speeding towards the group of zombies, just before they hit them, Alexis swerved, causing the zombies to move away. They then all jumped out of the van, and started shooting.

When they had killed them all, they walked over to the body they were surrounding, and looked down at them, and they all did a sigh with relief, to see that it wasn't anybody that they knew. Alexis then looked at the entrance of the building, to see the entrance doors were wide open, and the glass was smashed. They all got back in the van and Alexis sped towards the building.

She pulled up in the reception, before quickly closing the shutters. They all jumped out, and Alexis saw Frankie and Allie running towards them. "Alexis, they've been here, they broke in, they tried getting through the shutters but they couldn't. When they left, they were shouting your name" Frankie shouted. "I know" Alexis said. Alexis then locked the van doors, before her, Daisy and Danny ran off, and up to HQ.

When they got to HQ, Daisy stopped. "Oh my god, it's changed so much" She said. "No time to admire the surroundings" Alexis said, before pulling Daisy to her office.

"So, I'm guessing this is your boyfriend" Daisy said, pointing to Danny. Alexis laughed. "Yeah, this is Danny" she replied. "Nice going girl" she said. "I know right" Alexis replied, before winking at Danny. Danny laughed. "So, where's John?" Daisy asked. Alexis' eyes widened. "Didn't you know? John was in on the whole thing" Alexis replied. "No he wasn't? That was his twin?" Daisy replied. "What the hell?" Alexis replied, confused. "Yeah, they abducted John a few days ago, just after he retired. He found a way for us to escape yesterday, and he told me he was going to go and find you, to tell you their plan, but I got caught" Daisy continued. "This is crazy" Alexis replied, running her fingers through her hair. "Tell me about it" Daisy replied. Just then, Alexis' phone started ringing.

Alexis looked at her phone, "It's mum", she said, looking at Daisy. "Don't tell her, I want to surprise her" Daisy said. Alexis nodded. She answered the phone. "Hey mum" she said. "Where are you? Are you okay?" her mum replied. "Yeah, I'm alright, and I'm in my office with Danny" she replied. "Come to Bailey's office" her mum replied. "No, meet me in the conference room, I've got something important to tell you, we've had a major breakthrough" Alexis explained. "Okay, we'll go there now" her mum replied. "Okay, I'll be there in about 5 minutes, I need to change out of these clothes" Alexis continued. "Okay, hurry up" her mum replied. Alexis then put the phone down. "Okay, you go into the conference room and start explaining all of the clues to mum that you found at the house, then when you've told them the final clue, I will walk in" Daisy explained. "Yes boss!" Alexis smiled. She looked at Danny, "Come on you, let's get this party started" she said, she then walked over to him, and he put his arm around her shoulders and they walked out.

Alexis walked into the conference room, and stood in front of the table, Danny went and sat down. "Okay, me and Danny decided to take a quick stop at our house on the way to the warehouse. When we got to the door, it had been tampered with. We searched every room, and in all of the rooms, everything had been completely smashed up, and almost every room had a message written on the wall. The messages were *'Everything you have told has been a lie'*, *'Everything didn't happen the way you think it did'*, *'Things will become clearer soon'* and *'you were so young and naive'"* Alexis paused. "But then, I walked into Daisy's room" she continued, before pausing again. Her mum put her hands over her mouth, "Please don't tell me they ruined her things" she cried. "I opened the door, and there was a message on the wall" Alexis paused again. "What did it say?" her mum mumbled. "It said your sister isn't dead" Alexis said. At this moment, Louise burst into tears. Just then, there was a knock at the door, "Come in" Alexis said. The door slowly opened, then, a couple of seconds later, Daisy walked in. All colour drained out of everybody's face. Daisy walked over and stood with Alexis. "Daisy?" Bailey mumbled. Daisy smiled. "Hey sweetie" she replied. Bailey and Charlie then smiled, before running over to Daisy and hugging her. Daisy held them tight. "I've missed you both so much" she whispered. "We've missed you too" Charlie replied. They then stepped back, and went over to Alexis and hugged her. Louise then stood up and walked over to Daisy. She put her hand on Daisy's cheek. "Is this really happening?" Louise mumbled, tears still in her eyes. "I'm here mum" Daisy said, before smiling, "And I'm never going anywhere again" she continued. Louise then smiled, before hugging Daisy, holding on tightly. "Love you mum" Daisy whispered. Louise smiled, "Love you too sweetheart" Louise replied.

Chapter Thirty-One

"Where are Shay and Dylan?" Alexis asked. "Woah, Shay is here? Like, the Shay that used to live on our road?" Daisy asked. Alexis nodded. "Oh my gosh, I can't wait to see her!" Daisy shouted. Alexis laughed. "Oh and guys, big news, turn out John has a twin" Alexis said. Everyone looked at her in shock, "It wasn't him who was here the other day, it was his twin. Apparently, John only escaped yesterday" she then added. "We need to have a meeting. First off, let's go and surprise Shay" Daisy said. "What's the plan twinnie" Alexis asked. "Ring Shay and get her to meet you in the HQ lobby, then wait there for her, and when she gets there, say to her you need a meeting, then take her and that Dylan guy to the conference room, then I will walk in and just sit down, then we'll just have to see what her reaction is" Daisy explained. "Nice, let's do it" Alexis replied, before reaching into her pocket and pulling out her phone. She dialed Shay's number. "Hello?" Shay said. "Hey, It's Lex, you and Dylan meet us in the HQ lobby, we're going to have a meeting" Alexis explained. "Rightyo" Shay replied. Alexis then put the phone down. "Sorted" she said. "Let's do this" Daisy said. Alexis then saluted her, before walking out of the room.

Daisy then looked out of the gap in the door, and saw Alexis, Shay and Dylan walk into the conference room. She counted to 10, before taking a deep breath and walking into the conference room. "Hey guys" she said. "Hey Daisy" Alexis replied, Daisy then walked over and sat on the sofa in the corner of the room, "Oh, hey Shay!" Daisy shouted. Shay's face at this point was pale and she was speechless. "Daisy?" She mumbled. Daisy walked over to her, "Hey" Daisy replied. "Wha-how-when-what?" Shay mumbled. "Long story" Daisy replied. Shay then jumped up and hugged Daisy tightly, "Oh my god" Shay said. Daisy laughed. "Woah, is it just me, or am I seeing 2 Lexy's?" Dylan asked, confused. Alexis walked over to Daisy, "No, this is my sister" Alexis explained, putting her arm around Daisy. "Ah, I see, hey" Dylan said. "Sup" Daisy replied.

Everyone laughed. "Okay everyone, I have great news, I think I know the plan" Daisy said. Everyone sat down. "Basically, when they took me, John was forced into joining Ray and James' new gang, after Alexis killed them all, it turns out she missed the 3 main people coz they didn't come on the France mission, and they then formed a new gang. They told John, that if they didn't join them, and feed them inside information, they would kill me. The gang who kept me hostage were quite nice to me whilst Ray and James were in prison, they gave me things to occupy my time, and they made sure I had everything I needed, and they told me, that I had 5 chances, if I mentioned any of you, I lost one of my chances, and if I lost all 5 chances, they wouldn't ever let me go. I decided I would take matter into my own hands, and I tried escaping, but they had the whole warehouse on lock down, and it was covered with CCTV and they were tracking my every move, so I adapted to the surroundings, and get used to the fact that they weren't going to let me go. Because I thought, if I'm good, then they will let me go faster. They bought me magazines, CD's, and they even brought their kids in every now and then to keep me company. A few months ago, John broke down whilst he was supposed to be keeping an eye on me, and told me what they were planning, and he told me that he wasn't doing it because he hated me, he was doing it to save me, so I told him I forgive him. Then, Ray and James got out of prison, and everything went bad, he had me locked in a room for 3 months, before yesterday when I was told that they were letting me go. That's when John escaped and told me he was going to go and find you and tell you everything, but during the process, John's twin brother, Lucas, decided to pretend to be John, to turn you against him, then when Lucas didn't come back, it all got out of hand and John convinced them to let me go" Daisy explained. "That's mental" Bailey said. "Yeah, that's sick, keeping you away from your family but treating like that, I'm so glad that they didn't make you suffer, but just the thought of it makes me sick to my stomach" Louise said, "But at the end of the day, I'm happy that you're back with us" She continued. Alexis didn't say anything, and everyone could sense that she was angry. Danny turned to her, "Are you okay?" he asked. Alexis ignored him. "Which warehouse did he keep you in?" She asked Daisy. "The one near Range Road school" Daisy replied. "And when did you fly from the training base we were at?" she continued. "A few days after" Daisy replied, "Why?" she asked.

"So, you're telling me, not only was you probably on the same plane as me, with John knowing that you were on the plane, and in despite of the state I was in. Then, to top that off they kept you locked up in a warehouse that is a 15 minute drive from our house, for 5 years, whilst we thought you was dead? Not only that, you're saying that he kept you at the warehouse that was *opposite* the primary school that I went to, and Bailey and Charlie went too?" Alexis sneered. Nobody said anything. Alexis then stood up and threw the chair she was sitting on, across the room, causing it to hit the wall and break. Everybody lowered their heads, hoping that nothing hit them. Alexis then walked over to the door, before punching a hole into the wall next to it and storming out.

Everyone remained sat in the room, shocked at her sudden outburst. Alexis then walked into the lobby, and started throwing the chairs around, one of them getting stuck in the wall. She threw everything off the table, before flipping it over. She grabbed all the vases and one at a time, threw them at a wall, before standing in the middle of the lobby, holding a gun in either hand. In shock at the commotion, everyone ran out of the conference room. Alexis looked up at them, her eyes filled with anger, everyone looked around, shocked at the amount of damage she had caused in such a short amount of time. "Alexis!" Danny shouted. Alexis looked at him, "What?" she sneered. "What's wrong?" he asked. Alexis laughed, she put one gun back in her pocket, before walking over to the pieces of shattered glass from the vases she had broken, and looking through them. She found the piece that had "John" written on it. This was a gift from Alexis and Daisy for his birthday just before they left for the mission. She picked up the piece of glass, "What's wrong? Is that some sort of joke?" she sneered. Danny shook his head, "That was a stupid question I know, just please calm down" he said. Alexis shook her head. She then looked down at the glass in her hand, before looking back up, to see Danny walking towards her, "Babe, put the glass down, it's sharp and you'll hurt yourself" he said. Alexis shook her head, before closing her hand and squeezing it. Bailey gasped. After a couple of seconds, she opened her hand, and let go of the glass, it fell to the floor, part of it covered with blood. She looked down at her hand, "Compared to what he put me through, this is nothing, this causes me no pain" she cried. She then walked into her office, and over to a framed picture of her, Daisy and John when he awarded them with their agent license, she stood in front of it, staring at it. Everyone else then walked into the room. "How sweet is this?" she asked, smiling. She then put on a serious face, before punching the picture so hard that her fist went through the glass, the picture, the frame and the plasterboard wall. Alexis then looked at her hand, her knuckles cut and bleeding, "Oh look, it *still* doesn't hurt as much as what he's put me through" Alexis then walked over to everyone, shoving past them to make her way out of the room. Danny grabbed her wrist, "Alexis, you've made your point, please stop" he pleaded. Alexis looked past him and pulled away. She then walked into the lobby again, and she pulled out her gun, before starting to pull empty shots, she kept shooting until the gun ran out of ammo, before she turned around and threw it at a wall. Danny then ran up to her, "LEXY, JUST STOP, YOU'RE SCARING EVERYONE" he shouted, "NO" she replied. She then ran into her office, and grabbed 3 loaded guns off her desk, and ran back out, before running out of her office and down to the shopping centre, stopping at the entrance. Everyone followed her, scared of what she was going to do next. Alexis stood staring out of the shopping centre, she then ran and got into her van, before starting the ignition, without knowing, Danny and Daisy had managed to jump into the back, and Alexis slammed her foot down on the pedal, reversing out of the entrance, and spinning round, before speeding towards the gates of the centre, she increased the speed of the engines, and crashed through the gates, she then went speeding down the road, running over every zombie in sight. "ALEXIS STOP!" Daisy shouted, Alexis, startled, turned to see Daisy sat on the floor of the back of the van, tears in her eyes, Alexis then turned back to see where she was going, as she saw an incoming car, and she quickly tried to swerve it, unfortunately not being fast enough, crashed into the back of the car, before blacking out.

Chapter Thirty-Two

Alexis was woken to the sound of Daisy and Danny shouting her, "ALEXIS!!!!! PLEASE WAKE UP!!!!!" Daisy was shouting. Alexis then opened her eyes, and she was lay in the back of the van. She sat up and looked out of her window, "Thank god you're awake" Danny said, holding her and pulling her into his arms, "Please stop" he whispered. A tear rolled down Alexis' face, "I can't" she whispered back. Daisy was sat in the corner of the van, "Daisy" Alexis mumbled. Daisy didn't reply, "Daisy I'm so sorry" Alexis whispered. "It's not your fault" Daisy replied. Alexis moved out of Danny's arms, and sat next to Daisy. Danny reached out and held onto Alexis' hand, it was still bleeding and cut. He gasped; she looked at him and smiled, before looking down at her hand, "Oh my god" Alexis gasped. "What did I do?" she asked. Danny looked at her, "Wait, you don't know?" he asked. At this point, Daisy started crying, Alexis looked at her, "What's wrong?" she asked. Daisy ignored her. Danny moved over, before leaning over Alexis, "Do you know how you did this?" he asked. Alexis looked down at her hand, "It was from the crash?" she asked. Danny hoped that she was joking, but as he looked into her eyes, they showed genuine confusion. "Yeah babe, it was from the crash" he replied. Alexis nodded, "I'm so tired, please can we go back to HQ?" she sighed. Danny nodded. He climbed into the front of the van, and Alexis leant against the wall and closed her eyes.

When they had got to the shopping centre, Danny stopped as he just got into the entrance, and he jumped out and locked the gates with what was left of the chains, before jumping back into the van and driving into the entrance, he then got out of the van again, and lowered the shutters. He then opened the back of the van, finding that Alexis was asleep, he reached into the van, and lifted her out, and Daisy jumped out. He carried her up to HQ, and took her to her office. Daisy pulled the sofa bed out, and Danny laid her down on it. Just as he went to move, she held onto his arm, "Please don't go" she whimpered. "I'm not going anywhere, but we need to sort your hand out, before the cuts get infected" he explained. "Okay" she replied. Danny walked over to Alexis' desk and pulled out a first aid kit. He then walked over to her sat next to her. He carefully held onto her hand, and dabbed at the cuts with a wet piece of cotton wool, he wiped away all of the blood, before cleaning the wounds with antiseptic cream, to make sure they didn't get infected. Alexis just sat and watched him, completely numb to everything. "Does this not hurt?" Danny asked. Alexis shook her head, "I can't feel pain anymore" she whimpered. Danny didn't say anything. He put a piece of dry padding over the wounds, before bandaging up her hand, "All done, sorry I didn't do very well, I don't know much about first aid" he said. Alexis smiled, "Thank you" she whispered. Alexis then lay down on the sofa bed and closed her eyes, gently cradling her hand. Danny sat next to her, and stroked her forehead, and after a few minutes, she was asleep. He then stood up, and looked down at her, before leaving the room.

He walked to the conference room, where everyone was sat in silence. "Is she okay?" Daisy asked. Danny nodded. "What happened?" Louise asked. Danny looked down, "I don't know, she doesn't even remember smashing up the lobby, after we crashed, she thought that all of the cuts on her hands was caused by the crash" he said. "I think she's breaking down" he continued. Louise put her head in her hands, before looking up and wiping her eyes. "No, she isn't, she is strong, she'll get through this" she said, trying to re-assure everyone. Danny nodded, "She will get through it we just need to make sure that nothing stresses her out to that extent again" he said. Everyone nodded in agreement. "Okay, I'm going to quickly check on her, and then we'll have a meeting" he instructed. He then stood up and left the room.

As he walked back into Alexis' office, and he could hear her phone ringing. He looked in her pocket and pulled out her phone. "Hello?" he said. "Hey, it's Frankie, is Alexis there?" she asked. "Nah, she's asleep, why?" he replied. "Some guy called John is here to see her" she continued. Danny froze, "Hello?" she said. "Tell him Daisy will be down in a minute" he sneered. He then put the phone down. He moved over to Alexis, and looked down at her, before kissing her forehead and walking out of the room.

Danny walked down to the conference room, slamming the door shut. "John's here" he sneered. Daisy's eyes lit up, "Shall I go and get him?" she asked. Danny nodded, "Bring him up here" he sneered. Daisy nodded. "Wait, you are *not* going on your own, I'm coming with you" Louise said. Bailey and Charlie also stood up. "Same" they said. They all walked out of the room.

Danny walked over to Luke and Dylan, "We need to look after the girls, and we need to sort John out, I am not having him breaking my girlfriend. She's been through too much, I say we give him a taste of what will happen if he messes with any of us again. We're not going to kill him, just roughen him up" he said. Luke and Dylan nodded. Danny turned to Luke, "I shouldn't really do this, but here" Danny said, handing him a gun. Luke gasped. "You with us? You won't have to use it, it's just to scare him" Danny asked. "After seeing how much this has hurt them, yes, I may not have known Charlie for that long, but I care about her so much, I'm not letting anything hurt her, or her sisters" he explained. "Nice one bro" Danny said. "Okay, put your guns in your pocket and follow me" Danny said. They did as they were told, and they all walked into the lobby.

They waited for about 5 minutes; before they saw the girls walk through the doors with John following close behind. "You girls wait in the conference room, we'll be there in a couple of minutes, we just need to talk to John" Danny said, as calm as he could. The girls all walked into the conference room, and John stood staring at Danny. "Danny, I understand how angry you must be, they told me about what happened with Alexis, I'm so sor-" John started, but then, was interrupted by Danny punching him in the mouth, causing him to fall back. "Danny, I thought you wasn't going to hurt him" Dylan said. "No, I said we're not going to kill him" Danny sneered. Danny then grabbed John by the collar of his shirt and lifted him up, before pushing him back, causing his back to smash off the wall. "Bro, calm down" Luke shouted. Danny turned to him, "I've got this bro" he shouted. He then pinned John up against the wall, "Listen yeah, I don't care about what you have to say, if it was up to me, I would happily kill you right here, right now. I would happily make you suffer, kill you slowly so then maybe you might understand the pain you've put that family through" Danny sneered. "But I don't want to hurt her anymore, so for now, I'm going to let you live" he continued. Danny then stood back, and pulled out his gun, before shooting it directly next to John's face, missing his face by only a few centimetres. The sound of the shot causing everyone to run out of the Conference room, "Danny, don't" Daisy shouted. "I don't care about what you have to say, you don't scare me, you know nothing about anything that has happened, so shut your mouth" John shouted, wiping the blood off his face. Danny turned to him, he then walked over to him, before smacking John on the side of his head with his gun, causing John to fall to the floor. When John hit the floor, Danny kicked him in the ribs, causing John to curl up in pain, Danny then next to him, and pointed his gun at his head, "Do you understand how much you have hurt Alexis? just because you did it to protect Daisy, doesn't mean that you're a good person, I'm glad you protected her, but you didn't have to keep that away from Alexis, you could've told her the situation, you could've explained it all to her, instead of letting her think Daisy was dead, how would you like it if you was in that situation? Aye? Taking a little girl away from her family like that, and acting for all of this time that you were genuinely there for them, when really, you was plotting against them" Danny shouted. John laughed. Danny raised his fist to hit John again, before he was interrupted, "Danny!" Alexis shouted, he turned to see her stood in the doorway of her office. He looked back down to John, before punching him in the face again. Alexis to Danny and pulled him back, "Don't do this" Alexis whispered. Alexis then held out her hand to help John up. John grabbed onto her hand and Alexis pulled him up, he stood in front of her, "I'm so glad you're oka-" he started, Alexis then pulled back her fist and punched John in the face. "Why did you do it?!" she shouted. John wiped the blood off his face, "Please Alexis, you have to understand that I did it to protect you and Daisy" he pleaded. Alexis laughed, "To protect us? You were the one I turned to when I was told that they killed her, you comforted me until I got home, you gave me the base, and why? Because you are guilty, and you know you are!" Alexis shouted. "Alexis" Daisy shouted. Alexis turned to her, "What?!" she said. Daisy looked at John, "Tell her" Daisy said, tears running down her face, "No, don't!" Louise shouted. Daisy turned to Louise, "She has to know" she said. Louise started crying. "I'm your dad" John said. Alexis took a step back, "No!" she shouted. Bailey and Charlie looked at him, "What?" Bailey asked. Alexis turned around and ran into her office, "NO! NO! NO! NO! NO! NO!" she shouted repeatedly, whilst punching and kicking the desk, the pictures on her wall, the wall, everything she could see. Danny ran into her office and grabbed her, he then span her around and pulled her into a hug, he held her tightly. Alexis started to cry, "No" she whimpered. Danny held onto her, "It's going to be okay babe, I'm not going to let him hurt you" he said. Alexis started crying harder, "He already has" she whispered. Danny then started crying aswell, and he held onto her.

He knew that he would do anything to protect her, to keep her safe, and make sure she was happy. He looked down at her, her eyes were closed tightly, tears running down her face, he moved the hair away from her face, "look at me" he whispered. Alexis looked up, her blue eyes shining through the tears, "I'm never going to let him hurt you again" he said. Alexis smiled, before closing her eyes again, and holding onto him tightly.

After a couple of minutes, Alexis moved away, and wiped her eyes, she then looked up at Danny, "I can't do this anymore" she whimpered. "Can't do what?" he asked. "This, I'm not strong enough, I'm just letting everyone down and putting everyone in danger" she said. "No, you're not letting anyone down babe, you're allowed to have emotions, you're only 17 and you have so much responsibility, anyone else in your situation would react the exact same, if not worse. No matter what happens, me and your family will be proud of you, you're amazing and you're so strong. I won't stand here and let you talk bad about yourself, I think the world of you, you know that, I will do everything I can to make sure you're happy and safe" he explained. Alexis smiled. "I can't forgive him, not after everything he's done" she explained. "You don't have to" he replied. "What am I supposed to do? I can't hurt Daisy, he means a lot to her" she continued. "Listen babe" he said, he sat down and pulled her onto his lap, she wrapped her arm around the back of his neck and he rested his hand on her legs. "You shouldn't feel like you have to forgive him, you have your own mind, he's put you through a lot and he shouldn't even expect you to just forget everything. Just because he's pulled the dad card, that means nothing unless you want it to. You have the right to make your own mind up, and I'll support any decision you make" Danny said softly, kissing her forehead. "I'm here for you" he whispered. Alexis smiled, and a teardrop rolled down her cheek. She pressed her forehead against his, "Thank you" she whispered. "I'm going to go and make sure everyone is okay" she continued. Danny kissed her, "Hurry back" he said, before winking. Alexis blushed slightly, before laughing and leaving her office.

Daisy and John were sat in Baileys office, with Bailey, Charlie and Louise, whilst Shay and Dylan were asleep. Daisy was showing John the CCTV from when Alexis damaged HQ. "Wow, I can't believe I drove her to that" John mumbled, in disbelief. They didn't know that Alexis was stood at the door, watching it too. She ran back to her office, tears streaming down her face. "Babe, what's happened?" Danny asked. "Why didn't you tell me the truth?" she asked. "What do you mean?" he asked. "How did I hurt my hand Danny?" she asked. "Babe, I was just trying to-" he started. Alexis lifted her hand, "Save it" she whispered. Alexis then reached over and grabbed her gun, running out of the door and locking it behind her so that he couldn't go after her. He started banging on the door, and Alexis ran down the corridor and down to the entrance, anger completely filling her mind.

When she got to the entrance, she unlocked the shutters, before lifting them and driving out, she then locked the entrance back up, before driving out into the car park. She drove to the main gates, before getting out of her van and walking over to the gates.

"ALEXIS!!!!!!"

Alexis looked up to see Danny staring out of the window of her office, "PLEASE DON'T DO THIS" he shouted. Alexis turned away from him, before pulling out her gun, and shooting the few zombies that were surrounding the gates. She then unlocked the gates, and jumped into her van, and drove it out, before getting out, locking the gates again, and getting back in her van and driving off.

Chapter Thirty-Three

'Why did he lie? I don't see why he couldn't have just told me the truth, I would've handled it so much better if he would've just told me what really happened.', Alexis thought, as she continued speeding around the streets of Limebarn.

Looking out of the window, she saw how deserted it was, the floor was littered with bodies, everything was damaged, vandalised, puddles of blood covered the floor, it looked like something out of a horror movie. She kept driving until she got to her house. She drove into the garage, and jumped out of her van. She paced around for a while, then, she remembered that she had left 1 of her boxes of guns in the basement; she walked over to her van and grabbed a fully loaded gun, before walking back over to the door. She took a deep breath, before unlocking the door and walking into the kitchen. Closing the door behind her, she walked through the kitchen, and down to the basement and grabbed the box, before carrying it back up to her van.

Her phone then started ringing. She looked at the screen. It was an unknown number. "Hello" she spat. *"Now now now Alexis, no need for attitude"* the person replied. Alexis froze, "Who is this?" she asked. The person laughed. *"Not a very good idea leaving your family and your precious boyfriend all alone without safety"* they replied. Alexis didn't reply. *"What's up Alexis, cat got your tongue?"* they sneered. Alexis laughed, "Listen yeah, I don't know what you're talking about, I'm sat here in my office and they are all laughing and talking in another room, the whole of the floor is secured, so you try and get us, I dare you, because I will be waiting" Alexis replied. *"You can't trick us, we saw you leave"* he replied. Alexis laughed again, "Did you really?" she asked. *"Yeah, we saw your van"* they replied. "That wasn't me in the van" she replied. The person laughed. *"I don't think you understand Alexis, we know for a fact that you're not with them, because you've just walked past us*" he replied. Alexis froze, not saying anything. "*Did your mum never tell you about the monsters in the basement?*" they whispered. Alexis then put the phone down, before jumping into her van. She sped out of the garage, and she kept driving until she reached a gas station. She jumped out and grabbed the gas pump, filling up the tank with more petrol.

Whilst she was filling up the pump, she saw a poster stuck to a window.

IF YOU'RE ALIVE AND STILL HUMAN, RING US AND WE WILL ARRANGE FOR YOU TO BE SAFETY TAKEN TO THE SAFE ZONE, IT IS GUARDED BY MILITARY. WE WILL ENSURE THAT YOU ARE SAFE AND HEALTHY UNTIL THE EPIDEMIC IS OVER. CALL 0213 444 6798.

Alexis had an idea; she got in her van, before pulling out her phone, and dialing the number. "*Hello, Limebarn Military, if you are ringing for information of how to help the injured, press 1, if you are calling for transport out of Limebarn, press 2, and if you have any enquiries and want to be passed through to someone on the team, press 3*" an automated system explained. Alexis pressed three, "*Hello, how can we help you?*" the person asked. "I'm part of the secret services, I'm still in Limebarn, I have found where the infected are hiding, and I need help getting rid of them. I need you to plant a load of dynamite and activate when I instruct so. My family and friends are in danger and I need to get back to them, please can you help?" Alexis asked. "*Okay thank you for your call, we were trying to get hold of the secret services so your call has been appreciated greatly, please will you tell me your agent ID ma'am and we'll go from there*" the replied. Alexis told him her agent ID number. "*Okay thank you, we are entering your ID into the data base*" they replied. A couple of seconds later, they replied. "A*h, you're just the agent we've been looking for. We've been trying to locate your where-a-abouts since the epidemic started, thank you for ringing us. Now, please will you state the location in which you believe the deceased are hiding*" he replied. "They are hiding in the warehouse opposite Range Road School" she explained. "*Okay Miss*

Smith, we will have military in the area in around half an hour" the person replied. "Thank you, please will you text me when you're there? I'm going to go and confront the leaders, I will hold them off for as long as I can, text me when you are set up, and wait for my command to detonate" Alexis explained. "*Okay ma'am*" they replied. "What is your name?" Alexis asked. "*Terence*" he replied. "Thanks for this Terence" Alexis replied, "*Just doing my job, take care and good luck*" He replied. Alexis put the phone down.

Just as she was about to get into the van, Alexis heard screaming. It was coming from the shop in the petrol station. Alexis grabbed a gun out of the back of the van, before locking it and slowly, and quietly walking into the shop. "Hello?" Alexis asked. "HELP!" someone shouted. Alexis ran over to where the shouting was coming from. She saw a group of zombies stood around a large group of people. She quietly walked out of the shop, and walked over to her van; she opened it, pulled out another gun and locked it again. She then returned to the shop, and walked down the aisles. She then stopped when she saw them. She pulled out both of her guns. "Looking for me?" she shouted. They all turned to her. "Night night" she shouted, she then started shooting all the infected, and when they all dropped to the floor, she walked over to the group of people. "Thank you so much" one of them said. "Alexis?" one of them said. Alexis turned and saw a woman, who was her mum's best friend. "Oh my gosh, Paula" Alexis said. She then looked down to see Paula's daughter stood holding onto Paula's leg. Alexis put her guns into her pocket. She knelt down, "Hey Lucy, don't worry, the nasty people are gone" she whispered. Lucy smiled, before running over and hugging Alexis. Alexis lifted her up and swung her around. Paula walked over to Alexis and hugged her aswell, "Thank you so much" she said. Alexis smiled, "I'm glad you're okay, mum tried ringing you but you didn't answer" Alexis explained. "I know, I missed the call" Paula replied. "Well, all that matters is that you're okay, is everyone okay?" she continued. Alexis nodded. "Okay, let's get you lot to safety" Alexis explained. Everyone stood up, she walked over to one of the people, a woman who looked heavily pregnant, "Are you okay?" Alexis asked, helping her to stand up. The woman held onto Alexis and pulled herself up, "Yeah, I'm fine" she replied, breathing heavily. "How far gone are you?" Alexis asked. "Tomorrow is my due date" she said. Alexis raised her eyebrows, "Okay, we need to get you to safety, I'm Alexis by the way" Alexis explained, "I'm Sophie" she replied. Alexis smiled. She then turned to everyone else, "Come on everybody, I'll take you all to safety" She said. Everyone followed her out.

When they got outside, Alexis stopped. "Okay, there are way too many of you too fit in my van, does anyone else have a car here?" she asked. 4 of the people raised their hands. Alexis counted all the people. "Okay, there are 26 people here, all the people have a car step forward" she said. The people stepped forward, "Okay, you lot go and get into your car and drive to the main entrance, top up your cars with petrol and I'll send groups to each car and then you all follow me, okay?" They nodded and walked out of the shop. They all followed her outside. "Okay, Paula and Lucy you can come in my van, so get in the back, Sophie, you get in the passenger's seat at the front, but don't touch the box, it contains explosives" She instructed. She unlocked the van and they climbed in.

"Where is your boyfriend?" Alexis asked Sophie. "He went to the supermarket to get some food for the new house, and I came here to fill up my car with petrol, but then all of a sudden, a load of creatures started running towards me, I ran straight into here and I hid in the bathroom for a few hours, but then I heard people talking, and that's when I came out and found everyone, and we were just waiting for someone to find us and help us, then you came along, thank you so much" Sophie explained. Alexis smiled, "No problem, that's my job. Which supermarket was your boyfriend at?" Alexis asked. "I don't know what it's called, he just said he was going to the supermarket, I'm new around here" she replied. "What's his name?" Alexis asked. "Rick" she Sophie replied. Alexis smiled, "I have some good news for you, I rescued a man called Rick from a supermarket a few hours ago, he's safe and you'll be with him very soon" Alexis said. Sophie smiled, "OH MY GOD THANK YOU SO MUCH I WAS SO WORRIED YOU ARE THE BEST I CAN'T THANK YOU ENOUGH!" she squealed. Alexis smiled "No problem" she replied. Alexis grabbed her phone and rang Frankie, "Hey Frankie, it's Alexis" she said. "Sup girl" Frankie replied. "I need you to find a man called Rick, and tell him to wait in the main entrance of the shopping centre, tell him I need to speak to him" Alexis said. "Will do" Frankie replied. "Cheers, talk to you later"

Alexis replied, before putting the phone down. She turned to Sophie, "Thought you could surprise him" Alexis smiled. Sophie smiled.

When all of the other cars were topped up, and parked next to the entrance, Alexis put 3 other people in each of the cars. She then told the other 5 to get in her van. "Okay everyone, follow me" Alexis explained. She then got into her van and started driving back to HQ.

On the way, she found another group of people hiding, she told them to sit tight and that she'd go back and get them. She pulled out her phone and dialled Danny's number, putting it on loud-speaker and then placing it on the arm rest. Danny answered. "Oh my god Alexis, I'm so glad you're okay" he said quickly. "Open the gates, I'm coming back and I've found more people, do it quickly, spare keys for the entrance door and the gates are in my desk drawer, you and one of the girls bring your van, we've got more people to help, and get mum and the other girls and Dylan to come out to look after the new guests and tell them the rules" she explained bluntly. She then ended the call. Alexis then heard screaming coming from outside. She jumped out of the van to see that a group of people had been cornered down an alley by a small group of the infected. She pulled out her gun and shot all of the infected. She ran over to the group of people, and took them to a small house, she kicked the door down, "IS THERE ANYONE HERE!?" she shouted. "Yeah, please help us" she shouted. She ran into a room to see the room filled with people. "Oh lord" she muttered. "OKAY, HERE'S THE PLAN" she shouted, everyone stopped talking and looked at her. "RIGHT, I NEED TO GET THESE PEOPLE TO SAFETY, I WILL BE BACK FOR YOU GUYS AS SOON AS I'VE TAKEN THESE OTHER PEOPLE THERE, SIT TIGHT I'LL BE BACK SOON!" she shouted. "Thank you" someone shouted. Alexis smiled, and the people from the alley walked into the room with the others. Alexis ran back out and jumped in the van, and drove to the shopping centre.

When she got to the entrance, she beeped the van's horn, and the gates were then opened. She drove into the entrance; the other people following close behind. She jumped out of the van, and Danny locked the door behind them all. Alexis drove to the entrance, and got out of the van, helping Sophie out. "Shh, stay there, I'll bring him over" she whispered. Sophie nodded. Alexis walked into the entrance, and saw a man leaning on the counter, "Hey are you Rick?" she asked. The man stood up and looked at her, "Yeah, is everything okay?" he asked. Alexis nodded. "Come with me" she said. Rick followed her. When she got to her van, she stood her hand out, "Wait there" she instructed. Rick did so. Then, Alexis walked to the other side of the van, and walked back over to Rick, this time, with Sophie. Rick put his hands over his mouth. "Oh my God, Sophie! I've been so worried! I thought you was dead!" Rick shouted, Sophie smiled. Rick then ran over to Sophie, and hugged her gently. He turned to Alexis, "Thank you" he whispered. Alexis smiled, "It's fine". A couple of seconds later, Danny, her mum and sisters, Dylan and Shay walked over to them, with the other cars following close behind. Alexis turned to her mum, "Take Rick and Sophie up to HQ and get them settled in the conference room, and move all of our equipment into the cupboard in my office, then you, Dylan and Shay go into the furniture store and get some pillows and blankets to get them comfortable, get them a supply of food from the shops and get them everything they will need to ensure that they are comfortable. Sophie is due to give birth any day soon, so I'm going to ring the safe zone and get them to come and collect them both" Alexis explained. Sophie walked over to Alexis and gently hugged her, "Thank you so much, I can't thank you enough to be honest, you're an amazing person" she said. Alexis smiled, "We'll make sure that you, your baby, and Rick are looked after, and that's a promise" Alexis explained. Rick hugged Alexis, "Thanks love" he said. "It's okay" Alexis replied. Sophie and Rick then followed Alexis' mum, Dylan and Shay. "MUM, KEEP ME UPDATED" Alexis shouted. Alexis then pulled out her phone, and rang the safe zone back, "Hi Terence, it's Alexis, please will you send transport to the Limebarn Shopping Centre, we have a heavily pregnant woman here, she's due to give birth any day soon" Alexis asked. "*Okay love, I'll send someone now. By the way, the detonator is ready and awaiting your command*" he said. "Okay nice one. Ring 07979305443 when the transport is almost here, and one of my co-workers will get her to the entrance to make it easier, the shopping centre is very heavily protected" Alexis replied. "*Okay, will do*" Terence replied. Alexis then put the phone down.

Alexis then felt someone tap her shoulder, Danny was stood there, just as he was about to speak, Alexis quickly grabbed his face and kissed him. She then pulled away and smiled, "I love you" she whispered. Danny smiled back, "I love you too, so much" he replied. Alexis smiled and hugged him tightly. "Okay guys, we have a bunch of people in a house, we're going to need to make 2 trips" Alexis explained. Bailey smiled, "I have a better idea" she replied. "What's your idea?" Alexis asked. "Well, do you remember that film we watched, about those Egyptian mummies? And those people, who were running away from the mummies, stole a bus? I think we should totally do that" Bailey explained, Charlie and Daisy laughed, "That's a stupid idea" Charlie said. "No, I like it, let's do it" Alexis said, before high-fiving Bailey. "But we'll have to go on foot, because we can't leave my van anywhere. The bus depot is around the corner, we'll walk there" Alexis explained. Everyone nodded. "Has everyone got their guns?" Alexis asked. Everyone nodded again. Alexis smiled, "Let's do this" she said. She then parked her van in the reception, and closed the entrance shutter, before locking them. They all walked towards the gates, Danny unlocked them, and they all walked out, before Danny locked them back up, and they began walking towards the bus depot.

Chapter Thirty-Four

When they got to the bus depot, Alexis shot the lock, and opened the doors. There, were a row of about 15 double decker buses. "Which one shall we *borrow*?" she joked. She then ran down to the one right in the middle, pressed the emergency open, and climbed in. She jumped into the driver's cabin. She saw that there were a set of keys left in the ignition. "Result!" she shouted. Everyone jumped onto the bus, Bailey and Charlie sat down, "Nice one!" Daisy shouted. Danny laughed. When they was all sat down, Alexis started the engine and shut the doors, she then started driving, and set off towards the house.

When they got to the house, Alexis pulled over. "Okay, they're in there, go and get them all" Alexis instructed. Bailey, Charlie, Danny and Daisy jumped off and into the house. A couple of minutes later, they walked back out, followed by all of the people. Alexis got off the bus, "Okay, we need to fill out the top floor first, then the remainder of people can sit on the bottom floor" Alexis instructed. She then jumped back into the bus, before everyone else started getting on the bus, thanking Alexis, Bailey, Charlie, Luke, Danny and Daisy as they walked past. When they filled the top floor of the bus, the few people left sat at the back of the bottom floor. Alexis then shut the doors. "Okay, we're going to go for a little drive, see if we can find anyone else, then we'll go to the shopping centre with everyone else" Alexis shouted. "LET'S DO IT!" Daisy shouted. Everyone laughed. Alexis then started driving.

Through the journey, Alexis continually beeped the horn, to get the attention of any other people that are alive.

By the time they got back to the shopping centre, the bus was completely full of people.

When they got to the entrance of the shopping centre, Alexis saw a group of zombies surrounding the gates. She jumped off the bus, followed by her sisters, Danny and Luke. The group of zombies were chanting Alexis' name repeatedly. Alexis laughed. "LOOKING FOR ME?" she shouted. They all turned to her. Alexis smiled, and pulled out her guns, and so did the others. They all started shooting, and the live ones began running towards Alexis. One of them, knocking Bailey over, Bailey screamed. Alexis quickly shot them, and ran over to help her. Bailey stood back up and started shooting again. "Danny, unlock the gates and drive the bus in, quick" she shouted. Danny stopped shooting ran over to the bus, whilst Alexis, Bailey, Charlie and Daisy continued shooting at the zombies. Eventually, when all of the infected were dead, Alexis, Bailey, Charlie and Daisy ran into the car park of the shopping centre, Danny closing and locking the gates after them. Alexis then turned back turned to see a large group of zombies running towards the gate. "On the bus, now!" Alexis shouted. They all got on the bus, and Alexis sped towards the entrance. She then jumped off the bus and unlocked the shutters, lifting them quickly. "EVERYONE GET OFF THE BUS AND GET INSIDE!" she shouted. Everyone did so, and then Alexis ran inside after them and locked the shutters again.

"Okay, everyone, into the main hall of the centre" Alexis instructed. Everyone then walked into the main hall, followed by Alexis, her sisters, Danny and Luke.

Louise followed them all in, and everyone looked at them, quietly. Louise explained the rules.

They all then walked up to HQ, and John walked over to Alexis, "I know I'm not your favourite person right now, but please can I talk to you and the girls?" he asked. "What about?" Alexis asked. "Please, just come with me" he said. Alexis followed him, followed by Bailey, Charlie and Daisy. Everyone walked to the conference room and sat down.

John stood up, "Ok, I have something to say. First off, too you Alexis. I am so so so very sorry about all of this, I'm so sorry that I kept everything hidden from you, but you have to believe that it was for the best. Ray and James told me that if I told you anything, they would kill Daisy, and then they would kill you three girls, and I couldn't let that happen. I promised your mum when you joined the base that I would look after you all and keep you safe. I had to go along with everything they told me to do. You have to understand that the guilt ate me alive, I broke down every night crying because of the pain I felt, seeing you girls mourning and not being able to tell you what was going on. You have made me so proud over the years, and your strength gave me strength, I just had to do what I could to keep you all safe... I'm so sorry, and I hope that you can understand my reasoning. Next, Bailey and Charlie, I can't even begin to explain how proud I am of you girls, you started this at such a young age, just like your big sisters, and it must have been so hard for you to settle into this after everything that happened. You are both so strong and you are both amazing young girls. I'm sorry to you both of you aswell for hurting you and your family. Last off, to Daisy. Daisy, I am so sorry for everything I put you through, I can't believe that you're sat there, strong as ever, alive, smiling and back with your family. It seems so surreal, it makes everything I've had to do over the past 6 years, almost worth it. I promised you that this day would come. You need to understand that if I could turn back time and change how things turned out, I would, I am so proud of you and I'm so sorry, I love all 4 of you girls, you have all made me so proud. I hope that maybe one day, you can all accept my apology and we could start again, I know I've been a horrible father, but I am going to do everything I can to try and make it up to you, if you let me off course. I promise, I would give my life to save all of yours, you're all amazing, strong girls and I'm proud to say you're my daughters" John explained. A tear then rolled down his cheek. Alexis stood up and walked over to him, "Thank you" she said, she then hugged him. Bailey, Charlie and Daisy then walked over, and joined in the hug. "I love you girls, so much" John whispered. "We love you too" Alexis replied.

"Let's go back to the others" Bailey shouted. "To my office!!!" Alexis shouted. They all left the room. "Let's race" Alexis said. They all stood behind the line and John opened the door. "On your marks, get set GO!" he shouted. They all started running. When she was almost at Alexis's office, Charlie turned and laughed at Bailey, but just as Charlie turned back round, she ran into a wall. "OH MY GOD" she squealed. Alexis and Daisy turned to see Charlie sat on the floor holding her head in her hands. "What happened?" Daisy asked. "I ran into the wall" Charlie said, rubbing her eyes and shaking her head. Alexis and Daisy began laughing. "That's what you get for laughing at me" Bailey joked. Everyone joined in the laughter.

Danny, Dylan and Luke then walked out of Alexis' office, and all stopped to look at Charlie, who was still sat on the floor. "Charlie, you do know that there is a perfectly good chair over there to sit on?" Danny joked. Charlie smiled sarcastically. "She ran into the wall" John chuckled. "Yeah, thanks for the support, much appreciated" Charlie joked.

Luke walked over to Charlie and helped her up, before leaning in and kissing her. "Woah woah woah" Louise shouted. Charlie smiled, Danny then walked over to Alexis and grabbed onto her face, before kissing her. "STOP!" Bailey shouted. Alexis then laughed, before Dylan turned and kissed Shay. "Feeling a little uncomfortable right now" John joked. Everyone started laughing. "What now?" Charlie asked. "We need to have a meeting, I have an idea" Alexis said. She ran back to the conference room, everyone following close behind. When they got into the conference room, everyone sat down. "Right, you're all going to think I'm mad, but I say we just bite the bullet and attack" Alexis said. "What do you mean?" Bailey asked. "Exactly what I said, we attack the warehouse and kill as many of them off as we can, and when we've done all we can, I've got the warehouse wired up with explosives, ready to end this" Alexis explained. "Why haven't they just blown it up already then? Charlie asked. "Because we can't guarantee that they will all be in there. At least, if they know we're all there, then we can get rid of most of them, and it'll make getting rid of the rest of them a lot easier" Alexis explained. "Good plan" Bailey said. "I don't think that's a very good idea" John said. Alexis turned to him, "Why?" she asked. "Because they're already 10 steps in front of you" he replied. "How?" Alexis queried. "They've got armies ready" John replied. "I don't care, I'm not scared or intimidated by them" Alexis replied, shrugging her shoulders. "It's too dangerous right now, we don't know what they're planning, I think it's best that you hold back the attack plan" John explained. Alexis stood up, "Listen, I own this base, not you, you lost the right to tell me what to do a long time ago, you're either with me, or you're not" she shouted. Everyone stayed silent. Alexis sat back down. "Who's with me?" she asked. Danny, Dylan, Daisy, Charlie and Luke stood up. "I'm sorry Alexis but I can't" Bailey whimpered. "You'll be safer here anyway" Alexis said, smiling at her. "I'm too old for this" Louise said. Alexis laughed, "I know" she replied. "I'm too scared to even hold a gun, let alone shoot one" Shay joked. Everyone laughed. Alexis looked at John, "Thanks for the support, dad" Alexis sneered. "Right, you 5 with me, we need to get kitted up" Alexis said.

Everyone was handed a backpack. Each containing 2 machine guns, and 2 extra hand guns. Everyone was also handed a machete, safetly secured in a pouch. They threw the pouch over their shoulders, and the backpack onto their backs.

"Right here's the plan. Mum, Shay, Bailey and John keep an eye on the CCTV, and just make sure that the shopping centre stays safe and secure, beep me on the walkie-talkie's if you have a problem. You've got weapons if anything kicks off. Danny, Dylan and Luke go in Danny's van, Charlie and Daisy come in my van, we're going to park in the alley next to the school, and then walk from there. Me and Dylan are going to walk straight in and confront them, Danny, Charlie and Daisy stand out front, so that you can't be seen, I will beep you when I've done what I need to do. If anything kicks off, Dylan will beep you and you can back me up" Alexis explained. Everyone nodded. "Okay, Bailey, Mum, Shay and John, you guys go and monitor the CCTV from the shopping centre entrances security room. The closer you are to the main entrance to intervene in emergency, the better. Charlie and Daisy go to my van and wait there, Dylan and Luke go to Danny's van, I need to talk to Danny before we go" Alexis explained.

"What's up babe?" he asked. "As soon as this is all over, I've booked us a holiday to Paris" she smiled. "What?" he asked in shock. She nodded. "I'm going to show you where it all started, where we trained on our first mission, I'm going to take you to the most scenic places you've ever seen, everywhere I was taken on the mission, I'm going to take you" she smiled. "Are you sure you want to do that? Won't it bring back bad memories?" He asked. She shook her head, "That is my past, you are my future" she smiled, walking over and hugging him. He kissed her forehead. "I love you Alexis" he whispered. "I love you more" she whispered back. "No matter what happens, whether we kill them tonight or not, I promise that I will make them pay for the pain they caused your family" he whispered. "Likewise" she replied. Alexis kissed him softly, before he kissed her back. Alexis then pulled away, "Let's do this" she said. Danny let go of her, before walking over to the door, unlocking it and holding it open for her. "After you" he said. Alexis smiled, before walking to the door, "What a gentleman" she joked. She then kissed him, before walking out, and down the corridor. Danny followed her, wrapping his arm around her shoulders, pulling her closer.

When they got to the entrance, they walked over to everyone. "Good luck" Louise said, hugging her, "Stay safe" she whispered. "I will" Alexis whispered back. Alexis then walked over to Bailey and hugged her tightly, "Be careful Lex" Bailey whispered, tears running down her face. "Love you Bailey, I'll be back soon" she whispered back. Just as she moved her away, Shay pulled her into a quick hug, startling Alexis, "No crazy outbursts Lex, stay safe" she said. Alexis saluted her. Just as she was about to leave the entrance, John pulled Alexis aside. "I have nothing to say to you" Alexis sneered, "I know, but I have something to say to you, they know you're coming, they know everything. Their weakness is Ray, he is rubbish at trash-talking and he can't deal with confrontation, just thought I should let you know that" he explained. Alexis gave him a fake smile, before walking out of the centre and jumping into the van. "Let's go" Alexis shouted. They all drove off, and out of the gates, that were then locked by Louise.

And it begins.

Chapter Thirty-Five

They pulled up outside the house, and all climbed out of the vans, locking up behind them. They all walked over to Alexis, "This is it guys, I don't know what's going to happen, just stay strong and don't crumble under pressure, we need to end this, we need to make them pay for what they put us through" Alexis said. "I can't believe we're doing this" Charlie said. "We both know it needs to be done Charls" Alexis said. "I know, I'm just scared, what if something happens to one of us?" Charlie said. Luke held onto her, "I won't let that happen" he said to her. Alexis smiled, "He's right, nothing will happen, and I'll make sure of that" she replied. "Okay, Dylan with me, you guys follow behind shortly" Alexis said. Dylan nodded. Alexis turned to everyone else. Danny walked over to her and hugged her tightly, she hugged him back. "I love you" he whispered. "I love you too" she whispered back. Danny then kissed her, holding the kiss for as long as he could. Alexis kissed back, holding the kiss for a few seconds before pulling away. "I'll see you soon" she said. Danny nodded, letting go of her hand. Alexis walked over to Charlie and Daisy, and had a group hug, "They're going to pay for what they did to us" Alexis whispered. She squeezed them slightly, before letting go. She walked over to Luke. "Thanks" He said, "What for?" Alexis replied. "Everything you've done, you've made me feel part of something, and that's not a feeling that I'm used too… I just wanted to say thank you" he replied. Alexis smiled, before pulling him into a hug, "I will keep Charlie safe" he said to her, Alexis smiled, then pulled away. "Come on then Dyl, let's go" Alexis said. Alexis and Dylan then started walking towards the warehouse, and followed by the others shortly after.

When they got to the warehouse, Alexis stopped. She turned to Dylan, "You ready?" she asked. Dylan took a deep breath, "Yeah, he's gonna pay for what he put my little sis and her family through" Dylan said. Alexis smiled, before hugging him tightly. "Woah, what was that for?" Dylan asked. "To say thank you" Alexis replied.

Dylan smiled, "It's all good" he replied. Alexis took a deep breath, before pulling out a gun and holding it to her side. "It's show time" she said. She then turned and saw Danny, Daisy, Charlie and Luke hiding behind a wall. She smiled, "I love you" Alexis mouthed to Danny. "I love you too" he mouthed back. Alexis then walked to the entrance of the warehouse, Dylan following behind. "Get out a gun" she whispered. Dylan did so, as Alexis opened the door and walked in, Dylan close behind.

As soon as they walked in, the stench of death, and decaying bodies hit him. They held a hand over their faces. "Remember, it isn't airborne. The only way we can catch it is if their DNA gets into our blood" she explained re-assuringly. They quietly walked down the corridor, and to the end room. The doors for the end room had windows, so, staying low, Alexis and Dylan moved over to the window, slightly peaking over the edge. They saw a group of the infected stood in a circle that filled the room, around a chair. As they looked closer, they that someone was sat tied to a chair, with 2 of the infected stood behind them. Alexis kept staring, waiting for the 2 in the middle to turn around. After a couple of minutes, they turned around. Alexis cursed under her breath.

It was Ray and James.

Seeing their faces, brought her so much anger and her mind started racing, her heart beating faster. Alexis moved away from the door, she put the gun back in her belt, before opening her backpack and pulling out 2 machine guns. She loaded them with ammo, before putting her bag back on her back. Dylan copied what she did. "Kill as many of the zombies that are stood in the circle as you can, I'll deal with the two in the middle" Alexis sneered. "You ready?" she asked. Dylan nodded, and before he could reply, she stood up, and kicked the door open, and starting shooting instantly. Dylan copied her, and zombies started dropping to the floor, dead. Startled by the sudden outburst, Ray and James ran through the door on the opposite side of the room. Alexis and Dylan kept shooting, until their guns run out of ammo, Alexis then threw them out of the door, before pulling her machete out of its pouch. Alexis started running towards the remaining zombies, swinging it around and be-heading them. Dylan then pulled out his hand gun and started shooting them. "We need to find Ray and James" Alexis shouted. "GRAB YOUR MACHETE AND JUST RUN" she shouted again. Dylan quickly put his gun in his pocket, before putting out his machete, and running through the crowd of the infected, following Alexis.

Alexis swung the door open and ran inside, Dylan following. He then quickly shut the door, putting his machete through the door handles so the door couldn't open. "Well well well, if it isn't little Alexis herself" James said, smirking. "So, what's with you always killing my group? It's turning into a running trend with you. How would you like it if we did the same with your group?" he asked. "Try it, I dare you" Alexis replied. "Oh really, do you really think that I wouldn't figure out that the others are outside? Do you really think I would believe that you wouldn't come and attack without back up? Some super-agent you are" James sneered. Alexis froze. "Did I touch a soft spot there Alexis?" James joked. "Leave them out of this, it's me you want" Alexis said. "No, you're wrong, we don't want to kill you, not right now anyway, we want you to suffer" James sneered. Dylan ran towards him, "YOU CAN LEAVE MY BROTHER ALONE" he shouted. Alexis grabbed him and pulled him back. James and Ray laughed. Alexis ran towards the door, "Where are you going?" James shouted. "Where do you think? I'm not letting you anywhere near them" Alexis sneered. "Oh, well your too late" Ray shouted. Alexis turned, and before she could say anything, the doors behind James and Ray flew open, and in walked Charlie, Daisy and Danny, who were being held by 3 infected, and then Luke ran in and over to Alexis, "I'm so sorry, we didn't even know they were there, they just grabbed us, I tried fighting them off" he said quickly. "It's not your fault" Alexis said. "Let go of them" she shouted. "You see, these guys are different type of zombie. They operate through mind control. Like robots really. They won't attack unless I tell them too" James explained. "Let them go, we don't have to do this anymore. We've both got what we needed, I've got my sister back and you have caused me years of pain" Alexis sighed. "No, you have to choose" Ray interrupted. "What do you mean I have to choose?" Alexis mumbled. "You have to choose which 2 of them you want to save" James said, smiling. "No" Alexis whimpered. "You don't have a choice, you either choose 2, or we'll kill all 3 of them" James sneered. "ALEXIS PLEASE HELP US" Charlie shouted, tears running down her face. A tear ran down

Alexis' cheek, "Why are you doing this? You got your revenge, I've suffered, I don't understand why you're still trying to punish me for something that wasn't my fault in the first place" Alexis said. James and Ray laughed. "Chose now, time is ticking, you have sixty seconds to make your choice" James sneered, smirking afterwards.

I can't let them hurt Daisy again, I can't lose her again I've only just got her back.

I promised Charlie that I would keep her safe, she's so young, I shouldn't have dragged her into this… I promised my sisters, and my mum that everything is going to be okay.

I can't let them kill Danny, he's one of the best things that ever happened to me, I can't lose him and I can't make his family go through what they put my family through.

Why are they doing this to me? Why do they not just leave it, they got what they wanted, I suffered, my family suffered.

"Kill me" Alexis said.

"NO!" Daisy shouted, "Please no just kill me" Danny said, tears running down his face. "No, I have to chose who they kill, I choose myself" Alexis said. She quickly took a deep breath. "You should just kill me, I've been gone for so long, you thought I was dead anyway, it doesn't matter, just kill me, don't kill my sister" Daisy pleaded. Alexis turned to James. "Kill me" she said. "Is that your final answer?" James asked. Alexis took a deep breath. She then pulled out her hand gun, and put a single bullet in it, before sliding it across the floor to James. "Final answer" she replied. "No can do" James smirked. "Listen yeah, I said kill me, I gave you a gun, you can end this. You can make me disappear. Because I swear to god, if you so much as put a scratch on any of their skins, I will make you wish you'd never been born. I will have you tortured until you've got nothing to live for, until your begging me to kill you. I deserve this, like you said, I killed so many of the people closest to you, don't hurt them over a grudge you have with me" Alexis pleaded. "Please just kill me" she continued. James smiled. He picked up the gun and pointed it at her. "Are you sure about this? You can still change your mind" he said. "I'm sure" she replied. James then smiled. "Bye bye" James said, waving. Ray then waved at her and Alexis took a deep breath. James then pulled the trigger, the bullet flying from the gun, to Alexis' chest. Alexis fell backwards, and lay still on the floor. "NO!" Charlie screamed. "PLEASE NO ALEXIS" Daisy shouted. Danny broke down crying. Dylan and Luke ran over to Alexis' body, leaning over her, they pushed down onto the wound, trying to stop the bleeding. "No" Dylan whimpered. Luke put his ear to her mouth to see if he could hear her breathing. He then felt her pulse, nothing. He then slumped back. "NO" Danny shouted. Luke then took a deep breath, before leaning over and starting CPR on Alexis, he pushed her chest to try and get a heartbeat, before leaving over and giving her mouth to mouth. He then repeated the process a few times, he then saw Alexis' chest start moving up and down slowly. "She's breathing, we need to get help" he shouted. Just then, another 2 shots were fired. Ray and James fell to the floor, and the infected that were holding Daisy, Charlie and Danny back, ran off. Everyone turned to see Bailey and John, stood holding their guns up. "Where's Alexis?" Bailey asked. She then looked to see people crying, and then she looked around the room. After a couple of seconds, she stopped to see Alexis' body lay on the floor. She held her hands to her mouth, before collapsing. "No" she cried. Just then, they heard banging, coming from the doors, the infected were trying to get in. Luke and Dylan pulled Alexis' body away from the door, and to the other side of the room. Everyone then walked over and knelt next to her. Before anyone could say anything, the doors flew open, and a large group of the infected were stood staring at them. Everyone stood up and started shooting at them. Danny then ran over to Alexis' body, and lifted her up, before running out of the building. Everyone followed him, John locking the door behind him. They all ran to the van that John and Charlie came in, before jumping in and beginning to drive. They looked back, to find that they weren't being followed.

When they got to the shopping centre, the gates were already open. Danny sped the van straight in, and the shutters of the entrance lifted. When he stopped, he jumped out of the van, and ran to where all of the people were hiding. "ARE THERE ANY DOCTORS HERE? PLEASE HELP" he shouted. A man ran towards him, "I am, what's happened?" he asked. "Follow me" Danny instructed, before running back to the van. He opened the van, gently leaning in and lifting her out, resting her on the floor. "She got shot" Danny cried. The man leant down and knelt next to Alexis' body, he checked her pulse. "I can feel a slight pulse, we need to stem the bleeding, go and get some towels and bandages from the pharmacy" The man instructed. Daisy ran into the shopping centre and too the pharmacy, returning a couple of minutes later with the stuff. She handed it all to the man, and he started putting towels onto the wound, pressing it down. "I've rang the safe zone, they're sending another doctor and some equipment, they said they'll be about 5 minutes." John said. "They're also sending vans to take everyone in the centre to the safe zone too" he added. The man carried on holding own onto her wound, "They'll be able to do more for her, I don't have the right equipment" the man said.

A couple of minutes later, an ambulance drove into the entrance, 2 paramedics jumped out of the back and over to Alexis' body, "What's happened" they asked. "She got shot and her heart stopped but we give her CPR and she's breathing, but not very well. Her pulse is weak" Luke explained. The paramedics examined her. "She's having trouble breathing, we need to try and stem the bleeding, we need to keep the blood out of her lungs and out of her windpipe". One of them explained. They both stood up, and lifted her gently, and slowly and steadily carried her into the ambulance, "We need you to stay out there" they said. "Please save her" Daisy whimpered. "We'll do our best love" they said. They all walked into the main hall of the shopping centre. "OI, EVERYBODY SHUT UP" Danny shouted. Everyone stopped talking and turned to him. "Right, we've killed the people that caused the outbreak, but unfortunately, things escalated and Alexis was given a choice. They had me, Daisy and Charlie held back and she had to choose which one of us she would sacrifice, to save the other two" Danny explained. He then paused. "She chose herself" Danny continued. Several people gasped, and tensed up. "They shot her, but she's still alive and she's still fighting" Danny explained, he then turned and walked back away. He walked back into the entrance to see that the Ambulance had left. "Where've they took her?" Danny asked. "They have to operate, they've taken her to the safe zone, My mum and Bailey have gone with her, they said she'll ring us with any news" Charlie explained. "Where's Daisy?" he continued. "She's gone to

HQ with John and Luke" Charlie continued. "Okay, let's go to HQ" Danny said. Just as they were about to walk up to HQ, one of the people on guard ran into the building. "THEY'VE GOT THROUGH THE GATES" he shouted. Danny and Charlie ran outside. They saw a large group of the infected running towards them. "CHARLIE GET IN THE VAN!" Danny shouted. They ran back inside, and jumped into Alexis' van, before putting their seatbelts on. Danny slammed his foot down onto the pedal, causing the car to speed out of the entrance and drove straight into the group, knocking several of them over. He then lowered the window slightly, and pulled out his gun, before beginning shooting at the infected. Charlie did the same. "Danny, we're not going to be able to kill them all, we need to go back inside where it is safe" Charlie explained. Danny threw his guns onto the floor of the van, before slamming his foot onto the pedal and speeding back into the entrance.

Danny locked the shutters of the entrance. He turned to Charlie, "What do we do now?" Charlie asked. Danny rubbed his eyes, before running his fingers through his hair. "I have no idea" he replied. Charlie then put her head into her hands, and began sobbing. Danny put his arm around her, "What if she doesn't pull through? What if we lose her?" she mumbled. "She will pull through, we need to stay positive, she's a fighter" Danny said, attempting to re-assure Charlie. Charlie nodded, "Let's go up to HQ with the others" she replied. They walked up to HQ.

When Danny and Charlie got to HQ, Daisy, Shay, John, Luke and Dylan were all sat in the conference room, Danny and Charlie sat around the table, everyone stayed quiet. A couple of minutes later, Charlie spoke up. "Why didn't they bite her?" she asked. "What do you mean?" Danny asked. "Well, they're zombies, zombies bite people, they don't shoot them, so why did they shoot her instead of biting her?" Charlie asked. "She has a point" Luke pointed out, looking around the room at the others. Silence fell on the room again.

A couple of minutes later, John spoke up, "They weren't made to bite" he said. Everyone looked at him. "Care to elaborate?" Danny sneered. "I didn't come here to have to listen to your attitude" John shouted. Danny stood up and walked over to him, "Go then" he spat.

"No" John replied. "Well act like one of the team, you can't keep secrets, especially ones that are important. Now, either start explaining, or get out" Danny sneered. He then walked back over and sat down. "The infection was originally administered by injecting people with the virus, not biting them. Ray and James reached out to people that have a problem with Triple Threat, and the base, and recruited them as part of his army. He and my brother injected them with the toxin, then promised that he would then inject them with the anti-virus to remove the toxin, after they'd finished getting them to help him to destroy the base" John explained. "I don't understand" Charlie replied. "Basically, he recruited a bunch of people that hate you guys, then injected them with the toxin, to help them take down the base" John said. "How did he find so many people? Triple threat has only been active for 4 years" Charlie asked. "Something went wrong, and one of the people they recruited had a bad response to the toxin, this caused him to turn against Ray and James, and he started biting other citizens, so Ray and James, and their original gang went into hiding, and another league was formed" John explained. "So basically, we've only got rid of the leaders of one of the two groups that are after us?" Daisy asked. "Yes" John replied. "Ray and James only recruited 6 people, and none of them have gone after you all yet" he continued. "Who do we need to worry about more?" Danny asked. "Ray and James' side, without a doubt, they are a lot smarter than the others, the good thing about when it comes to fighting them though, is they can't pass the toxin on to you, it's impossible. They can only fight with their fists, or any weapons that they obtain" John explained. "So, we have to fight off two armies, and there is only us 7 left" Danny stated. "Pretty much" John replied. "Do Bailey and Louise have weapons?" Danny asked. "Bailey has her backpack, and I gave mum my backpack" Charlie replied. "Okay, well we're going to have to deal with this tomorrow now, it's our turn to go on lookout" Danny explained. "You don't need to worry about that, I rang the safe zone, they are sending vans to come and collect everyone in the centre, to take them to safety. Also, we need to make sure that we get plenty of sleep, so that we can keep our energy levels up" John explained. Danny nodded. "Okay guys, I know this is going to be difficult but you guys need sleep, I know you're all so worried about Alexis we need to stay strong, for her, and we need to keep our energy up. Louise and Bailey are going to ring us with any updates.

Tomorrow is where the action begins" John explained.
"I'm gonna crash in here, Danny, Luke and Dylan you can stay in Alexis' office. Daisy, Shay and Charlie, you girls go into Charlie's office" he continued. Danny stood up, "Woah woah woah, since when was you in charge?" he said. "I never said I was in charge, I'm just-" "No, just nothing. You don't give us commands, you've done enough, this isn't your base anymore, it's Alexis', Daisy and Charlie are in charge now, got it?" Danny sneered. John, speechless, just nodded. Then Danny, Luke and Dylan walked out of the room and to Alexis' office, and Charlie, Daisy and Shay walked out of the room, and to Charlie's office.

Danny swung the door of Alexis' office open, before walking over to the other side of the room and punching the wall. "Bro, you need to calm down" Dylan shouted. "How can I calm down? He's walking around, acting like a hero, giving out his orders… After everything he's done, my girlfriend is fighting for her life, and he's only just told us that we've still got another group to deal with" Danny shouted. "I know all that, but he's right in the sense that you gotta stay strong man, if not for yourself, do it for your girl" Dylan replied. Danny took a deep breath. "I'm gonna go and ring Louise and see how Alexis is" Danny muttered, he then walked out of the office, and down to Charlie's office. "I'm gonna ring your mum to see how Alexis is, is it okay if I do it in here? So then you guys can speak to her aswell" he said. Daisy nodded, "Sure, we was just about to ring her anyway, I was gonna send Charlie to get you" she explained. They all walked over to Charlie's desk, and dialed Louise's number into her phone. It started ringing.

Louise: "Hello?"
Charlie: "Hey mum, It's us, and Danny, we just wanted to see how Alexis is"
Louise: "Oh, hey guys. She's just come out of surgery, the doctor said it went well, they removed the bullet from her chest, and stemmed the bleeding, she responded well to the surgery.
She's gonna be fine, we're just waiting for her to regain consciousness"
Everyone smiled.
Daisy: "That's great! Are you and Bailey staying there for the night?"

Louise: "Yeah, is that okay with you girls?"

Daisy: "Yeah, that's fine, we'll stay here with Shay and the boys, how's Bailey?"

Louise: "She's asleep at the moment, she's still a bit shaken up"

Charlie: "I can imagine, well we're gonna try and get some sleep, we'll ring you tomorrow"

Louise: "Okay sweetheart, night everyone"

Charlie and Daisy: "Night mum"

Louise: "Night girls"

Danny: "Night Louise"

Louise: "Night Danny"

Charlie ended the call.

"Thank god" Daisy said, before sighing. "I know right" Charlie replied. Danny smiled, "Told you girls she was going to be okay" he said. Everyone began to feel cautiously optimistic. "I'm gonna go and get some rest, I'm exhausted" Danny said. "Okay, night Danny" Charlie said. "Night Charls" he replied. "Night" Daisy said. "Night buddy" he replied. He then walked out of Charlie's office, and back to Alexis' office. "How is she?" Dylan asked instantly. "She responded well to the surgery, they're just waiting for her to regain consciousness" Danny replied. "That's great news!" Dylan replied. Danny sat on the sofa, with his head in his hands. "I know bro, I don't know what I would have done if anything would've happened to her" Danny explained. Dylan walked over and sat next to him. "I know bro, I know, just focus on the positives, she responded well to the surgery, so she's on the mend" Dylan explained, trying to re-assure Danny. "Thanks bro" Danny replied. "It's okay man, you need to get some sleep and we'll sort stuff out in the morning" Dylan replied. Danny nodded. "Okay man, let's crash" he replied. They then both got comfy, as well as Luke, before falling asleep.

Chapter Thirty-Six

RING RING! RING RING!

Danny opened his eyes slowly, before sitting up and rubbing his eyes. He then stood up and walked over to Alexis' office phone, picking it up. "Hello?" he said. "Hey Danny, it's Louise, are the girls awake? They aren't answering their phones" Louise said. "I'm not sure, what's up, has something happened?" Danny asked. He heard Louise sniffling in the background. "She's slipped into a coma, Danny" Louise whimpered. "What? When? How?" he asked. "Early hours this morning. She opened her eyes for a couple of seconds, but she didn't respond to anything anyone was saying, then she closed her eyes again. The doctors said she should be conscious by now, then they told us a couple of minutes ago that she's gone into a coma" Louise said. He then heard her break down crying in the background. Tears started building up in Danny's eyes. He sniffled a little. "Louise, we need to stay strong, for her, all of us! I'm going to sort this okay, I'm going to make them all pay for what they've done to your family, I'm going to get justice, for Alexis" he said, anger building up inside him. "Thank you Danny, I'll call you when I get any new information" Louise replied, sniffling. "It's fine, and thank you, talk to you soon, stay strong!" Danny replied. The line then went dead. Danny turned and grabbed a stapler off her desk, before throwing it across the room. The loud nose waking Dylan and Luke up. "You okay mate?" Luke asked. "She's gone into a coma" Danny replied. "I'm so sorry mate, she'll be fine soon, I guarantee it, she's a fighter" Luke replied. "Cheers man" Danny replied. "Luke's right bro, she's a fighter" Dylan interrupted. "I know" Danny replied. "I gotta go tell Daisy and Charlie" Danny said, running his fingers through his hair. "Want us to go with you? To help you comfort the girls?" Dylan asked. Danny nodded. Dylan and Luke stood up. They all the walked down to Charlie's office.

Danny knocked on the door. "Come in" Charlie shouted. They walked in, closing the door behind him. "What's up?" Charlie asked. "Your mum just rang me" Danny said. Everyone stayed silent. Charlie gulped. "What did she say?" she mumbled. Tears started building up in Danny's eyes again. He took a deep breath. "She's gone into a coma" he said. Just then Charlie burst into tears, and collapsed to the floor. Luke ran over to her and held her tight. Dylan walked over to Shay, and hugged her tight. Daisy didn't say anything, she just stood staring at Danny. "Are you okay?" He asked. "We need to end this, we need to make them pay" Daisy sneered. "I agree" Danny replied. "For Alexis" he continued. "For Alexis" Daisy repeated. "We need to have a meeting, now" Danny shouted. He then walked out of Charlie's office, followed by Daisy, then followed by everyone else.

"What's happened?" John asked. "Alexis has gone into a coma" Danny replied. "I'm so sorry to hear that mate" John replied. "I'm not your mate" Danny sneered. "I was just trying to be-" John started, before Danny interrupted. "Just don't bother" he hissed. John rolled his eyes. "Right, so who's the leader of this other group?" Danny asked. "A man called Mark Rayborne" John replied. "And who's that?" Danny asked. "He was one of the most feared men in the country. He caught his wife cheating on him, so he killed his wife and tortured the man she was cheating on him with. Then he went on a 48 hour drug binge, and killed a group of tourists in a hotel lobby in the city, before going on the run for 9 months, before we finally caught him", John explained. "Oh yeah, I remember hearing about that! But why is he teaming up with Ray and James against this base though?" Danny asked. "He's after the agent that caught him and got him put in prison" John replied. "And who's that?" Danny asked. "He's after Bailey" Charlie interrupted. John nodded. "What I want to know, is how you can be so calm about all of this?" Danny shouted. "One of your daughters is lay in hospital, in a coma, and another one of your daughters is possibly in danger, and you're sat there, being so casual, acting like you don't give a shit" he shouted. It stayed quiet for a while, before John spoke up. "They're in a safe place, nobody from the outside that could be a threat to them in anyway, or get to them, there are military protecting the safe zone 24 hours a day" John explained calmly. "That's not the point" Danny sneered. "Well, what is the point then? Being angry will get us nowhere, we all need to stay calm, and figure out a plan" John replied. "Being angry shows that you care, about what's happening and what's happened to Alexis. Being calm makes you look like you don't care" Danny replied. "Well I guess we both have our own ways of responding to situations" John sneered. "Whatever", Danny replied. "Guys, we're gonna get nowhere if you two are always at each other's necks" Daisy shouted. "What do we do now?" Danny asked. "The shopping centre isn't safe anymore, we need to get everyone who we have here, to the safe zone" John replied. "I rang them just before you guys walked in, they're sending trucks to come and pick everyone up" John replied. "We need to go and let everyone downstairs know what's going on" Danny pointed out. They then all walked down to the shopping centre.

Danny whistled, and everyone turned and looked to him, quieting down. "So, here's the plan, we rang the safe-zone, and they're sending trucks to come here, and take you all to the safe zone" Danny shouted. Some of the people started cheering. "When they are here, we will show you out of the back entrance and we will get you all onto the vans. I just want to say, thank you all for co-operating with us whilst you've been here, we were all afraid that you lot would trash the place and run riot, but you've followed the rules we have set and we are all very grateful for that, especially considering the situation with Alexis. The safe zone is monitored and guarded 24/7 by the military, and some of the people that are part of the navy, and it will be a lot safer there, than it is here" He continued. "Oh, also, I need to talk to Vicky" he shouted. Everyone went back to doing what they were doing, and Vicky made her way over to them. Danny turned to Vicky, "Do you want to stay here with Luke? We have a place on a higher floor that the infected won't be able to get to, you're welcome to stay if you want" Danny explained. Vicky laughed. "Are you kidding me? You've just said that this place isn't safe, do you think I'm an idiot? Luke might be stupid enough to believe you, but I sure am not" She sneered, her breath reeking of alcohol. Danny stood speechless. Vicky looked at Luke, "Look at you, stood there with a gun in your hand, I always knew you was a waste" she sneered. Danny spoke up. "Listen, if I would've known that you would have reacted like this, I wouldn't have bothered asking you. How dare you stand there and call him a waste, he's stepped up to protect the other people in this community, whilst you've been down here, drinking alcohol. If anyone here is a waste, it's you" he sneered. Vicky rolled her eyes. "Whatever, have a nice life Luke" she shouted, before stumbling off.

Danny turned to Luke, "I'm so sorry man, I didn't know she would react like that, just ignore what she said, you're not a waste, you're a hero. She's not worth it. You can stay with us, we'll look after you" Danny said. Luke then smiled, "Cheers bro" he replied. They had a quick hug.

They all went back up to HQ, walking back into the conference room.

Not long later, John walked into Alexis' office. "The trucks are here" he said. "Okay, start getting everyone onto the trucks, do it as fast as you can" he instructed. John nodded, "Will do mate" John replied. Danny smiled, he then turned to the others "Right, we all need to make sure we are fully kitted up with weapons, we need to reload" Danny continued. "Kitted up for what?" Charlie asked.

"We are going to end this" Daisy interrupted.

Danny and Daisy re-loaded everyone with weapons.
"And Shay, I've got something for you" Danny continued. He then walked out of the room, and to the weapon room, before coming back carrying a machete. He handed it to Shay. He then put it in a pouch, and handed it to her. "I remember how you said you don't like guns, so I thought you would prefer this, put it over your shoulder and you can pull it out easily whenever you need to" He explained. "Thanks, Danny" she said, before swinging the machete over her shoulders. "You lot ready?" he asked. Everyone nodded. He then grabbed his phone off Alexis' desk and put it in his pocket, before pulling his backpack onto his back. "Let's do this" He said. He then walked out of Alexis' office, followed by the others, he then walked out of HQ, locking the main doors and closing the shutters after them, he walked down to the entrance of the shopping centre.

When they got to the entrance, he walked through to the shopping centre, he saw John stood waiting. "Everyone gone?" Danny asked. John nodded. "Okay, in the vans, let's go. John, with me. Daisy, Charlie and Shay in Charlies van, Luke and Dylan in Alexis' van. They all jumped into the vans, and drove out of the carpark, down the road and to the warehouse.

"We need to explain to Bailey and Louise what's going on, and we need to tell them about Mark" Danny explained. He then pulled out his phone and handed it to Dylan, "Call Louise and put it on speaker" He instructed. Dylan did so. "Hello?" Louise said. "Hey, it's Danny, any news?" Danny said. "Oh, hi love. And no, she's still the same. The doctors said she should be conscious now, her breathing is normal, and everything about her is normal, but she's not awake, I don't get it" Louise replied, sorrowfully. "She'll be awake soon, don't worry. Louise, we got something to tell you" Danny replied. "What is it? What's happened? Is everyone okay?" she asked. "Yeah, everyone's fine, but the thing is, the infected got through the gates, so we had to ring the safe zone to come and get all of the people who we were holding here, to take them to safety, and we've left" he replied. "Oh, are you coming here?" Louise replied. "No, we're going to the warehouse" Danny replied. "What!? You better be kidding me Danny" Louise shouted. "No, we need to end this Louise, we both know that. We need justice, for Alexis" he replied. "You've got to promise me that you'll look after Daisy and Charlie, and yourself for that matter! And the others! Promise you'll all be safe?" She replied, her voice shaking slightly. "I promise" he replied. "Oh, and there's something else" Danny continued. "What?" she replied. "We found out that there are two different army's out to get us, and Bailey's in danger" Danny replied. Louise squeaked slightly. "What do you mean?" she asked quietly. "Ray and James infected around 7 people originally, and the toxin he infected them with, turned them into zombies, but they won't pass the toxin through biting. However, one of the people he infected; their body rejected the toxin, and it had a different affect on them. It turned them into actual zombies, that bite to spread the toxin. The leader of that army is a man called Mark Rayborne, he is after revenge on the person that had him put in Prison, which is Bailey" he explained. It all stayed silent. "That's why they're here" Louise whispered. "What do you mean?" he replied, started to get worried. "They got into the safe-zone, we're on the top floor and they can't get to us, their making their way up and killing everybody" she replied. "Why didn't you tell me this sooner?!" he replied. "They can't get to us"

Louise replied. "How do you know?" he replied. "Because they've quarantined the whole of this floor, we have military at every possible entrance" she replied. "Okay, call me if anything gets worse and we'll come and get you" he replied. "Okay, stay safe" Louise said. "You too" Danny replied. He then ended the call. "We need to do this quick, then go to the safe-zone, it's under attack, but Alexis, Louise and Bailey are safe on a quarantined floor" Danny instructed.

A couple of minutes, later, he pulled up outside the warehouse.

It's time.

Chapter Thirty-Seven

Bailey and Louise's P.O.V

Bailey and Louise were stood around Alexis' bedside, they could hear the infected outside the room, banging on the door and making strange noises. "We're not going to be safe in here for much longer, they're going to get in" Bailey mumbled. "We've got to protect your sister" Louise replied. "I know" Bailey replied. Bailey held onto Alexis' hand. "Please wake up Alexis, we need you, it's not safe here anymore, they're going to get in, if you can hear us, please fight this, please wake up, Danny, Charlie, Daisy, Shay, Luke, Dylan and John are on their way to the warehouse, none of us are safe, we need you, we need your bad girl attitude, your sass and your amazing aim, we all need you. I'm scared, I'm so scared, please wake up, please" Bailey begged, tears running down her face. Just then the door slammed open. Stood in the doorway, was a group of the infected. Mark was in front. "There she is" he smiled, showing his razor-sharp teeth, blood dripping out of his mouth and down his face, dripping onto the floor. Louise smiled, shooting Mark between the eyes. "There he goes" she joked. Bailey looked at her in amazement, "Nice shot mum!" she shouted. Bailey and Louise stood up and grabbed guns off the table next to Alexis' bed. They both started shooting at the zombies, Bailey was screaming, and a group of military ran in and started shooting at the infected. Some of them started getting closer to Bailey, she was shooting as many as she could, but there was too many. "MUM HELP" Bailey shouted. She put her guns on the bed next to her, and grabbed her machine gun and started swinging at them. Louise grabbed another gun, and started shooting in two different directions. She was shooting at the infected in front of her, and the ones that were now cornering Bailey. Just then, Bailey dropped her gun, "I'VE RUN OUT OF BULLETS, PLEASE HELP ME" she screamed, tears running down her face. "KEEP USING THE MACHETE, YOU CAN DO THIS BABE, I BELIEVE IN YOU" Louise shouted. She put her machine gun on the bed and grabbed her machete the same as Bailey. They both started swinging the machete at the zombies, beheading them. Just then, shots were fired. Bailey turned to see Alexis sat up with guns in her hand. Alexis then pulled her backpack out from under the bed, she pulled out two guns and started shooting the remaining zombies. She got out of bed, unplugging the needles in her arms from the machines. She walked towards the door, shooting at the zombies who were trying to get out. She then pushed the door shut and grabbed the chair from next to the door and put the chair leg through both handles, jamming the door shut. She then turned to her mum and Bailey. She was about to say something, but then she collapsed. Bailey and Louise ran over to her, and helped her up, before helping her to walk over to her bed. They sat her down and Alexis grabbed her air mask, and put it over her mouth, she took a few deep breaths, before taking it back off her mouth. "Get me some bandages" she instructed, before putting the mask back over to her face and breathing in and out some more. Bailey ran over to a drawer and pulled out bandages out, before running back over to Alexis, she handed them over to her. Alexis then wrapped a bandage around her arm, which was bleeding because she pulled the needles out of her arm. She put the other bandage on her hand, to hold her canular in place. She then grabbed her air mask and put it back over her face, before taking some deep breaths. "Get me those needles and medication pots" Alexis instructed, pointing over to the tray at the end of her bed. "Put them in my backpack" she instructed. Bailey did so. Alexis put the mask down and took a deep breath. "Hey guys" she said, smiling. "I'm so glad you're okay" Louise replied. Alexis smiled. "Get me my clothes" Alexis instructed. Louise grabbed her clothes, and helped her get dressed.

When Alexis was fully dressed, she stood up, with her air mask in her hand, and carefully pulled her backpack onto her back. "Let's go" she said. She then slowly and carefully started walking towards the door, she grabbed a wheelchair from behind the door. She pulled it out and sat in it. Still holding her air mask, she put it over face and took some deep breaths. She pulled out her guns. "When I say so, Bailey, pull the chair leg out of the door and open the doors, then we'll all start shooting and run, stop at a lift and we need to get out of here" she instructed. Bailey walked over to her mum and Alexis, and they walked out of the room. They ran down the corridor, Louise pushing Alexis in the wheelchair, Alexis strapped her mask over her face, and took deep breaths, whilst shooting at the zombies. They then stopped at the lift and Alexis pressed the button, whilst they were waiting, Bailey and Louise carried on shooting towards the infected. When the lift opened, they quickly ran in and pressed the button, and the lift doors shut. Alexis leaned over and pressed the ground floor button. Whilst it was going down, Alexis pulled her mask out. Louise looked at her. Alexis looked pale and ill, her eyes showing she was in pain. "Pass me both of your machetes" Alexis instructed, breathing steadily. They did so. "When the lift door opens, it will probably be swarming with zombies, I'll hold a machete to the left and to the right, and mum, run, I will chop their legs off so they can't follow us, mum stay low when you're running. Bailey, you sit on my knee and shoot as many as you can, till we get to the exit, then look for a van" Alexis explained, before putting the air mask back on, and breathing into it. Alexis pulled the machetes out of the pouches and got them ready, Bailey sat on Alexis' knee with 2 guns pointed in front of her.

Ground 4, 3, 2, 1.

The doors opened. Louise began running towards the zombies, there weren't as many as expected. Bailey shot at them, and Alexis held the machetes to her sides, cutting the legs off any of the infected that were in her way. When they got to the exit, Louise looked around, she saw an ambulance, and she ran over to it, she opened the back of it, and pulled the ramp down, they wheeled Alexis up the ramp and into the back. Louise and Charlie jumped into the front. Louise turned the ignition, slammed her foot onto the pedal, and the van went speeding forwards. She drove out of the gates and drove towards the warehouse. She pulled her phone out and handed it to Bailey, "Ring Danny" she instructed. Bailey rang him. "Hello Danny, its Louise, where are you?" she said quickly. "We're stuck in a room in the warehouse, there's more of them than I thought" he replied. "On my way now" Louise replied. "Where's Alexis?" he asked. "She's safe" Louise replied, before ending the call.

About half an hour later, they pulled up outside the warehouse. Louise turned off the ignition before jumping out of the ambulance, along with Bailey; they walked to the back of the ambulance and opened the doors. They saw Alexis stood there holding two guns, her machete around her shoulders on her back, along with her backpack. She still had the mask over her mouth. She nodded and slowly climbed out of the van. They then all walked to the exit and into the warehouse. They walked into a room which was full of zombies. They hadn't seen Alexis, Bailey and Louise. Alexis pulled her mask off, "Give me your machete again Bailey, we're going to do the same as we did at the safe zone, except you're gonna run in front and shoot them, I'm gonna hold the machetes, and mum will shoot the ones behind her" Alexis whispered. Bailey nodded and handed Alexis her machete, and Alexis held them either side of her. She then put her air mask back on. Bailey nodded. Bailey then took a deep breath, before she started running and shooting. Alexis and Louise followed her, they killed off as many zombies as they could, before stopping at the other side of the room. Alexis then dropped her machetes, before pulling a machine gun out of her backpack and starting shooting at the infected. "In here" someone whispered. Alexis turned around to see John stood at the door behind them. "Oh my god" John mumbled. Alexis pulled her mask off her face and took a deep breath, "Hey dad" she muttered. Before turning to Bailey and Louise. "You two first" she mumbled, she then put her mask back over her face. Louise and Bailey walked into the room, Alexis then followed.

Chapter Thirty-Eight

When they walked into the room, everyone stopped and stared, saying nothing. Danny was sat against the wall, his head in his hands. Dylan nudged him, "Bro" he mumbled. Danny looked up. Alexis took her mask off her face, before smiling at him. Danny quickly stood up. "Hey" Alexis mumbled.

Danny stood staring at her. Alexis then walked towards him, stopping and standing in front of him. She put her mask on and took a couple of deep breaths, before taking it back off. Danny looked at her, she looked so pale and ill, ghostly almost. He looked into her eyes, he could see that she was in pain, but somehow, she was still managing to smile. He didn't know how it possible, he thought she was dead, but now, she's stood in front of him. He reached out and stroked her face. She lifted her hand and put it over his, holding onto it. Danny then smiled. "Say something then" Alexis muttered. Danny just smiled, he then gently wrapped his arms around her, "I'm so glad you're okay" he whispered. Alexis didn't say anything, she just held him back. She then collapsed and fell onto the floor. She put her mask back over her face and sat on the floor, breathing in and out. Danny sat next to her and put his arm around her, she was shivering. He took his jacket off and wrapped it over her shoulders. "You should still be in hospital, you need to take it easy" he whispered. Alexis smiled. Daisy and Charlie then walked over her and sat in front of her, Alexis took her mask off. "Hey" she mumbled. Daisy and Charlie both smiled, before carefully both hugging her, Alexis hugged them back, before putting her mask back on and taking a few deep breaths. "We need to get out of here" Alexis mumbled. "It's safer here" Danny replied. "I know, but I need to go back to the hospital, if I don't get back to the hospital, I could die" Alexis said. "Does anyone have my phone?" she asked. "I have" John shouted. "When we get out, send "red1" to 999 and that will detonate the dynamite that the military set up for me" Alexis quickly said, before putting her mask back on, finding it harder to breath. Alexis then held her arms up and Danny pulled her up. She put her arm round Danny's shoulder, and Dylan walked over and put her arm around his shoulder, "Hey Lex" he said gently. Alexis smiled. "Put my guns in my hands" Alexis mumbled through the mask, Daisy handed her two guns, and Alexis held onto them. "Okay, Louise open the doors, and Daisy and Charlie go in front and shoot as many as you can, Alexis will shoot some, Louise and Shay come behind us with machetes, Luke behind with a gun, then John follow with a gun aswell, and when we're all out, John, send the code" Danny explained. Everyone nodded.

Louise then walked over to the doors, and they all got in positions. "Go" Danny said. Louise opened the door, and everyone made their way out in formation. They all made their way through the infected, they were surrounded, the room was filled with at least 120 of them. When they all got out, they all turned and started shooting at the infected that were trying to get out. "They're gonna get out, the code takes 2 minutes to detonate" John explained. "Just keep shooting" Danny replied. Alexis then passed out and collapsed onto the floor. Daisy ran over to her. "I'm gonna get her into the ambulance and get her on some proper oxygen, you guys keep shooting" she shouted. She then lifted Alexis and slowly carried her over to the van.

John turned to the others. "I have to go in and distract them" he said. "No you can't, the place is going to blow up in less than a minute, just keep shooting" Danny replied. "Danny, I have to, we can't hold them back, there's too many of them" John shouted. Danny looked to the door, he saw a large group of zombies stepping out. "No, you can't" Danny replied. "I have to" John shouted. "It's the only way we can get them to stay inside" he continued. John looked at Alexis' phone. He started counting down."10, 9, 8, 7, 6", he then ran into the building.

Danny tried running after him, but Dylan held him back. "NO!" Danny shouted. A couple of seconds later, the whole warehouse exploded into to flames, the impact causing everyone to fall back. Danny stood up and put his hands over his mouth. He tried to look into the doorway, all he could see was flames. He tried walking towards the door, but Dylan grabbed his arms, "He couldn't have survived that" he said. Danny shook his head, and pulled out of Dylan's grip. He walked closer to the door. Just then, the building started collapsing. Danny took a few steps back. They stood staring at the building, in shock. "He gave his life to safe ours" Danny mumbled. "He's a hero" Dylan replied. Danny turned to see Luke holding onto Charlie, who was crying into his shoulder. Dylan walked over to Shay and pulled her into a hug, trying to comfort her. Danny walked over to Louise and Bailey, who were hugging and crying. Louise then let go of Bailey. Bailey turned and hugged onto Danny. "He's a hero Bailey" Danny whispered. Bailey nodded and pulled away, and Danny put his arm around Louise's and Baileys shoulders, before they all walked towards the ambulance. Danny climbed into the back and stood next to Alexis. She pulled her mask off. "What happened?" she asked. "John ran into the building in the last couple of seconds, I couldn't stop him, I'm so sorry" Danny explained. Tears then started building up in Alexis' eyes and Daisy burst into tears.

"We need to get Alexis out of Limebarn" Danny instructed. He then jumped out of the ambulance and over to his van, followed by the others. Louise and Bailey got back into the ambulance, and they all just carried on driving.

When they got to the outskirts of Limebarn, the road was blocked off by police and military. Charlie jumped out and walked over to them, she showed them her agent ID and a couple of moments later, a group of forensics followed Charlie over the van.

Everyone was checked, to make sure they weren't infected.

A while later, and an officer walked over to them, he looked to the military who were guarding the gate. "All clear"
The officer shouted.

The gates opened, and they all drove out of the city, escorted by a police car to a hospital.

Chapter Thirty-Nine

When they got to the hospital, Danny walked over to the ambulance. Louise and Bailey jumped out of the front, whilst Danny opened the back doors. He climbed in and looked down at Alexis. "She's still unconscious" he whispered. He then reached over and gently lifted her up off the stretcher, and carried her into the hospital. He then laid her down on one of the hospital beds. "What do we do now?" Danny asked. A doctor ran over to them, "What happened?" he asked, examing her. He opened her eyelid, shining a light into it. "She was shot, the safe zone operated and removed the bullet and she went to a coma. She came out of the coma for a while, but she must have tired herself out whilst she was fighting off the infected" Danny explained, holding onto her hand. The doctor nodded, writing notes. "We'll take her to a cubicle for examination.

A nurse then pulled the stretcher down the corridor, into a room, followed by the doctor. Danny stayed behind with the others.

They sat in the waiting room for a while, before the doctor came back out. "She's recovering well from the surgery at the safe zone. Luckily, a nurse had updated her medical records. We've put her on oxygen, as her pulse was quite weak and it didn't appear that her body was producing enough oxygen. She's very weak and her body is very tired, but she is going to be okay. The painkillers should kick in very soon" the doctor explained. "How about her wounds?" Louise asked. "Everything looks to be healing okay" the doctor replied. "Thank you" she said. "Can we go and see her" Louise asked. The doctor nodded, and Louise and the girls followed the doctor. Danny walked back over to Luke and Dylan, sitting with them. "Are you not going with them?" Dylan asked. Danny shook his head, "I'll go and see her after they have, she needs her family right now" he smiled.

An hour or so later, and they all walked out of the room. Daisy, Charlie, Bailey and Shay walked down the corridor, and Louise walked over to Danny. "We are going to go and get something to eat. You should go and sit with Alexis, she's still unconscious but it's best that she has a familiar face there when she wakes up" she said. Danny nodded, standing up. Louise pulled him into a hug. "Thank you for everything" she said, rubbing his back. "What do you mean?" Danny asked. "You kept your promise. You looked after my girls, everything is going to be okay" she said. Danny smiled. "I would do anything for you and your family" he said. "I'm proud to call you my son" Louise said. Danny gave her squeeze, before moving away. She then followed the girls, to the canteen. "You guys coming?" Danny asked. Dylan shook his head, patting Danny's back. "We'll go with the girls to the canteen, you go see your girl" he said. Him and Luke stood up, and they formed a group hug. "Thanks boys" Danny said.

Danny walked into the room, pulled up a chair and sat next to Alexis' bed. He held onto her hand. "I love you" he whispered, before lowering his head and leaning it onto the bed. Everything stayed completely quiet for a couple of minutes. Danny then felt Alexis squeeze his hand, she mumbled. Danny quickly stood up and looked down at her, he lifted off her air mask. "What did you say babe?" he asked. "I love you too" Alexis whispered back. She then opened hereyes and looked at him, smiling. Danny smiled back at her. "You okay?" he asked. Alexis nodded. "Are you in any pain?" he continued. Alexis shook her head this time. "Good" he replied. He then stroked her face, "I thought I'd lost you" Danny said. "When he shot you, I thought you was dead, your heart stopped I thought I was going to lose you" He continued, a tear rolled down his cheek. "I knew he wouldn't kill me, I knew he'd hurt me, but he wouldn't kill me, and I knew I'd be able to fight it" she replied. Danny smiled. "You're so strong" he replied. Alexis smiled back at him.

She then pushed herself up so that she was sat in an upright position on the bed, before leaning back onto the headboard of the bed. "Do you have your phone?" she asked. Danny nodded. "Please can I borrow it?" she asked. Danny pulled it out of his pocket and handed it to her. She then dialled a number and held it to her ear. "Hey Pete, it's Alexis" she said. "Hey love, how's things?" he asked. "Not too good, please can you send 3 helicopters here, we're at the Royal

Cross hotel, just outside Limebarn… to take us to Spain?" she asked. "Yeah, but it may take an hour or so. There are 5 out at the moment, so I'll send 3 of them to go and pick you lot up" Pete replied. "Thank you" she replied. "I'll get the pilot to ring you on this number when he's almost there, so then you lot can get ready" Pete replied. "Thanks" Alexis replied. "See you soon sweetie" Pete replied. Alexis then ended the call. She handed Danny his phone back. "We're going on holiday" Alexis said, smiling. Danny laughed. "Go and tell the others" Alexis instructed. Danny saluted her and walked out of the cubicle.

A couple of minutes later, he walked back into the cubicle, to see that Alexis had fallen asleep, and she had her air mask back over to her mouth. He walked over and sat next to her bed on the chair, and he just watched her sleep, watching her chest move up and down at a steady pace, showing that her breathing was getting better. He was just so happy that she was alive and still breathing.

A while later, Danny got the confirmation call that the helicopters were outside waiting.

"Alexis, Alexis" Danny said, nudging her slightly. Alexis shot up and opened her eyes, pulling off her mask, swinging her arm in front of her, holding a gun. "Sorry babe, I didn't mean to scare you" he said, kissing her cheek and taking the gun off her. "Where did you even get this" he joked. "I don't know, must have been in my pocket" she shrugged. "The helicopter is here, time to go" he said. Alexis rubbed her eyes, before holding her arms out. Danny laughed. He then leant down to Alexis and put her mask back over her face, before gently lifting her up. She wrapped her arm around his shoulders. He then carried her out of the hospital and into the helicopter, where her mum and sisters were, waiting for them.

Danny then sat Alexis down, before putting her seatbelts on, and then putting her headphone and headset on for her. "Hold on tight" the pilot said. Danny then pulled the door shut, and the helicopter slowly began to lift off, and it set off to Spain. Alexis pulled her mask off and turned to Danny, "Danny" she said. "Yeah babe?" he replied. "November 15th, put it on your calendar" she smiled. "Why?" he asked. "That's when we are going to France" she said. Danny smiled, before holding onto her hand. "It's a date" he replied.

NEWS REPORT

Limebarn is now officially under quarantine. Military have worked around the clock to get the last remaining survivors out of town, taking them to the military base, where they are offering temporary accommodation to those affected by the epidemic. The previously titled 'Safe-zone' came under attack shortly before, however the military were luckily already at hand to evacuate everyone to a more permanent, and safe location. Over 350 people were saved from the small town of approximately 400 residents. The rate of death is low, and people are starting to recover from the ordeal. The police and military are working together to provide treatment to those affected, both physically and mentally, and the government are already working on a plan to renovate the town. £3.5 billion has already been put in place for repairs, and the work is looking to take around 9 months to complete, on a fast-track basis. They are currently working on a long-term housing solution for the residents of Limebarn. Plans are underway to get as much of people's belongings out of the quarantined zone, and back to their rightful owners. The whole country is working together to help the people unfortunately affected by the recent events. Upon inspection, police have found that most of the infected were somehow trapped in a warehouse, which was then detonated by explosives. Reports say that the agent group Triple Threat ABC are responsible for saving, and evacuating the people of Limebarn. We want to thank those anonymous agents for everything they have done to protect the community. Stay tuned for updates.

26382982R00104

Printed in Great Britain
by Amazon